AF145977

Joe Dexter
Prisoner Zero

Limited US Patriot Edition

Steve Schild

Joe Dexter
Prisoner Zero

Steve Schild

Special thanks to:

Andrea Rohpeter
Kay Radzik - Mars 100 Candidate
Leo Kopka

And of course, to the best girls in my life:
Corinna – Elvira – Yanika

Thank you to all my fans and followers. You are
the best.

Phone: 0041 79 783 03 06
steve.schild@bluewin.ch
www.steveschild.ch

Bibliografische Information der Deutschen Nationalbibliothek: Die Deutsche Nationalbibliothek
verzeichnet diese Publikation in der Deutschen
Nationalbibliografie; detaillierte bibliografische
Daten sind im Internet über dnb.dnb.de abrufbar.

1. Auflage, 2019

Herstellung und Verlag:
BoD – Books on Demand, Norderstedt
ISBN 978-3-7357-8471-1
steve.schild@bluewin.ch
www.steveschild.ch

My dear daughter Elvira,

Since I was a little boy, I have been dreaming of two things, the colonization of the universe with spaceships, and a girl who changes my life forever and makes me happy.

For years these dreams grow up in me; I did not know what I would find and how I could progress. Then in 2012, I accidentally discovered the Mars One project and immediately knew that this was my way.

Even now that I'm writing these lines, the project is up to date and I'm one of only a handful of applicants worldwide. This year, it will decide how the mission will continue.

The second dream is about a mysterious girl. Today I know that this is you, my wonderful daughter. My dear companion Corinna gave birth to you, a source of great joy.

It took me years to realize what was going on inside me. In 2016, I met a master who introduced me to mystical rituals and showed me how to find myself. Unfortunately he can not physically read these lines anymore. But he will always be close to me.

Prior to that, a friend had explained to me how to create an imaginary world in which one has access to his subconscious: In my personal mystical world lived a great dragon. I entrusted my secrets, fears and desires to this dragon. One day an egg lay in its nest. A few months later a dragon baby had hatched from the egg. At that time, I began to hear in my dreams a voice that kept calling me. And it was this call that I will never forget: "I want to go to Earth, Steve! It is time for me to arrive. I am a soul that wants to incarnate and you will be my physical father. I am the Dragon Warrior."

You must know that at first I was unsure. For such intensive messages from the realm of the unconscious often have a violent effect on people. But after a lengthy period of testing, going in and out, Corinna and I agreed that motherhood was the right decision.

On the 6th of November, in 2016, you, my beloved Dragon Warrior, were born. Your birth, which was not easy to start, was such a touching moment for me as I had never experienced it before. Not without reason are birth and death the most important events in a person's life. In between lies life, which can be so unique for everyone, as long as you become aware of it.

Another friend had contacted me. He is a member of a centuries-old order in the background and has encouraged me that this kind of humanistic work is also the right path for me. Members of this community have always closely followed and logged world affairs. It is also revealed to those who want to know this: Over the next decades, political, economic and social systems will change globally. This new order involves the establishment of three competing world powers. These three large blocks will also have colonialism unprecedented in order to meet their peoples' huge resource needs. This especially in inhospitable areas, such as in desert areas and in lonely mountain heights. But these efforts will also reach the deep-sea regions and the interior of the earth.

In particular, however, the advance into space will be massively forced.

Such colonies are usually populated by people who for some reason can not cope or are no longer welcome in their hometowns. Often they can then escape reprisals and persecutions only because they declare themselves ready for colonization and the concomitant exploitation of foreign territories. Over time, former colonies gradually develop into independent social structures. This story is full of examples.

I am not a clairvoyant, but I still maintain visions. That's why I can well imagine that the Mars One project is an important part of this future. As a result, I try to contribute to this development through my work. For all visible difficulties and always for the benefit of the people.

My first novel certainly does not claim to be included in the canon of world literature. The story should be entertaining in the first place. Importantly, I wish that the issues raised in the story also give reason to think seriously.

Of course I do not see the future as gloomy as it is described in this novel. But it is true that on our planet there are destructive groups at work, which strive to promote only the materialistic and thus the control over the power. Joy, compassion, empathy, charity and tolerance are values that mean nothing to them.

But as always, goodness tries to defend itself against evil. So the world is not a vale of tears, it always offers individuals the opportunity to reform themselves in order to take the constructive path.

In this novel quite stereotypical assignments are made. But I do not blame anyone. It's all about showing that history repeats itself if you do not stay vigilant and handle resources carefully. What happened in the past can not be reversed. But we must no longer blame today's generations for what had been. On the contrary, we should primarily work on ourselves to lead a meaningful life. A blessed existence, which is loving, appreciative and constructive.

I hope for this for my Elvira as well as for all other children in the world. My thanks for the past, ongoing, or future support therefore applies to my partners and friends, my family, and in particular my parents, who enabled me to have a beautiful youth. For their trust and their encouraging confidence, I especially thank my partner Corinna.

My dear daughter, I hope that one day you will read this book and understand why I do it all. I also hope that you will be a little proud of me.

Thanks Corinna, Kevin and Felix

Steve Schild

At Home

The morning was dark. Even before Vivianne could look out of the window, she knew it was raining. Shortly before, she had roused to the terribly shrill ringing of the alarm clock. Joe, who was lying next to her, had not been bothered by the alarm clock. Calmly he slept on; he did not have until 09:00 to drive to work.

Half sleepy and with glued eyes Vivianne ran into the bathroom. She was still too tired to notice the puddle on the floor, and when she stood in front of the mirror and felt something thick between her toes, the smell of fresh dog feces hit her. Matador had once again made a mess. Diarrhea.

"What a day!" She thought. "It can hardly come any worse."

Vivianne washed her feet, fetched a rag to cleanse the floor, and opened the windows wide enough for the smell to escape. Then she washed her face and put on fresh clothes. What was missing was a coffee. While the coffee was out of the machine, she heard internet radio on her cell phone. Another attack in Israel, the weather misty and cold. A start of the day like any other. With a few swallows she drank the pick-me-up. That was good. But now to work quickly.

Vivianne was a computer scientist. Only recently she had completed her education and found a good job by luck or chance. Working as an IT-Support at a well-known fiduciary office was fun and the working atmosphere was very pleasant. Nevertheless, she did not feel the need to go to work that day. Fortunately, it was Friday and the weekend was not far in coming.

Vivianne hopped down the stairs to her car, an old Toyota Carina that had 250,000   Kilometers on the speedometer but behaved like a new car. No rust, no bumps and dents, no other problems. Joe, her husband, who enjoyed making things, had converted the interior into a high-tech cockpit, and even had a DVD player and rear view cameras. But that did not impress Vivianne, she just wanted to get the car to work. On the way she realized that people were driving once more, as if a rhino were after them. Besides, at the roundabout she would almost have been rammed from the left by a guy who seemed to be sleeping. When Vivianne turned on the radio, she realized she was not getting to work on time. It was reported there was a more than three kilometers long traffic jam.

It was now 08:00 am. Joe crawled out of bed and looked into the same rainy sky that his wife had seen before. After putting on some old shorts and a T-shirt, he went to the office where he started his computer and checked his e-mail account. There was not a single E-Mail. Apparently, there was no one in the big world who thought of him. Well, what should it be, he was used to getting only a few e-mails. Joe was playing some music, it was a group from the 1980s: Kraftwerk. How beautiful these sounds came from the six loudspeakers. He enjoyed the music, he was fine today.

At the same time, he logged into his online shop, where he offered science fiction figures, games and merchandise, and went through the new order entries. The e-shop went well, soon he wanted to open his own shop with Vivi, as he called his love. After processing the orders, he switched off the device and got ready for work.

Joe was employed as an electrician at the company Megatron Robots. The company was only five minutes on foot down the street, so he had no stress and could enjoy the morning. He was even fine with the fact that it was raining, it always raised his mood, it just was missing that it was thundering. Lightning and thunder fascinated him so much that he had hung pictures of weather lights and thunderstorms all over the office. How impressive these huge energies were. Joe jogged to his desk, drank a hot Ovomaltine there, and then went to the lab.

When Vivi came home in the evening, it smelled delicious of fish and spinach. As soon as she closed the door behind her, the dog came rolling up, a mixture of Appenzell Mountain Dog and German Shepherd. Vivi had long disliked dogs, but when, on a Sunday morning, a stray, slightly limping dog had run into her. she had immediately enclosed him into her heart, given him the name Matador, and taken him home. He was a sweet, old, dorky guy, and Vivi liked him immensely. Shortly after the welcome by Matador Joe came and hugged her. Finally they were together again. Such a day could last forever; every minute they were without each other was like an eternity to them.

The evening was spent with reading and meaningless discussions about the food. Vivi thought again that she was too fat and Joe just did not want to have a salad for lunch the next day. Vivi constantly complained that she was too fat, but in actuality her body was so well-formed that you could not even say the word "fat" Joe had other worries, as usual. After reading his book, he tried to install a new program, but it did not work. Hammering against the keyboard, he almost knocked the new flat screen to the floor. It was enough for him, Vivi just had to look at it! She took care of the problem and quickly solved it. Joe had forgotten to set the compatibility properly, so it was no wonder that the program had not run. Normally, Joe could not be upset so fast and Vivi was the one with the fury, but today it was the other way around. After everything was installed and running properly, Vivi turned off the PC. She wanted to watch another movie with him, and the next day they both could sleep in. They chose "Virus", a blockbuster that was about an alien computer virus that infected all the PCs on a research vessel. The virus was so advanced that it made the entire crew their own by killing all members and providing their bodies with electronics, turning them into bio-mechanical robots. The movie was already running for an hour when Vivi turned to Joe and realized he was sound asleep. So She watched it alone, until only trash was on the screen Then she woke him up, so they could go to bed.

Joe woke up early the next day. He could not help it and tried to wake up ~~woke~~ his wife. Instead of a "good morning", however, her only answer was a mumble He knew how he could get her to open her eyes. In the kitchen he prepared breakfast to bring her in bed. As Vivi smelled the coffee and the baked rolls, she was immediately wide awake and began to eat heartily. Now the day was saved, it only needed feeding the dog and walking it. Breakfast overtook

Vivi, so Joe was forced to get up and go out with Matador. But it was a wonderful day. Joe sang to himself while the dog played with stones out in front. Again and again he came to his master and urged Joe to play along. Every now and then, Joe was persuaded and threw the stone somewhere in the bushes, where Matador could not find them so fast.

Meanwhile, Vivi was at home and ironing the laundry. In the background was a radio station with modern, bland music. In the evening, she and Joe planned to go to a special 80s festival and she was really happy because she had never been to such a big event. In Nesslauen, an insignificant village in Germany, where they lived in a house on the edge of the forest, there had never been a similar event. At 8:00p.m. the spectacle would start.

When evening came Vivi was in the bathroom, getting ready for the festival, while Joe, who had already taken a shower, was impatiently waiting for her.

The Party

In their old car, Joe and Vivi set off. They had agreed
that Joe would drive today and not drink alcohol. The
journey took only about ten minutes. The marquee
was set up outside the village, on the opposite side of
the village from Joe's and Vivi's house. For the
relationship of the 2000-soul community, the tent was
very big. It seemed that the visitors had come from far
away. Old cars parked around the grounds, including
Pontiac's and Dodges. Their eyes immediately fell on
an 80's Pontiac Fire bird Trans Am, her dream car.
Vivi shot a few dozen photos of the cars and Joe
meanwhile got the tickets. 40 Euros were more than
enough, but it was not something to see every night.
And once a year they could afford it, because the
couple lived thrifty. Joe and Vivi entered the tent and
they were surrounded by freaks with fancy hairstyles
and suits. The band Kraftwerk just started their show
on stage and thrilled the audience with the song »Wir
sind die Roboter«. (we are the robot`s) The crowd
began to dance, moving monotonously to the rhythm
of the music as if on drugs. It looked amusing, no one
danced out of line.

But the couple wanted to first have a drink and sat
down at a table. Vivi had long been enjoying an Irish
whiskey, Joe was drinking a mineral water. Rocking,
they let themselves be carried away by the sound of
the music and enjoyed the show. When the concert
was over, they moved to the bar and ordered drinks
again. As much as it was possible in the roar of
loudspeaker music, they talked. As always, her main
topics were computer and the future. What would
happen if in 50 Years, all raw materials would have

been used up and there would be no oil left? There were theories about nuclear fusion generators, which released a tremendous amount of energy. Maybe there would be lightning generators that could store all the energy of a thunderstorm for years. Vivi was talking confusedly, the whiskey seemed to work, because she told of flying saucers, of which she had read. She said that the Germans built some of them during the Second World War, then she talked about their whiskey and how good it was. Joe smiled and listened to her gibberish. Since Vivi almost never drank alcohol, two glasses were enough to make her drunk. They continued to talk and some interested young people sat down to talk with them eagerly. Vivi was the highlight of the evening. She talked incessantly about her experience as a computer scientist, and that she had read that in the Arctic there would be a civilization that had settled there towards the end of the war in 1945. She claimed that the Illuminati ruled the world, and from then on they could no longer be taken seriously. Joe had also read into those books that lay around their homes, but he did not like that, for him it was all nonsense and mental spin. He preferred books about Arthur and his Knights of the Round Table. Everything old had done to him, the Middle Ages fascinated him.

However, the listeners at their side also turned out to be mentally disturbed persons who had something to report about UFOs and aliens. Joe tried to touch on another topic because it became so absurd that he could not stand it any longer, because once Vivi got drunk, it was no pleasure to argue with her. No one spoke and Vivi talked so fast that one hardly understood anything.

Time passed and Joe gave up giving the conversation a different direction. Gradually they got tired. Their conversation partners had said goodbye and the two strolled once again on the festival grounds. Finally, Joe had to drag his wife to the car. She was still able to stand on her feet, but the mixture of fatigue and alcohol had got to her. As they sat in the car, Joe put a DVD in the player and played a movie to distract Vivi, who was too upset. After a few minutes she fell asleep. Joe started the engine and slowly rolled down the compound to the road. The night sky was clear, no clouds could be seen. Joe decided to drive over the highway that passed by the edge of the village. That was the shortest way to the other side of the village. When the short news came on the radio, it was reported that an unusually big storm front approached and could be expected with rapid weather change. Hail was predicted and it was advised not to take the highway. Joe was on the exact highway at that time. No cars were visible, and it was ghostly quiet out there. His gaze wandered to the dark, cloudless starry sky. There was no sign of a storm front. Which direction would she come from? Joe drove on. It was only a few minutes to the exit. As the radio began to rustle, he turned it off angrily and blamed the high-voltage lines that stretched on either side of the road.

Just before the highway exit, Joe looked up into the sky again. He tilted his head and peered up from the windshield, where he actually saw a storm coming up. It was pitch black within a few seconds, the moon, which had been so bright before, was suddenly covered by a black cloud cover. Joe turned on the fog lights so he had extra light and massively slowed down the speed. And then - completely unexpected a first lightning strike lit up the area. It was followed by a second, a third and finally a dozen. Lightning hissed past them everywhere. The surroundings were lit as bright as day and now Joe also saw why he should have avoided this road. In the car, which could serve as a Faraday cage, they were safe from electrical discharges, but what should they do if a power pole were hit or the wind was to buckle one of the isolated trees and throw it onto the road? The lightning whipped more and more furiously through the air, but this did not seem to bother Vivi. Snoring softly, she leaned her head against the windowpane.

The Lightning Strike

Shortly after Joe left the highway, it started to hail. He watched the storm with increasing displeasure. Such a storm could be very dangerous if you drove. He wanted to get home as soon as possible to bring himself and his sleeping wife to safety. Joe accelerated, concentrating on the lane, which was almost swallowed by the darkness. There it happened: an inconceivably bright light shone and a terrifying roar, a hiss and a humming, a drone as loud as 1,000 aircraft that started at the same time were heard. Joe was blinded. He hit the brakes and came to a halt on the curb. Lightning flashed simultaneously, the pylons some distance seemed to burst, the road wobbled as if the world were ending Sparks flew through the air and a few bushes on the roadside blazed in flames. The air around the old Carina was burning hot, the warmth seemed to scorch her. At that moment, a stone broke through the right-hand window, like a tennis ball, and hit Vivianne's head. She was bleeding and Joe was horrified tried to wake her, but had no success.

"My God, is she dead or just passed out?"

Suddenly, the car was set in motion without his intervention and Joe saw something indefinable. Starting from a point in front of them, the whole environment gradually became a viscous, sticky mass, not solid, but not liquid, and they moved right to the center. Reflexively Joe put the reverse gear in and accelerated. All attempts to get away from the disaster, however, were unsuccessful, the car was sucked faster and faster forward, although the engine was no longer running. Joe flowed down the sweat on his body, his hands clinging to the steering wheel and the noise did not stop. But the lightning storm had dried up and the surrounding darkness had enveloped them like a black cloth.

A jolt - and Joe fainted.

"Am I dreaming or am I dead?" Joe thought as he slowly came to himself. Through the car window he saw strangely glowing, white, red, violet, and yellow bullets that flashed past them at a furious speed.

With horror he suddenly remembered what had happened to his wife. "Vivi!" He turned to her. Still she leaned asleep at the car window. A fine, red trickle flowed from her long, brown hair and slowly dripped on her pink top, which she had put on for the 80s festival. He tried to wake her up, but once again was unsuccessful. At least she was not dead, he felt her breathing.

"What happened? Where are we?" He thought desperately.
Slightly hysterical, Joe laughed. The festival! Now he remembered clearly the incidents events of the night. They had been on the way home from the 80s festival. Interestingly enough, this seemed endlessly far away now. As if it were 100 years before It had not been more than half an hour since they had left.

If one believed the accounts of many people, he would probably soon have to see a white light at the end of a tunnel. But he saw nothing. He heard strange noises. Maybe someone had dumped something in the mineral water and he went crazy. Nothing seemed normal to him and again he fainted.

When Joe awoke, the car had come to a halt. The colored bullets of light had said goodbye and made room for a yawning black emptiness. Vivi was still unconscious beside him. He undid his seat belt and tried to get out of the car. The door was easy to open, but when he carefully put his foot on the ground, he did not feel it. The light inside the car was not enough to break the dense darkness that prevailed outside, so Joe decided to stay in the car until his thoughts cleared. Confused, he rubbed his eyes, then looked at his watch and noticed that it was not working anymore. There was only a black thing left on his wrist, completely burnt. Strangely enough, the interior of the car was not damaged at all. Only on the bonnet did he see a few black stripes in the spotlight and the window on Vivi's side that was broken by the stone. Joe tried to turn on the radio, but only biting noises came from the speakers. The device searched for frequencies and for a short while Joe saw MF on the screen 215.0 light up, a frequency he did not know, then the display went out and the radio gave up the ghost. "World class," he sighed.

The Awakening

Gradually it became light and outlines of the surroundings became visible. But everything was covered in a strange haze, so Joe could not get a clear picture. He felt as if he was slowly awakening from a deep dream. Had he just imagined everything? Had he passed out? He saw the contours of hills and shrubs begin to emerge and everything became sharp again. At that moment, Vivi woke up from her impotent sleep. Irritated, she looked around and held her head, which hurt.

"Where are we?" She asked. "What's happening?"

"I have not the slightest idea! You missed the best of the movie," Joe said ironically. Vivi looked at him questioningly.

"Sorry for the stupid saying. Honestly, I'm glad you're alive!" He leaned over and took Vivi in his arms. After that he described to her as well as he could the events that had occurred, even though he himself could scarcely believe what he was telling. But the strange environment was proof enough that something incredible had happened.

The street they were on was gone. Only a few concrete places between the stones testified that here - a very long time ago - once had to have been a paved road. The entire landscape was littered with these rocks. They were overgrown with moss and between them some small bushes kept themselves. The horizon was swallowed up by a hazy soup, and there were no elevations in the landscape except for small, moss-covered hills in the area. The sky was gray and foggy. Here and there were cable remains in the stone columns. The landscape looked completely impassable, abandoned and neglected. Now Joe also realized why he had not been able to feel any ground before: the left front wheel jutted into the air, as the car was stuck on a large chunk of stone.

Hesitantly, they hopped out of the car. Although the landscape looked rugged and craggy, they sank into a soft moss rug. The plants made a comfortable pad over the rocks.

"Where are we?" Vivi repeated.

Joe shook his head in disbelief. "Hit me as hard as you can. I think we only dream that."

Vivi responded to his request.

"Too hard," Joe said, rubbing his cheek, "I never thought you dare."

Vivi could not believe that she had just rocked Joe with full force. Apparently she was in shock. So it really was not a dream; it was reality. But where were they? Still on the highway, or what was left of it...? Had this storm destroyed the whole landscape or were they somehow catapulted into another dimension with their car? Only, how was that possible? And how on earth would they come back to their normal life? By no means with the car, the Carina could not cover a meter on this rough terrain. Here you would have needed a bulldozer.

"We can stay here," Joe said hopefully. "At some point, the rescuers will search the area. There is not such a storm every day, sweetheart. Someone's coming. Someone will come"

Both looked instinctively at the sky to see if they could see or at least hear a helicopter, but in vain. Not even birds were seen f in the gray haze, which surprised her. It was dead quiet. Vivi started to move restlessly. She did not want to wait for someone to come. In addition, she was hungry. Determined, she headed for one of the higher hills. "I'll be back soon," she called to Joe. "Wait in the car for so long!"

When she reached the top, the sight took her breath away: in front of her was the circular rim of a huge crater that looked as if a meteorite had hit where the little village once stood. But there was something else that caught Vivi's eye, something as bizarre and unexpected. On the horizon, she noticed the diffused image of several metallic-looking objects, which were almost swallowed by the fog. It seemed as if flying saucers the size of a soccer field were floating in the sky. This evoked a picture in her, she thought of old science-fiction movies from the 1950s and was even more confused than before. In vain she looked for the sun. She would like to approximately know what time it was about. But the whole sky lay under this strange veil of mist that dipped everything in a gray twilight.

"My God, how long have we been unconscious?" Vivi thought as she staggered down the slope back to the car.

Joe had run the heater to warm up the interior of the car. Fortunately, he had found remnants of the last purchase in the trunk. He was waiting for Vivi grinning with two 1.5-liter bottles of sweet drink and a bag of nacho chips with cheese flavor.

"Welcome to lunch, sweetheart," he greeted her as she returned from her trip after over an hour. This instantly lifted Vivi's mood and hungrily made their way over the chips. With the drink they were more cautious, who knew how long they had to endure far from civilization-?

Vivi told Joe everything she had seen up on the hill, and how absurdly the situation seemed to her, so strong was the tiredness that overcame her while discussing ~~her~~ their situation.

While they slept for a long time, the dim light outside became weaker and was replaced by the deep darkness. Towards morning, the dim light of the gray haze slowly reappeared.

Joe woke up first and everything was just as it was the day before: they were trapped in the same dimension, at the same time, in the same post-apocalyptic place. They had no food left and only about 2.5 liters of liquid left.
"Let's go," Joe announced, "I do not think anyone is looking for us here" So they set off on foot.

On the way they came across a smashed billboard made of plastic. It read "Tel Community for Live. Reserve your new iPhone Quantum now. For only 300 euros you are in the future! Offer valid until December 2050."

Without a word they exchanged a look. As they walked on, they saw the wreckage of an indefinable vehicle in front of them. It was also covered in moss like the boulders that lay everywhere, and with this camouflage integrated perfectly into the environment. They did not discover it until they were very close.

The vehicle resembled a car, but this form was unknown to them. At most in In sci-fiction magazines, they had seen such futuristic designs. The wreck had wheels that were stored in the fuselage. It looked like they were only released when needed. The cabin looked very battered. Vivi walked over to the part of the vehicle that looked like a door and clawed at the joints. She squeezed and pulled and heard a faint hiss and humming - and suddenly something moved. Part of the outer shell disappeared and you could see the interior.

Vivi screamed.

"Oh, God!" She called, turning her face away.

Joe pushed her aside to catch a glimpse. In the driver's cabin, in a decayed chair, perched a crooked skeleton. It bore a uniform with the inscription "New Germany, No. 1202," and on its right arm was a symbol that bore a strong resemblance to the swastika from Hitler's time. But they could not precisely define or classify the sign, it was too abstract, too unfamiliar.
Joe gently grabbed the skeleton by the arm and pulled it out of the vehicle. He dragged it behind a bush and left it there. They breathed deeply.

Vivi muttered, "Out of sight, out of mind."

Reluctantly, they sat down inside the vehicle. If they could get the thing going, this would be their chance to finally leave this endless rocky desert. At the point where the steering wheel would have been, there was an elongated keyboard with several buttons and switches. Suddenly the doors closed. The hologram of a woman's face appeared on the darkened windshield and a voice asked if the pilots wanted to activate the emergency program and send out an SOS message. Helpless, Joe looked at his wife. The moment he said to her, "I'm trying to activate it somehow," the computer recognized the speaker's intention by modulating the voice and confirmed, "SOS is being sparked. Emergency program is activated."

Something happened. The vehicle rumbled and in front of them, where the black windshield had previously been, a display appeared depicting the external environment. The inner part of the vehicle was very solidly equipped, even the largest crash could damage the capsule and the controller. Once the main power source failed, it seemed, an emergency generator automatically started. A note on the display showed Joe and Vivi that this was the case. Likewise, they saw on the control display that two drive nozzles were activated. Slowly the vehicle rose into the air and hovered slightly above the surface of the earth.

Impressed, Joe and Vivi glanced at each other. This technique fascinated her very much. You could only control the vehicle with your voice. Vivi asked the computer for the time and the answer was: "Current time: 12:07 noon." Next she asked for the date and other stored on-board data.

"Today's date: July the 21st of 2150. Launching of the Hovercars: 2110. Mileage: 1,380,024. Use: police cars. Current status of the emergency generators: 100 % charged. Emergency signal status: on air."
"We're in 2150?!?" Joe almost dropped his eyes out nearly as he looked at Vivi. This swallowed only empty.

"Give us general information about the year 2150!" Joe demanded.

"Average level of radioactivity: 0.4 Sievert. World population: 4.12 billion. Acute danger from C17 pandemic on the southern hemisphere. World power: New Germany."
"There are only 4 billion people left?" Joe asked Vivi questioningly.

Immediately the computer commented: "World population drastically reduced towards the end of the 2070s. Up to then, the world population had increased exponentially to its capacity limit. System collapsed. Acute scarcity of resources and food as well as epidemics, fueled by overpopulation, led to mass extinctions. Re-decimation of the world population in 2079, caused by global explosions of nuclear fusion reactors, sabotage is suspected."

"Stop!" Joe said, asking the computer, "How far back is your personal database?"

"Year of enumeration: 1900. All human beings have been recorded since January 1, 1900."

"Looking for Joe and Vivianne Dexter."

"Please specify."

"Joe Dexter, born in 1984, and Vivianne Dexter, born in 1986. Living in Nesslauen. No children, no criminal record. Parents Peter and Miriam Dexter. Died January 2023 in a car accident."

"Joe and Vivianne Dexter, disappeared in 2016. Wanted by New Germany, unauthorized experiments with time are suspected."

"Wow!" That overwhelmed Joe, so they were being searched on suspicion of having built a time machine? And sometime in the future, you noticed that? The situation was paradoxical.

"Search for Nesslauen!" Joe ordered.

"Village in Old Germany Population in 2052: 3212. Destroyed by a meteorite in 2053."

So that was the crater Vivi had seen from the hill. Curious, Joe continued, "Since when is it known that Joe and Vivianne Dexter have done time experiments?"

"First Findings: 01 August 2021. Unfortunately, the necessary technology to locate the two persons was missing."

"What's to happen if Joe and Vivianne are found?"
"Deportation to New Berlin. Subsequent interrogation. Death penalty."

"Death penalty?" Vivi stood up in horror.

"The whole thing is getting weirder," thought Joe. "We're looking for a time crime in the future!"

Stunned, the couple stared at each other. They were sentenced to death and did not even know what had happened. Or else might happen...

They Are Coming

Dejected, Joe and Vivi sat in the hovering vehicle. The computer patiently waited for further instructions.

"Why did this have to happen to us? How I would like to be at home in our beautiful home," Joe said in frustration.

Vivi remained silent, she could not speak. What the computer had just revealed was too much at once. When she got a little restrained, she answered softly, "Yes, Joe...Our dream of a shop disappears. Everything we wanted to build. The whole thing is suddenly worth nothing. Why did we set such plans and goals? Should we have enjoyed it more, Joe?"

Joe gave a resigned shrug. "It's too late for that. Let's look forward! What can we do? I just know we're wanted." At that moment, he got shivers up on his back.

"Vivi, we sent a distress signal before! Who will find us? What if it's a New Germany? We have just delivered ourselves to the enemy!"

"Let's get out of here. We need to get rid of the vehicle, they can locate us by it. Then we'll look for a suitable hiding place!"

Joe and Vivi strapped themselves in and then Joe started the vehicle with his voice. Slowly it flew silently over the rocks and bushes. He had specified a minimum speed. First he had to familiarize himself with the controls. The computer asked for the destination.

"Just go straight, eight, nine kilometers, I'll stop."

The computer voice replied, "Please specify."

"All right, go straight for eight kilometers. Increase speed."

"Please choose speed."

How fast would this thing go? Vivi ordered: "80 km/h!" And the computer accepted. Grinning, Joe looked at Vivi.

"It seems to be easy to drive this thing."

In between, information about the condition of the vehicle and the battery level of the emergency generator came from the loudspeakers. The display, which showed the environment, continued to show only stones and bushes. There was no other flying object in sight. Secretly, they breathed lightly. Nevertheless, they could be caught up quickly if someone searched the place from which they had sent the signal. Suddenly the vehicle slowed down.

"Target reached," the computer reported.

"Continue. 30km straight, speed 120km/h," commanded Joe.

As it looked, this stone desert was quite large. There was no sign of a civilization far and wide. For a brief moment, a green dot appeared on the far side of the screen, but it disappeared as quickly as it had come. Halfway there, the two of them suddenly recognized on the screen that a kind of airship was revealed close to them. Joe had read that they were investigating camouflage, but that they had actually done so well astonished him very much. The airship had perfectly integrated into the area until it was revealed.

A voice came from the speakers in the cockpit, and a man's voice said: "We've got your distress signal, please identify."

What now? What should Joe answer? Was that the police? Vivi recognized the same symbol on the strange ship as she had seen on the officer, and she whispered in Joe's ear, "It's you. There. The same sign as the dead policeman."

Joe was startled. "Are you sure?"

"Yes, look, it's clear."

"What should we do?" Joe asked his wife. "What do you think, how fast can we go with this thing?"

"No idea," Vivi replied. "Let's try it, it's definitely better than being captured."

Again, the alien ship said, "Please identify."

Joe ordered the computer full acceleration.

"Danger! Not recommended for full throttle," the on-board computer replied.

"Well, what do we have to lose? Are you ready?" Joe told Vivi.

"Yes, Joe."

"Full throttle, manual control," he ordered. The vehicle accelerated and both were pushed into their seats. They saw the display show a speed of 1,500km/h. Next to it was a kind of map.
Despite manual control, the ship avoided small obstacles, but still flew straight ahead. Joe ordered a course change to the right, the computer re-calculated and flew the modified route, but something did not seem right, the police ship was still right next to them.

"Oh, shit, we're too slow! Computer, identify the ship that follows us."

"Ship of Haunebu Class 6, small fighter, maximum speed 4,300 km/h."

"Well, we should have known earlier, so of course we have no chance."

Vivi hesitated: "Let's stop...Maybe the ship has something like an ejection seat, but that could be the technique."
"Wait a minute, I'll answer the fighter-hunter," Joe said, remembering the nameplate on the skeleton policeman's uniform. "Can you hear me? This is Mark Meier, No. 1202."

For a moment it was quiet, then the pilot of Haunebu responded.

"Mark Meier has been missing for six years. We will now take control of your capsule. Do not try to escape whoever you are, it would be pointless."

The alien ship was now steering their aircraft, and Joe could not even try to figure out if it had an ejection seat.

The two ships landed gently on the ground. With the high speed they had been able to maintain for such a short time, they had traveled a considerable distance within minutes. The area no longer resembled a rocky desert, but consisted of grassy areas and small wooded areas. In the background they could make out a civilization. Here, too, the sky was gray and overcast, and if you looked closely, you could see flying objects that were swallowed in the horizon by the haze.

The door of the small aircraft opened and Joe and Vivi got out. Out of the flying disk came three people clothed in black coats, with a swastika-like sign on their right upper arm.

"Oh, you shit, Vivi, what's this club?" Joe whispered.

A voice came to them: "Surrender, in the name of the Führer.(Leader) "If there is resistance" we use violence."

The couple could not believe it. Had a second Hitler come to power 200 years after the demise of Nazi Germany? Was that the future? Joe was just about to surrender, but suddenly there were shots from all around and the three strangers were hit and collapsed. Several people stepped out of the woods and dragged them away to a flying ship, well camouflaged in a small forest clearing. An explosion lit up the area and destroyed the Haunebu of the New Germany. Vivi called for Joe, and Joe called for Vivi. But before they knew it they were struck on the back of their heads.

The Anti-Technician

"Where am I?"

Joe looked for his wife, but there was no one except for a person wearing a sort of doctor's tunic.

"You're safe," the stranger said, "do not worry. You were not approachable for almost two weeks. The blow to the back of the head was necessary, but unfortunately you fell into a coma, I'm sorry, mister. Good that you're back among the living." The doctor winked gently.

"Mister? My name is Joe, Joe Dexter. Where is my wife?"

"Your wife is fine, she's recovering too. As soon as you come to power, I will take you to her. She's resting for now." The doctor began dribbling a serum into his veins with an infusion of jelly.

"I'm fine," Joe said. "I want to get up and go to my wife!"

Sighing, the doctor gave in. He did some more tests, then allowed Joe to get up slowly.

Joe looked around stealthily as he followed the doctor in a white flannel pajamas. The interior of the building looked like it had been built in earlier times - possibly from the 20th century. Considering that they were in 2150, Joe would have expected a more futuristic design with a lot of technology. But there was nothing like that here. The doctor's room alone was equipped with just a few technical items At the entrances stood guards everywhere. Joe wondered if the building was an old World War II bunker fortress.

"Sir," Joe said to his counterpart, who had also addressed him with an English title, "where am I?"

"Patience, patience, we'll explain everything to you, but first you should regain your strength. You have to eat, get fit." The doctor led him to a room where Vivi was waiting.

"Joe, there you are, finally you woke up! For nights I sat with you at your bed. I thought I'd lost you." She set aside the book she had been immersed in and ran to meet him.

"Now I am with you again, my dear. Are you alright?" Joe asked after hugging her tightly.

She nodded. "Yes, darling, everything's fine. Now eat, Joe, it's quite edible, the food here. And on an empty stomach you will not stand the news I have to tell you."

Three of them went to a dining room and sat down at one of the tables. There was a kind of stew. What was in it, Joe did not care, he just ate and it tasted good. In the meantime, the door had opened and a young man with black hair had approached them.

"Let me introduce our leader, Albert White," said the doctor.

"White? A German name?" Vivi asked, horrified.

"That's the way it is, yes. I am New-German.. But do not worry. I'm not behind the regime, I'm working for the antitank technicians, and maybe "leader" is a bit over the top because I'm just recruiting the recruits and keeping the personnel records. Well, Joe, now it's your turn, unfortunately I can not spare you, as I could not spare your wife. She already knows everything, and now it's your turn."

Joe finished the last bites and followed the young gentleman with Vivi into another room. The doctor had gone back to the infirmary. The room looked comfortable and even had a sofa. It was beige and reminded Joe of old movies from the 1950s.

"Joe, listen to me," the leader began. "We know you and know what happened. Investigations in various databases have shown that you disappeared during a thunderstorm, which happened almost 140 years ago. For some years you did not know what had happened to you. Even your car was untraceable. But then investigators found out that you probably fell into a time-lapse. Favored by an extremely strong lightning strike, which hit one of the overhead lines. Next to it was probably your car. They found shards of a car window in this place. When the lightning struck with such high energies that two of the opposite lines coupled ~~to~~ with one another, it must have resulted in a magnetic field, which tore a hole in ~~the~~ time, and you were pulled in. That you landed in our timeline is probably because you were trapped for some time in a dark room, the so-called Time Hole, which spit you out in the year 2150. Surely you are wondering what happened during that time? You certainly read a lot about oil shortage and scarce resources in your time. To prevent a shortage of energy, the first nuclear fusion power plant was commissioned in 2025. The widespread expansion of this technique was pushed forward, but nobody knew that the earth would endure only a certain number of such power plants. The production of these plants continued so rapidly that by 2050 already 75% and in 2057 nearly 100% of the earth could be supplied with nuclear fusion energy. It was an energy technology breakthrough. The reactors did not produce waste and it was mostly clean energy that was released. In the development of new cars and aircraft, a lot of money and effort was invested, so that the technology pace rapidly progressed. What no one knew was that the Earth's magnetic field changed due to the high level of nuclear fusion energy. 20 more years passed before the danger was eventually realized. But it was already too late. The necessary shielding would have taken another ten years, and shutting down the plants was impossible as it would have triggered a worldwide power outage. This would not only have meant crime and chaos, but also global terrorism and war, because all security systems would have been limited. In 2079, scientists tried using a new technique to bring the magnetic field lines back on track. The experiment went awry: one of the power plants exploded, or, one might say, imploded. It was followed by a chain reaction, which was unstoppable, but could be slowed down. Humanity had been granted two days to hide deep inside the mountains before the second explosion. The following detonations were within a few hundred Kilometers so strong that nothing and nobody survived on the surface of the earth. The force of the explosion was unprecedented, stronger than countless atomic bombs. When all the power plants were destroyed, after a few months they dared to go back up into the open air. It was a sight of the horror that offered itself to humans. Everything was desolate and bare. Since then, the sky has been permanently covered by a gray haze several kilometers thick, and we now suspect that the power plants were manipulated years before by the New Germany. We know clear weather only from old photos in databases. A miracle that the world has survived, and strangely enough, nature recovered faster than anyone had ever hoped. No one knows why, but only a short time after the explosions, nature began to sprout again. Tree growth exploded and within a few years they formed magnificent crowns. However, the fauna had suffered a powerful setback. Countless animal species were extinct because of the misfortune. There are almost no free-living mammals and birds left on earth today. Only insects and worms could stay alive along with marine animals, which had had a natural shield by the water masses. In reserves, clones of most mammals were raised from stem cells. So you could artificially rebuild the wildlife. But in the wild I have met no animal for many years. There are almost no free-living mammals and birds left on earth today.

"On the political level, too, a lot has changed. Unfortunately, not for the better...perhaps in your time you heard the conspiracy theories about the National Socialists. These have proven to be correct. In the Antarctic a civilization ~~has~~ had formed after the Second World War. They called themselves New Germany and their leaders stated that they came from the Third Reich. To date, however, this has not been proven. Nevertheless, followers of the theory believe that the New Germans already had fabled technologies. Allegedly, they are said to have owned flying discs, and it is believed that behind many UFO sightings were actually those flying discs.

"Whether this is all correct or not is an open question. In any case, after the global explosions, a far-right group has cold-bloodlessly exploited the vulnerability of the population to the catastrophic conditions and seized power. They call themselves New Germans and established a steel-hard regime throughout Europe. The political borders, as you know them from your time, no longer exist. Today Europe is called New Germany. The regime has annexed innumerable lands. Only the Ukraine and some Balkan countries did not bring them into their possession - the Russians were faster.

"The new regime was able to build an incredibly strong army within a few years. Those who did not voluntarily follow ideologies were forced to do so when tortured. So they soon had over a million warriors. These were mixed with clones that have pronounced genes of aggression and no compassion. The New Germans also upgraded massively. Today they are in possession of airships as big as several football fields, a huge combat aircraft fleet and various beam weapons.

"Unfortunately, there are very few people who fight back against the New Germans, only the New Allies and of course we anti-technicians..."

The leader was interrupted by Joe. "What's the name supposed to mean, anti-tech ...?" he said curiously.

"Well," Albert White continued, "we call ourselves that because we oppose the technology of the New Germany. What the New Germany have already developed since they took power is dizzying. They have extremely well-trained engineers, programmers and technicians in their ranks. The rest of the world lags far behind them in terms of innovation potential, know-how and state of development. But we doubt that this know-how is good...ultimately, the increasingly extreme technologies will bring the world to an end, we are convinced. We have already seen it in nuclear fusion reactors. At the beginning it was a noble idea...to produce clean energy and to relieve the environment. But man is insatiable. He could not stop building some power plants. No, the whole globe had to be tapped. And now we've paid the price." Albert White shook his head sadly, then started to speak again.

"Basically, we can not do anything about the New Germans. They are far superior to us. The only organization that can possibly hold its own against the regime is that of the New Allies, also called the Rebels. They have bases all over the world and have allied themselves with all countries that have not been taken over by the regime of the New Germany. Their goal is a fall of the regime. Already for the near future, attacks on New Germany by the rebels are planned. At the moment, however, they are not yet ready for a large-scale deployment. They are still struggling with the losses of the first wave of attacks six months ago. At that time, they made painstaking acquaintance with the high-tech weapons of the New Germans and had to flee much faster than planned. Russia is not interfering yet and America remains neutral until now. We're in the middle of a war here, Joe! At the moment it is relatively quiet, but who knows when New Germany strikes again..."

Joe had to swallow empty. It was really hard food to digest. He looked at Vivi from the side and she looked up at him with a raised eyebrow.

"And what about the New Allies as anti-technicians?" Vivi asked.

"Well, we're doing some kind of cooperation. We supply them with information. We anti-technicians are specialists in research, you know. Fighting is not our thing, we leave that to the rebels. But in obtaining information, we are unbeatable. Our archives and databases are the most comprehensive in the world and are maintained very accurately. We have a complete collection of all knowledge on earth that includes all the facts and historical data as well as a database that is updated with personal data every second. The only area where we use technology." Albert White smiled apologetically.

"So why did you find out so quickly that we're talking about Joe and Vivi Dexter in 2016?" Vivi asked.

"Very attentive, young lady," replied Albert White. "We overheard your distress call. We always do that..." the leader smiled. "How else should we stay up-to-date?" The last statement sounded like a justification to Vivi.

"For some time now we have been able to connect to the radio system of the New Germany. So far unnoticed, though they have such good technicians," the leader smiled. "That's how we absorb very important information. When your emergency call came, our database immediately found out that it had been sent by a ship that was missing with the pilot.

For six years. This irregularity has triggered an alarm. But not only with us. Through our interception system, we've seen the New Germans scan your aircraft to decrypt your DNA. You did not notice that," Albert White said as he saw Joe and Vivi's questioning faces.

"Your DNA was then matched against the database and yielded a hit. As simple as that."

"Where did our DNA come from in the database?" Vivi continued. "In our day, there was still something like privacy, because you could not just take DNA samples from people and thus fill a database!"

"This was taken for granted after you two had disappeared from your time. You were searched for, for many years, and were considered missing. Forensics has had taken your whole house apart to get clues. At the time, your DNA data was decrypted and stored on the basis of hair and dander that they found."

"Well, I'm really impressed!" Joe said appreciatively. "But why are we here? You saved us from the New Germans..."
"That is correct. Well, actually it was the rebels. After we identified you, we immediately informed the rebels. They had to act extremely fast, as it was clear that the New Germany would be on the spot immediately. The verdict that would have been imposed on you two would have been interrogation and capital punishment, as you already know. It was therefore essential that the rebels arrived at your whereabouts before the New Germans or at least at the same time as they. Fortunately, the rebels were on the spot in

good time before the New Germans could put them in their aircraft and deport you to New Berlin. Why do we do this for you, Joe? Well, everyone who is against New Germany is our friend. And we're keen on your account of the journey through time!" Albert White looked expectantly at Joe.

Almost as extensive as the leader had previously told his account, Joe described Vivi's and his experiences. "Well, so here we are," he concluded. "What can we do for you, Albert?"

"It's best you keep quiet and do not let yourself be seen outside. Haunebu 6 and 7 fly everywhere. You have already made acquaintance with a six, the sevens are a lot faster. It flies up to 70,000km/h faster. However, this is just the maximum possible speed. Throughout the globe there is a speed limit of 9,000km/h. These are guidelines for international air traffic and even the New Germans have to adhere to it, because if this speed is exceeded atmospheric disturbances occur which also affect the New Germans. They use the sevens mainly for exploring Europe and the rest of the world, as well as for space travel, where the speed limits are unlimited. Then there is also the Achter series, which is used exclusively for space travel. We do not know anything about it, but there are rumors that the Moon Station Alpha Two will be upgraded on the far side of the Moon for interplanetary flights. The aircraft of the Achter series can reach almost the speed of light. We suspect that the New Germans are still looking for the 67 light years distant star system Aldebaran, or the theoretical ancestors who they suspect are there. They have not given up hope of meeting Aldebaran's one day. If it is up to the theories of the New Germans, that is, our forefathers.

"Joe, we'll bring you back from this fortress to the rebels tomorrow, since tomorrow is a holiday and the circumstances are very favorable. The patrols that fly are heavily reduced. The rebels will then try to bring you to America and to safety. There your chances of survival would be many times higher and you could lead a reasonably normal life. We are here in the middle of Europe, in the fortress of the New Germans. Although we antitank technicians live in well-secured bunkers deep inside the earth and have a well-functioning self-sufficiency system, I still think you'll fare better in America than a lifetime in our bunkers. We're used to it, Joe, but you do not know how to be locked up. *You* were really lucky that you entered the year 2150 in an abandoned wasteland. The New Germany avoid this place due to the topography. This may also be the reason why no one had discovered this officer's ship earlier. There are no patrols flying there. Imagine that you appeared in the middle of New Berlin. Then the rebels would not have had a chance to bring you to us. I'll show you our whole complex, and tomorrow you'll have to get up early and travel to a secret meeting place. Luckily we were able to get a Haunebu 7 in our possession. We've discovered how to change its disguise and managed to bypass the automatic tracking system, but we did not get any further, the technology is just too advanced. Our scientists work on it day and night. At some point we will have encrypted its functionality and handed it over to the rebels so they can use it to attack."

After heading through the huge complex and all the breaking information, Joe's head was full *and* he needed to rest. Politely, he inquired if it would be possible to retire to the bedchamber. He talked to his wife about everything they had learned and tears came to Vivi.

"Do not worry, we can do it. I'll always be with you and take care of you. Let's go to sleep. Tomorrow we have to be fit to make the dangerous transfer to the rebels," he said, lying in his arms on the comfortable double bed offered to them.

The professor

Despite the softness of his bed and exhaustion, Joe could not sleep, and he kept seeing the thunderstorm. Why did this happen to us? He still could hardly believe it. As he rolled around in bed, he tried everything to finally reach the land of dreams. Astonishingly, Vivi slept well for a long time. What did she dream about? The thought of what would happen next morning did not release him from his worry. What if the New Germans saw them? What had happened to her house, the dog and everything else? Did a meteorite actually pulverize all its belongings? Was it still at the same place at this time? I hope someone had offered Matador a good home. How did your parents feel? Or have they been dead for a long time? His head was full of questions. Even though he was very tired, Joe straightened himself, put on his shoes, and searched for the snack room.

Everything was quiet, only at a distance he heard some guards chatting. The light burned everywhere in the corridors. A short man with long hair and glasses came towards him. His appearance reminded Joe of that of a zombie.

"Good night, you're the new one?"

"Right, Joe is my name, I'm glad to meet you."

"Everyone here calls me the professor. I saw on the surveillance cameras that you came out of the dorm, what's going on?" He shook hands warmly with Joe.

"I'm on my way to the lunchroom," Joe replied.

"I'll accompany you, if that's all right with you. Since you are still awake, I can discuss some details with you tomorrow. By the way, I'll be on the whole mission."

The professor was like able to Joe at first sight. However, he looked quite young for a professor. He could hardly be older than 38 years. But they would definitely get to know each other better.
Arriving in the lunchroom, the professor approved a bar of chocolate and a glass of coke. Joe was content with the drink.

"There's still Coke after 130 years?"

"Yes, at least it's almost the same as in the 21st century. Now and then the rebels can attack a transporter of the New Germans. In exchange for our information, we sometimes receive deliveries of goods. Coke is rare. It is still very popular. The recipe contains small amounts of cocaine, but also a substance that prevents you from becoming addicted. So you have fast power when you drink the stuff. Incidentally, the sugar was replaced by artificial substances. It has almost no calories, but that was already the case in your time. Only the chemical additives are quite different today."

"Well, it tastes the same," Joe remarked.

He enjoyed the cool drink. Maybe it was the last time he could consume such a thing. Who knew what would happen tomorrow?

"Well, Joe, I can give you some more information," the professor continued the conversation. "The more you know about the New Germans and their practices, the better. You have already been informed about a few copies of your fleet yesterday. There are, however, other models with which they operate. The first series of the Haunebu for example. These aircraft are only three meters in diameter, but should not be underestimated. They act as small guardians of buildings and are very agile.

"You should also beware of the "peace birds". The name should not be taken too seriously, as they are by no means peaceful. It's a new kind of drop-wing type airplane, something similar to a plane from your time, I think the F-14 as it was known back then. The soldiers who jump out of it carry "wing suits", which they can open in free fall. So they are able to land almost anywhere. Since the "peace birds" need little fuel, the New Germans have massively increased their fleet with these models and recruited thousands of soldiers as jumpers. The planes look like huge birds of prey and are also extremely dangerous. Do not even try to shoot at them, you would just waste ammunition." When the professor noticed Joe's questioning look, he added, "Well, Joe, it may be necessary to fight back. Do not think that your flight to America will be a picnic.

"The rebels have already managed to shoot down some "peace birds", but they still have too few effective weapons to do any significant damage. The best they have in their arsenal against the flying birds is the microwave weapon n. They send - similar to your time the microwave ovens -   short impulses that can put the enemy aircraft out of service. If you point

50

this weapon at people, they are dead within seconds. Unfortunately, you can only fire three shots per minute, the energy requirement is enormous. So think twice about firing on three people, or on a spaceship that's out of action for at least 30 seconds, out of which as many as 100 soldiers could get out. The rebels did it on a successful mission which they stunned the ship first - that's what we call the 30 second dysfunction - and then destroyed it with a ray torpedo. Without the deactivation by the microwave-drops, that's our nickname for the weapon, the ray torpedoes unfortunately do not work. Around the aircraft exists a kind of force field from which the rays bounce off. Unfortunately, both the microwave-drops and the beam torpedoes are hard to come by. So always use it sparingly! By the way, have you been informed that you will be killed if the New Germans get hold of you? First, your knowledge is sucked out and stored in a mainframe and then you get an injection and are dead within milliseconds. The bodies are plasticized and put on display. Above you would be a big inscription: These were time manipulators. That's what happens to anyone who spies on us."

For a while they sat in silence at the table. The professor had a melancholy expression. With sad eyes he just stared into space.

"What's up, Professor?"

The professor answered with a shake of the head. "Nothing. Everything in perfect order. Well, more or less. I know how you must feel to have lost a loved one. For some time now, my wife Mary has been imprisoned by the New Germany. We were there when the rebels raided a van. I could escape, but unfortunately not her. I do not even know if she's alive. Most likely her head has already been severed, which is the maximum punishment for us opponents. Other crimes, such as theft, burglary and so on, are punishable by lethal injection or life imprisonment. But secretly, I hope she is still alive. They will try to catch me as well. All coordination is over here, you know, Joe. If they catch me, they would still lack the mainframe of the anti-technician."

"I'm so sorry for you." Joe knew exactly how he felt. But at least he had not lost his wife. That made the whole situation reasonably bearable. That Vivi was at his side gave him strength and hope. Tears ran down the professor's cheeks, and Joe did not know what to say. As the man regained his composure, he started to report details: "We'll leave at 08:00a.m. tomorrow and walk, that's safer. The path leads 20 miles to a remote place, which is very rarely monitored by patrols. We have to travel ten kilometers before we can go into a dense forest. There is a base of rebels in an abandoned bunker. We will spend the night there and the next day trek over a mountain range to the whereabouts of Haunebu 7 arrive. The march will be exhausting. We will only be three, because with any more, the sooner we will be noticed. We will bring three small beam weapons, which in case of emergency are not efficient enough. They are only sufficient for rudimentary self-defense. Should it come to an attack and the New Germans massively outnumber us, it is best to shoot yourself. Otherwise, they will arrest you and torture you until you confess. These are torture methods that in the 21st Century you did not know of. For example, they are connected to a computer, and your brain is stimulated so much with impulses that it feels like you're arm is being cut off. Neither do you die or there is any mess that you have to clean afterwards. You will, however, feel unbearable pain. It is your decision."

``How do you know all that, Mr. Professor?'' Joe asked skeptically.

"I was captured myself, but I managed to outwit the guards, and so I took over the entire Haunebu. That is the ship we own. That was before my wife Mary met her fate."

"Oh, you are the hero who managed to capture such a ship? The leader told me about it."

"That's how it happened Unfortunately, I and my team have not yet been able to replicate the technique, if one wants to say so. The New Germans are working with systems I am not familiar with, and neither databases nor historical documents have anything to suggest. Unfortunately, much of the data was destroyed during the big explosions. I just managed to turn off the tracking system and change the cloaking device. That's not how they usually see us. If we manage to reach the Haunebu 7, we have a chance to escape the New Germany! You can trust me, Joe. But when it gets serious, I'll save my own soul, understand?"

"Yes, understood."

"You should do the same."

Joe was shaking.

"Here, take one of these. This pill will help you fall asleep. However, you should go to bed shortly thereafter, otherwise you will fall over. The stuff works well."

"All right, I'll go. Good night, Professor, thanks for everything. I'm sorry about your wife."

"It's okay."

The professor remained alone in the lunch room, his head lowered. Joe went back to the bedroom. Vivi was still asleep, and Joe looked at her, so happy and satisfied, her long, brown hair lightly covering her face. Her mouth was half open and from time to time a few indefinable sounds came from it.

"How beautiful she is," Joe thought as he lay down next to her. Slowly his eyes closed.

The Walk to the Bunker of the Rebels

"People, get up! It's 7:00 am, we're leaving in an hour!"

It was the professor who woke them up. He looked relaxed. "You have plenty of time to freshen up. I have already packed your things, the contents of the backpacks consists of five cans of energy drinks, two vitamin pills and two food preparations. The small, cheap-looking box that you will also find is a mobile navigation device that shows you the surroundings on the display. You will need it and it can be mounted on the wrist."

The device actually did looked cheap, but when Joe turned it on, it amazed him. In the highest resolution on the display appeared the space in which they were, and he could manually select the indicator radius, so Joe could look at the closer and wider environment.

"Wow, not bad a hologram projector, only that you can also look into the buildings, awesome, I've always dreamed of something like that," he said enthusiastically.

The professor smiled. "Now you're coming, we're leaving at 08:00a.m.."

But Vivi resisted. The day before, she had agreed to flee, but today everything seemed different.
"What's going on, Vivi?"

"I can not go, I do not want to."

"We already discussed that yesterday. Everything is prepared, we can not help it. What else should we do here?"

"I'm not coming." Vivi's tone became aggressive.

Joe did not like the sudden change of heart. Everything was prepared and now she would back down at the last moment? She knew he would not leave without her. How could she endanger her whole future? He had thought she would stand by him any time. Joe felt a nervous discomfort that made it rumble in his stomach. Stressed, he shouted at her: "Dammit, do you want to die here? What about our future? Did not you even want kids? Be reasonable!"

Vivi went pale. Joe did not respond for a while. "I'm scared, Joe. I do not wanna die. Of course I want children. How many will we have, honey?"

"If you want, we'll have a dozen."

"Joe, I love you very much, you should know that I will always stand by you."

"Yes I know."

He took Vivi in his arms and hugged her tight. "Come on, we have to go."

Just before the march, they were given their weapons, and the professor told them what to look for. "All you need to do is aim well enough, the things are set to automatically detect people or other objects and make corrections of their own accord. Note, however, that continuous firing is not possible, the energy storage must be recharged again and again. This is done automatically with the integrated micro generator, on the integrated display you can see the status of the weapon. So shoot at short intervals. Along the way, you can take a few test shots. Now go!"

They walked together through the corridors of the complex and approached a gate that led into a tunnel. At this point, the leader said goodbye, who had previously accompanied them for a while.

"Take care of yourself!" He said as he squeezed their hands. "We will not contact you, that's safer. Otherwise, the New Germans could hear the message and locate you. Only when you reach the rebels will the professor send us an encrypted message."

With a queasy feeling, Joe and Vivi set off in the tunnel accompanied by the professor. They had known that the anti-technician complex lay beneath the earth's surface. Now they were extremely glad of this fact, as they were now able to march underground through the Neo-Germanic territory, without the risk of being seen by anyone. Only after four kilometers the tunnel would lead to the earth's surface, but they would be in an unpopulated area. Then to hope that no aircraft discovered her.

After almost an hour's walk through the straight tunnel, a gate blocked their way.
"This is the end," the professor said. "Now it's daylight. Let us be careful!"

With his strong flashlight, which had served them well all the way, he shone it on a niche containing a device with a keypad. After the professor had typed in a code, the heavy door silently slid aside and disappeared into the tunnel wall. Behind the hatch was a small room. Bars of iron led up the wall. The professor did not hesitate and started to climb. Vivi followed him and Joe was below her. Just before they reached the surface of the earth through a shaft, the professor again typed a code into a device mounted in the wall. With a soft sound sibilant, the lid of the shaft unfolded.

Carefully, the professor pushed the lid a little further and peered into the area. It was quiet, there was no aircraft noise. The likelihood was great that there were no living things nearby.

"Let's go," the professor muttered, swinging to the surface. When Vivi and Joe stood beside him on the ground, they saw that the manhole cover they had just climbed through was well camouflaged by moss and vegetation. If you did not know exactly where you were, you could never find the secret entrance to the anti-technician complex. Fearfully, Vivi looked around. Her heart was racing wildly. If the New Germans would discover them, their chances would be zero. She figured that any second an aircraft would pop up and shoot her down. There were not even many ways to hide. They were in a plain sight in the open field, and except for a few trees there was no shelter.

"Now comes the dangerous part," the professor said. "The next kilometer and a half we have to walk almost without cover. Then we get to a hill where there are at least a few boulders. If any enemy appears, you must be prepared. It would be good if you did some more target practice. Do you see the two trees over there? Joe, shoot it. Just a quick push on the trigger."

A bit awkwardly, Joe picked up his beam weapon and aimed at the nearer tree.

"Sllllllrr!" The stream was fast, hitting the tree trunk in the middle so that it immediately pulverized at the struck spot and the rest of the tree fell to the ground a ~~lot~~.

Perplexed about the weapon's efficiency, Joe turned to the professor.

"What, this weapon is not meant to cause much damage? A large part of the tree was simply pulverized."

"That's the way it is. You'll soon realize that the New Germans own weapons that far exceed the firepower of this one here. They also have guns to stun you. They can only fire them from a short distance, so watch out for your navigation device, it will warn you as soon as anyone moves around them. Well, Vivi, the second tree is yours", the professor told her

Vivi shivered, but she kindly performed her test shot and realized it was not that difficult. The weapon corrected the run itself and hit the target in the middle. As the second tree lay on the ground, they moved on.

"You're probably wondering about the helmets," the professor said as he walked across the plains at a swift pace.

Joe nodded. "Yes, what do you need them for?"

"Helmets only have the task of hologram projection and information display via head-up displays. Some soldiers also have a mobile force field, but we do not know much about that. We saw rebels firing at officers who did not move. Everything bounced off of them. The only weak point these force fields have, we suspect, are old weapons from your time. These penetrate the force field effortlessly due to the low bullet velocity. For reasons unknown to us, the force fields do not recognize the old lead bullets as a threat. Unfortunately, these weapons are hard to come by. But our leader, for example, owns one."

On the way, they suddenly saw some slices circling in the sky far away. Vivi's blood froze, but the planes were too far away for them to be discovered.

"What's the range of this scanner?" Joe asked.

"About 500 meters, but the stunning rifles have to go down to 300 meters close before they can shoot with them. So you have a little more time if you are discovered. If there is a river nearby, jump in. For some reason, the detection systems of the New Germans can not find us in it, maybe the water acts as a mirror and deflects the beams of the search devices", the professor explained. "Maybe the New Germans have fixed that mistake now, but I'd try. Oh, I almost forgot. Here,an earpiece we can use to communicate with, should we not be able to get that close together." As he spoke, the professor reached into his pocket and handed Vivi and Joe a small button each.

"There's a small push button, you see, so you can choose between two variants, Talking Normal and Talking Thought Funk. We communicate with each other by thinking. But do not worry, the device only recognizes thoughts that want to be sent. For example, if you want to tell Vivi how much you like her, just think: Send to Vivi. I like having you. The simulation is so real that you might think that the other person is standing next to you. This technology replaced the mobile phones and all other communication devices 80 years ago. It is also possible to transmit picture messages. The recipient sees the picture in front of him - great right? A multi functional toy with some interesting additional options, even controlling vehicles is made possible by wireless connection. Your current physical condition and vital signs are also recorded and can be transferred to partners. However, you will hardly need most of the functions, the complete infrastructure like your Internet does not exist any more, even friendship networks like your "Facebook" no longer exist. The New Germans abolished everything and built their own networks. Ingenious toy or what?"

"Absolutely," Joe nodded enthusiastically as he put the button in his ear and passed the second to Vivi. "That's what I wanted in my time." In front of them they already saw the slope of the hill, which they had to ascend.

"In an hour and a half we reach the highest point, from where you can survey large parts of the area. The reception is particularly good at altitude, so we will pair our three sat nav devices there, so that the receive power will increase tenfold. Within five kilometers, we can then locate all living things. This is the best way to secure ourselves and get a good picture of the surroundings. On the other side of the hill begins a large forest. As soon as we are in the undergrowth, we can take a break and have something to eat. Unfortunately, we can not risk that before. After another ten kilometers march we will reach the bunker of the rebels."

Silently they began the ascent, but the professor was apparently in a narrative mood. It rarely passed a few minutes without him speaking.

"Do you remember what I told you about the peace birds, yes? If they come, don't shoot them, as I said. They are way too fast. Hide and wait for the soldiers to jump off. But remember, if peace birds do come, there is always somewhere a small or a larger mother-ship nearby. So you do not really have time to wait, you will be located right away. Run as fast as you can. Seek protection in a body of water. And throw away your scanners, the New Germans will find them first. Although the scanner does not send a signal, it emits a small magnetic field and they think they are human. This detracts from your own magnetic field. You then stay maybe two to three minutes. Unfortunately, it is not much."

After drinking a can of energy drink, the three marched on. Suddenly they heard music in the distance, which the wind carried to them It was a kind of trance mixed with old songs from the Wehrmacht. "Be glad we're not around, this music is brainwashing, it puts you in an indefinable state of happiness and obedience. The music has some wavelength that stimulates the happiness hormones. It is addictive. It all sounds very confusing to you, but a lot has changed in those 150 years. For example, the year 2042 was the motto of technology worldwide. There was a fund, and anyone who had invented anything could submit their project and, when approved, received the necessary financial resources for development. Patents were abolished and everyone had access to the latest technologies. This should have helped poverty reduction in the world. Well, as you can see, technology has become the biggest danger...Duck!" The professor shouted.

A Haunebu 6 flew over them.

"Did they see us?"

"I can not say for sure, but we'd probably be dead or captive if they saw us."

Joe and Vivi shuddered as the professor continued, "Normally such a ship would not miss any opponents. Perhaps an urgent mission was in progress."

The ship had already vanished from sight,and the three of them took a deep breath.

"Go on!" Vivi urged. "We're almost to the top of the hill."

After calibrating their sat nav devices, they began the descent. Soon they came into a dense forest. The tall firs and undergrowth gave them the feeling of security. Nevertheless, a scanner of the New Germans would be able to locate their magnetic fields. They were safe only in the bunker of the rebels. Fortunately, the ten kilometers through the forest ran without incident.

Destination Haunebu

With aching legs and tired from the long march, the three arrived at the bunker of the rebels in the evening. The entrance was well camouflaged and was under a natural cluster of bushes. The professor activated the opening of the trapdoor with a code. They climbed the metal rungs down into the depths of the forest floor and entered a large, underground bunker. It smelled rotten and it was wet and cold.

"This is where we set up camp, they will not be able to locate us here, the bunker walls are insulated so there is no radiation to scan us. It all looks like a natural collection of water on their scanners."

"Great, we're sleeping in the water," Joe grinned.

"What's weird about that?" Vivi responded defiantly. She was hungry and exhausted.

"Oh, come on, shall we spoil our spirits because of these new Germans?"

"Joe,You must be crazy You should be beaten up, you idiot."

"All right, I'll shut up, excuse me."

"Is there something to eat in this bunker?" She asked the professor, without acknowledging Joe's apology. "We should be able to get something edible," the professor said. On the one hand he was amused by the small quarrel of the two, on the other hand he missed his wife.

Together they walked through the only door that led out of the great room to find a kitchen or pantry. They did not have to search for a long time, they found what they were looking for in the next room. Each took a few of the packages that were stored on a shelf, then returned to the large room and began eating the dietary supplements. Each piece was in a sealed foil and resembled a compressed protein bar. It tasted like nothing, but it was filling.

When they had filled their bellies, they took the sleeping bags out of their rucksacks and made themselves comfortable on the empty cots in the room as best they could. Joe cuddled up to his wife and both fell asleep exhausted. The professor had taken a book with him and read a little more in the light of his flashlight. It bore the title of "Expelled from Home" and dealt with the 20th century and an Iraqi refugee who later came to power. He glanced at the screen, which was mounted in the wall and connected to a night-vision camera that showed the exterior around the manhole. Soon, however, the professor nodded, half-sitting, half-lying, the book slipping from his hand.

Joe woke up in the middle of the night. "What was that?" He mumbled and sat up.
"Nothing. Go back to sleep," Vivi said, half asleep.

"I heard something!"

"Then check the screen."

It rustled again. The camera not only delivered a high-resolution picture, but also an impressive sound quality.

"It's an animal, a fox! Professor!" Joe whispered excitedly. The Professor woke up, yawning heartily and blinking at Joe, who was fascinated and pointing at the screen. "Look at this! Their leader told me there were almost no animals left."

"Yes, that's right, I have not seen a single mammal in the wild since birth."

"There you see one."

The professor's eyes almost dropped out of his head, so overwhelmed was he.

"Nature seems to recover quickly, there are still wild animals," he exclaimed enthusiastically. He quickly grabbed a notebook from his backpack and began to sketch the look of the fox, fascinated. He could not wait to report this to the anti-techs. His people would become jealous and question him. Again a reason to stay alive.
Joe smiled. "We have seen many foxes in our time. Our house was in the immediate vicinity of the forest edge. In the evening they often came very close."

The professor was impressed by this story. "If this war comes to an end, I will come to America and we will try to open a window of opportunity. I wish I was in your time. It must have been nice."

"Yeah, that's it." Only then did Joe realize that you should enjoy every situation and be grateful that you were allowed to live. Even if you had no food, you still had something to enjoy. Vivi, however, had not been enthusiastic about the fox, but slept on, turning her back on Joe. Joe also soon fell asleep. The professor, however, watched the fox until his eyes closed.

The next morning, Joe woke up first.

"People, wake up, it's bright out there." The professor and Vivi slowly opened their eyes and stretched. After drinking a squeezed bar and a drink, they rolled up their sleeping bags and climbed to the surface of the earth. Outside, they received a pleasantly warm summer's day when the sun was swallowed by the dense haze.

"It would have been better if it had rained," the professor said. "The last section will be dangerous. The festival is over today and the New Germans will fly many patrols again. All right, let's go."
Resigned, Joe and Vivi looked at each other and started silently. Joe had a slight sore muscles, Vivi blisters on both heels. After two hours of permanent marching, they emerged from the forest and came to a large, grassy plain.

"Now it's only two more kilometers," the professor said. "We going to make that! The Haunebu is hidden in an underground bunker. The path leads along a river, an ideal location. Should the New Germans approach before we get to the bunker, we can save ourselves in the river and swim away."

What they did not know was that the river was no longer a river, but an illusion. A deceptively real one, and one would only notice if it was too late. Nor did the three suspect that the ship that had flown over them yesterday had tracked them down. However, the day before had actually been involved with an order and had no time to land immediately and capture the three strangers. But the New Germans had recorded and calculated the marching speed and direction, where they would find the approximate location of the trio again. They had expected the three to march through the forest and were already in position in the haze with their airships. Thanks to their scanners they could see through the fog very well. They had also placed ground troops. Thanks to their cover, they were invisible, so to speak. They had not taken the loss of their Haunebu with ease. They knew the ship needed to be hidden somewhere in the area, but so far they had not been able to find a trace of it. Who knew, perhaps the three figures were anti-technicians and would now show them the way.

The three hikers walked along the riverbank. Everything had gone well, they were almost at their destination, so they thought they were safe and their precautions suffered. Nobody looked at the scanner. The New Germans were everywhere, well camouflaged. Nothing was heard, nothing was seen, not even the wind whistled. There was deathly silence, only the crackling of the shoes of the three on the stony ground could be heard.

"How fast everything passes," Joe thought. "Just now we were at this party, enjoying ourselves, and now we're here, in a future 150 years away from home. Time travel is possible, God! What you could prevent with it all! What if the Allies had acquired this technology? Could you have used it to defeat the New Germans?"

He felt disgusted by the fact that the future had actually achieved nothing better than creating another power-hungry, brutal dictator. Anger rose in him, a rage he had never felt. All the equal rights, the tolerance and the good intentions of the 21st Century had not come to anything. It was hard to believe that humanity had once again embraced such a person; one should have learned something. Joe had always thought that all that UN and EU nonsense did not help. The people would always run after the person who felt safest. Now it was this new leader. Joe did not know his name, and he did not want to know him either. One thing he realized, he wanted to change something. He would not retire in America, he would build up a new force against the New Germany

The three approached their destination.

"We made it quickly." The professor stopped, pointing to a spot in the grass that looked like any other. "Look, there's the secret entry at the front. The Haunebu awaits under our feet."

But just then Joe felt a slight blast and fell over. The others did the same, as the New Germans shot and stunned them. All of a sudden, three soldiers came out of nowhere and seized the companions. They dragged them into a flying machine, which had also been discovered shortly before, and flew away

Almost at the same time a deafening noise sounded. An explosive charge had been dropped and ripped open the ground. As a result, the underground bunker was exposed, in which the Haunebu 7 had been kept safe until that day. There followed a ray torpedo, which hit the flying disk and it burst apart with a huge explosion. It was the last thing the professor saw when he regained consciousness for a short time. Any hope was lost. The only ship they had was destroyed. Then he was stunned again and lumped down. Joe, Vivi, and the professor were dragged to a small cell protected by a force field. It was no larger than two by two meters. They were not even able to stand in it, it was probably a cargo space. Unconscious, they layed on the floor of it and were shipped to New Berlin. They did not even have the time to shoot themselves to avoid the threat of torture.

Captured

It was pitch black. Slowly Joe felt for his flashlight and lit up the room. He was blurry and shook oddly. But gradually the outlines became clearer again. The veil slowly moved away from the eyes of the three, a stabbing headache remained. They realized what had happened: The mission had failed. No one had looked at their scanner, they had been so sure of victory, so that all caution had no meaning.

"What happened?" Joe asked.

"No idea," Vivi replied.

The professor, however, knew exactly what had happened. "We have been captured, the worst has come true. Now we will need a lot of energy and strength, they will not give us the opportunity to die until they know everything about us. I also heard that a body search will be done upon arrival. We will be searched from head to toe and we will go through a kind of x-ray machine. I will try to use a piece of clothing to insulate the ear-chip so that I can hide it without being seen by the X-ray, because it will certainly be helpful. How good that our clothing was treated with nanotechnology-lead-titanium. It's a wonder they have not taken the chip from us yet. Probably the soldiers were so excited to have caught us that in their haste they forgot to search us."

"And how's that going to work?" Joe had no idea how the professor wanted to do it.

"Look, my clothes are finished with an ultra-thin lead alloy machined using nanotechnology. The fabric thus remains elastic and we are still a little protected from the radiation. I will wrap the ear device with it and, well, hide in my rectum. When it comes to x-rays it should not be possible to distinguish it from normal feces, at least I hope so. Our last chance..."

"Yes, and how are you going to do that? How do you slice the fabric?" Joe asked.

"I'll show you." The professor raised his arm and held it out to his friends. "My arm was created in the lab," he explained. "Bred genes. As a result of the terrible explosions, many babies with missing limbs have been born. That was also the case for me. There was only one arm. But today this is no longer a major challenge for medicine. My arm was artificially made. During the growth process, a kind of chamber was inserted. My parents thought that might be useful to me later. On the x-rays, the chamber just looks like a normal vein. There are, however, some emergency tools, one of which you can use as a pair of scissors, for example. Look! Everything made possible by nanotechnology and nanobots."

He pressed a spot on the left upper arm, whereupon some round, very small, elastic objects pushed out of the flesh. However, they looked more like a kind of fabric, and how they could be used as a tool, Joe did not have any idea.

The professor explained, "When I bring these objects near a force field, their structure changes, they magnify, and they become rock hard. The process can be reversed as soon as the tool comes close to a force field again, inside the vein, force fields have no influence on the tools, the veins are isolated. That's awesome, don't you think?"

"Amazing, yes," Joe nodded. "It makes no sense to me and I have no idea how it all works. I'll leave it that way and marvel at the technological possibilities, dear Professor."

Meanwhile Vivi sat in the corner and cried softly. When Joe wanted to calm her, she sobbed even more. She began to scream hysterically and beat wildly. Suddenly she stood up and rammed her body against the force field that made up the wall of her cell. Immediately she was thrown back. However, she did not let herself be tempted to try again, got up again, roared around in the chamber and pounded at the force field. A second time she landed on the floor. Her expression was apathetic, her complexion pale, Joe had never seen his wife like that, and when he tried to reassure her, she backed away and struck him. Outside, the guards were aware of the altercation. One of them briefly deactivated the force field and stunned Vivi with one shot, so she collapsed within seconds. She lay motionless on the floor.

"Oh my God!" Joe exclaimed in horror. And turning to the professor, he said desperately, "What is going on with her?"

The professor said she had a typical anxiety syndrome. "I do not have to explain that to you," he went on. "A human who freaks out for a few seconds. You can call it psychosis for my sake. Anyway, she will not say a word for the next few minutes."

Meanwhile, they had arrived in New Berlin. The force field was deactivated and the men were dragged out of the room like animals, while Vivi was left lying there they would come for her later]+. When the men got out, they saw that their aircraft had landed on a kind of platform, in the midst of a large audience.

"What's that?" Thought Joe, startled. "Are we on display here?" He whispered to the professor.

"Oh, my God!" The professor paled. "That looks like it."

A soldier stepped next to the prisoners and, with a sweeping gesture, shouted loudly, "Here are the traitors, the time manipulator Joe and the famous professor. We finally have them, as we promised you."

The crowd cheered and screamed, "Kill them, let them suffer..." And while the people screamed, the soldier pushed the two prisoners. "Come on, you dogs!"

The soldier shocked both of them with a small device he held in his hand, forcing them to march off. Wistfully, Joe glanced back at the aircraft they had arrived with. Vivi was still unconscious on the floor there. What would they do with her? He did not want to think about it, otherwise he would feel sick.

Behind the grandstand towered a gigantic tower in the sky. Its tip reached into the haze, it looked like it had no end. "What the hell is this crazy tower?" Joe said softly to himself. They came to a metal bridge, which was a passage to the tower. Joe looked up the dark steel walls of the complex. At intervals of about 50 meters, along the whole height, huge, old German imperial flags stuck out of the side walls. At about 200 meters altitude, there were four turrets, each pointing in a different direction.

"See, you dogs, this is your prison. Up there are old, German Reichsfahnen, they should remind us of the old times. And in the gun turrets underneath are antique 88s weapons, they are to testify to how large and powerful the German-Germans were and are still. At night, huge holograms are projected into the air, so that the guns are even seen from a distance of over five kilometers. This complex is the nation's tallest and best armed building. So do not try to escape, it would be pointless. Come on, you'll have plenty of time to see our logo later."

"For someone who wants to hate and kill us, the soldier is quite talkative," wondered Joe. He did not know at the time that he was dealing only with a clone that felt no emotion. Neither hatred nor pity.

They reached the huge entrance hall. In front stood two old tanks, brightly lit as decoration. Joe knew them well, they were the once-feared Tiger tanks, marked with the SS sign. In the hall they walked past a cordon of ten soldiers, each standing as stiff as a mannequin. The walls were decorated with old paintings and pictures from the Third Reich. "Is that the resurrection of National Socialism?" Joe wondered. And addressing one of their guards, he said, "Will we see the leader?"

"Silence, son of a whore. You will never have that privilege."

Joe spat reflexively at the soldier, and immediately a slap hit him in the face, the soldier's fist was rock hard. Joe was bleeding on his right eye.

They pushed on, driving straight ahead for about 100 meters. At the end of it, a door opened and behind it also stood ten guards on each side of the room.

"Well, you dogs. Stand there in the middle and take off your clothes, immediately."

Reluctantly, they undressed. Suddenly, some people appeared in white coats and sprayed them from head to foot with a remedy, a kind of disinfectant solution. "That you're not bringing vermin into the Reich."

Then they had to go through an X-ray machine and were subjected to a body search. "They seem to be alright, but keep a close eye on them," one of the white-robed men shouted.

"Why does everyone have to scream here?" Joe turned to the professor.

"No idea, maybe they're deafened by the continuously playing music. Pure idiocy. Where did we land? I hope that will end well."

"How long does it take to become addicted?"

"No idea, I guess, about three to four days. After that, we are lost and will never be the same again without help from others. But they will kill us anyway, because there have been relapses in the past."

Before they knew it, more doctors came - or whatever they were, because somehow they all looked the same, the soldiers and the doctors: all had bright blue eyes and blond hair: this was the new race. Only their clothing differed.

The doctors injected them with a chip by holding a small device to their heads, which automatically located the desired target in the head and then triggered itself. It was not even painful. Joe could not believe it, now he had a microchip in his brain that he might never get rid of.

"Oh, goddamn shit, what are we going to do?" He said faintly to the professor. The soldiers could not understand his words, the confusing music surpassed the murmurings.

"Trust me," whispered one of the doctors flatly, who had just passed them and walked around them, as if he wanted to inspect them again "You will be led back to your cell. All your actions are monitored. In your cell there is a recycling machine. That will be enough for you."

"What does he mean by "recycling machine", a sort of recycles?" Joe asked the professor as the man in the white coat returned to the other doctors.

The professor shook his head. "I have no idea, I've never heard of it."

They were led by another soldier to an elevator, with which they rode up to a height of 400 meters. That lasted only a good 20 seconds and Joe felt an ear pressure because of the rapidly changing height difference.

"Get out, you sons of a freak. Impure race. Dirty pack. Here is your cell. Enjoy the view!" The soldier grinned smugly. He seemed to enjoy his power and insult the prisoners, but perhaps he was just a prisoner of the music. It ran constantly, if only quietly in the background. German music mixed with modern trance. They called it Klance, a word re-creation of trance and classical music. Disgusting to listen to.

"Look at this," the professor muttered as they stood alone in their cell. "But watch out, it's also secured with a force field."

He pointed to the window, which let the misty daylight fall into the gray room, and drew his attention to the view, and what it offered. The professor stood in front of it and let his eyes wander. Joe stepped closer and also looked out the window, it offered an incredible sight. As far as he could see, there were houses. From up here, everything looked like a model. In the distance he could see tiny flags on the walls of the houses carrying the new banner. New Berlin was a futuristic city, with a hint of the old Reich. In the air were zeppelin-like airships. Around the prison were smaller Haunebu, one-man flying ships, but still dangerous.

"So it happened. We're prisoners," Joe pronounced the facts. "Do we have a any chance of escape?"

"I have no idea, Joe." The professor shook his head resignedly.

Joe pointed to a device on the wall.

"Should that be the recycle? It's just a box, what's on it?" He stepped closer to the square box of white plastic. As Joe pushed a button, a white plastic wall slid down and opened a toilet bowl. Then Joe saw the sign with the imprint, which was fastened above the bowl.

"Impure race, eat your recycled shit, or die of hunger," it said. "God damn it! That can't be serious...?" As always, Joe swore. "Are we...?"

"Yes, that's exactly what we should do. It just costs the electricity and they have enough of that. Incidentally, such systems have long been used in space travel. It's not that bad. The output is a kind of compressed protein bar. You can stay afloat for weeks like that."

"Still disgusting, those damned bastards!" Joe revolted.

"Not too loud. Otherwise they will beat you once more. By the way, Joe, now that we are cellmates, I would like to introduce myself once correctly. My name is Julian Schneider. Professor is just my nickname because it is rumored that I have a strong mind. Actually, I'm not a professor at all."

"However, for a professor, you seem quite young, Julian." Joe grinned. "On this occasion, maybe we could drop the formal courtesies and talk, what do you think?"

"With pleasure. To be honest, I was not sure how to address someone from 2016. Maybe you had other habits and courtesies," the professor said.

Joe had to laugh again. "Actually, the culture of the 21st century is very open. It's common to make people you know a bit."

"Well, good prisoner, then," the professor said ironically.

"Honestly, this is a modern concentration camp," Joe said.

"What is a concentration camp?"

Joe answered the professor and told him some more about the Second World War, the downfall of the empire, the new beginning, and how the EU and the UN should have prevented new wars. He talked about his house, his family and his job. He missed Vivi insanely and felt an inner restlessness and melancholy. Now he was in the same boat as Julian. Both had been separated from their wives by the New Germans.

Joe looked around. "I do not see cameras or anything else here."

"Yes, that's understandable, they do not need that anymore, we have the chip. So they always spot us, without the chip they are almost blind. New-Germans are implanted with such a chip from birth. Most do not even know it. Theoretically, you can even tap into our optic nerves and see what we see."

"And why did not you have such a chip so far?" Joe asked.

"Well, I am a new German citizen, but, as you know, belong to a different political group. In today's New Germany, people are not classified according to ethics, religion or origin, but according to their political views. My parents were already anti-technicians and they were not as controlled by the regime as the people in their own ranks. As good Germans, they left us mostly alone. In recent years, however, they have aggravated their mind towards us. Having been able to secure significant war victories against Russia and the West, they have for some time been focusing increasingly on the disruptive factors in their immediate environment. They want to wipe out the anti-technicians and the rebels. They have me now."

As they spoke, all of a sudden the force field that had blocked the way to the corridor disappeared. A soldier came in and behind him the force field closed. Joe recognized him again. It was the same man who had previously told them to trust him.

"Prisoners, I'm going to tell you something," he opened his speech, "if you try to attack me, the chip will kill you immediately. If you try to overcome or touch the Force field, you will be killed. If you do not eat, you will die yourself."

"Why were we captured?" Joe asked the guard. "We have not undertaken any hostile actions against the New Germanic Empire. Why should we be killed? Do not we have the right to a lawyer to explain our situation?"

The guard remained silent. Then he turned and said as he went, "You'll see."

The force field opened and closed.

"What does he mean by , 'you'll see'?" Julian asked. "Well, maybe he wants to help us. He said at the visitation that we could trust him. He makes a different impression on me than the others," Joe replied.

"They're all alike," the professor replied. "I do not trust these whore sons in the least. I'll lie down for a bit, how about you?"

Julian sat down on one of the bunk beds and yawned heartily. Joe did not feel tired. The whole thing had upset him a lot, and he felt a constant fear and nervousness about Vivi.

"I can not sleep now," Joe replied, staring out the window.

Julian lay down, closed his eyes and let his thoughts slide. So far they had gotten off lightly, but the threat of torture and death floated over them like a sword of Damocles. It would start soon.

Was there no way to escape from this prison? The fox in the forest came to mind, as he had crept away quietly and they had barely noticed him. He crawled out of his burrow at night when everyone was asleep. Was that the solution? Escape in the night? But the chip would betray him immediately. In addition, they were 400 meters above the ground. You would need an aircraft. However, the only Haunebu that existed in

their circles was destroyed. It seemed hopeless. The
professor pondered. After a while he fell asleep.

The interrogation

After a not so good night on a mattress, which was not much thicker than a towel, Joe woke up. His stomach growled louder than a lion about to attack. Through the window came the familiar gray glow of daylight. Julian had been awake for some time and kept pondering the fox. They had to somehow disappear from the building. Doing this silently was not a problem, he could disable the force field under certain circumstances, even the problem with the chip he had now solved.

"But how do we get down 400 feet from here, and how can we get over the many miles to the city limits?" He thought. Everything seemed to go down the drain again. It was really impossible. The area stretched 100 times 100 kilometers, the only chance was to grab a new Haunebu, but this idea was too fantastical.

As he thought about it, the force field opened.

"Get up, you dogs, and follow me," commanded the soldier, who had appeared. It was the same one who had talked to them yesterday.

They were taken to an empty interrogation room, and the guard whispered conspiratorially to them, "I'm not what I look like. I have been an overseer here for 20 years, occasionally helping rebels to escape, yet I have to do everything I can to be unrecognized. I will help you in due course. Julian, your wife is fine. You will see her soon. Just hold on. Do not betray anything so you can live longer. You'll be in pain, but they'll just be imaginary, caused by the computer, never forget that."

"How did you overcome the music?" Joe was curious. "How did you manage...?"

"No, you'll see." The guard said nothing, raised his right arm, and slapped both of them in the face so that it looked like he was interrogating them in a conventional way. Sometimes he had to cut the throat of a prisoner, this was necessary to survive and to save many others. But they were fortunate enough to be important. There were other times and other circumstances. In 2016, such interrogation methods were unimaginable.

The soldier wanted during the interrogation, above all, technical information about the time machine, which Joe and Vivi had allegedly built. Even if Joe wanted to, he could not have given the soldier any information. He repeated again and again that there was no time machine and he had no idea how it had been possible to get into this current time.

After the interrogation, they were dragged back to their cell. They had been given a few surges from strange weapons and Joe had fallen to the ground. Julian was more resistant to the pain, his genes had been positively influenced before birth, as was common among the well-off people. Thus, the children of the new generations were almost immune to infectious diseases and infirmities, a kind of genetic vaccine. When Joe came to, he was still slightly dizzy and his head was throbbing. He walked over to his cellmate, who was standing by the window, staring into the fog, still searching for a bright idea for escape.

"Will we manage to get out of here? What's up with that guard?" He began.

"No idea, maybe we'll know, maybe not."

It gave the two a little hope. "He managed to break the music," Joe continued, "we can do it too. But a simple earplug in the ear probably does not help, probably the addictive rhythm will be planted into our brains over some frequency, so even if we could not hear anything, we'd become addicted. They must have a knowledge, these fanatics! How do they know so much? Are they in possession of the hermetic key to wisdom?" Joe laughed at his joke, but basically it was by no means amusing.

When he got serious again, he said to Julian, "What are they going to do to us?"

"We'll probably find out early." The professor remained calm. "Do not think about it."

"I'm glad to have met you. What would have happened if we had fallen into the hands of the New Germany without you?" sighed Joe.

"What will you do if you make it to America, Joe?" Julian asked back.

"We will start a family. Vivi wants kids, and I'll do some work. "Joe looked thoughtfully at he wall. Tears shimmered in his eyes.

"How about you supporting us?"

"Look, Julian. Maybe it could actually become something. I have the greatest desire to kick these New Germans powerfully in the ass. I just do not know what Vivi would think of this idea. She is such a soft girl. She is in need of harmony, I do not really want to involve her in a war. I hope she is fine. Which cell she is in? Do you think that your wife is also in this building? Or are both already dead?"

"You must not think so, Joe, they're still alive, believe me, and we'll come out together here. I promise you."

"Do not make promises you can not keep, Professor."

"We can do it, Joe," the professor repeated confidently.
"Julian, you're a good person. I only hope that you keep your character, and are not subjected to this music. This addiction turns everyone into a mindless zombie who submits to a single man. Whether he wants it or not."

"Joe, the music recently gave me an idea of how to break out of this cell," the professor remarked.

"How so?"

"Do you see the force field?"

"Yes of course."

"I have my tools here...If I can create an extremely high-pitched sound using the force field and my tool, it should be possible to disable the chip. It is only a guess. It could kill us as well. I'll think up different frequencies and make calculations."

"And where will you write your calculations?"

"I do not need a notebook, I still have my communicator, so I mean my ear-chip as a trump card, I'll project everything and find a way through my thoughts. But even if we can deactivate the force field and the chip, we still have the task to solve how we can disappear from the height of 400 meters. I need a moment to get a sparking idea. But we'll make it, believe me."
"Professor, you're a brilliant mind, where did you learn all that?"

"Well, I'm New-German, my boy, remember? We have the hermetic key to wisdom." Julian grinned.

"Well, that was just a stupid saying. Seriously, where does your intelligence come from?"

"My grandfather was a leader of a science troupe," the professor began to tell. "He began to work on a method by which he could pass on his knowledge to his son. He carried out the experiments immediately on his own. He managed to transfer his know-how to a server. This could feed the knowledge of electrical impulses of another person. As a teenager, my father used to have my grandfather's experience and intelligence. In a second step, my grandfather activated and changed the knowledge cells in my father's head so that they penetrated the genetic material. When my mother became pregnant with me, I had the knowledge of father and grandfather in me. Unfortunately, my grandfather never realized how the flying disks were constructed, only cloned scientists had access."

"Why don't you use your knowledge to build better weapons?"

"We're trying, but we do not have the raw material. If I had made it to America, I probably could have started it, but when I realized all this, my wife was captured and they learned that I am the grandson of this scientist who had operated on the New Germans. That's why I'm so important to the regime. I'm too dangerous for them because I know too much. In addition, they absolutely want the scientific work of my grandfather. To date, his method has not come to the public and it is not yet possible for humanity to transfer knowledge. My grandfather hid his research somewhere and never published it. I'm sure they'll interrogate me soon. We have to make sure we get out of here right away, otherwise we'll be exposed to music too long."

At that moment, a patrol marched through the corridor. This happened exactly every six minutes. There was a big antique clock in the corridor, so Joe had been able to count the minutes between the checks. The soldiers had always arrived on time.

The second interrogation

Time passed slowly. Hunger and thirst grew stronger, but Joe resisted the temptation to use the recycle. At some point, however, he would not be able to escape the urge and go to the bathroom. Over a loudspeaker they suddenly heard the sounds of the crowd, which had to be outside in the arena. The detainees had to deliberately overhear the sounds when new arrivals were humiliated or tortured. This served to reinforce one's own fear. It sounded like a prisoner was being tortured or killed. The crowd cheered and whistled, they were thrilled. How could an interrogation, murder or even torture trigger such feelings of happiness among these people? They were all trapped in the frenzy of heteronomy and manipulation.

The same people in the twentieth and twenty-first centuries had considered the EU and the UN the best, and now it obeyed the voice of a single man. It was unimaginable. Would they shout and cheer like that? Would even a descendant of the Dexters watch and also applaud?

"Professor, what do you think, how long will we be interrogated?"

"As long as the crowd amuses them, or until they've sucked the desired knowledge out of us, I think. After that they will kill us. I do not know, Joe. I have not seen my Mary for a very long time, I just want to hold her in my arms once more. But she probably will not even recognize me. That's what scares me most."

"She will recognize you. Once you have freed her from the addiction. Once you've disabled your microchip, then yes, she'll remember."

"I've already calculated the possible frequencies, Joe. As soon as I have an idea how to overcome the altitude, we are gone. But I want to find my Mary first. I can not leave the building without her."

"And I'm not leaving without Vivi. We have to talk to this guard again. Maybe he can do something for us!"

"Yes, we do. As soon as he shows up. At the moment my ideas are exhausted. I can not do more right now. It's all up to this watchman now. I hope we can trust him. Without him we are as good as dead. Are you hungry as well?"

"Yeah, damn hungry, but I'm not going to eat from this recycle yet. I'm not a dog, I'll endure it for a few more days."

At that moment, the force field went out and a guard came in. "Here's a bowl of fresh water and a piece of bread, make sure you get ready for the interrogation. And do not come unwashed."

Most prisoners, stupid enough, ate the bread at the same moment. Greedy, Joe also wanted to get over the provisions, but the professor held him back.

"Joe, just leave it and hide it in the recycle. It will only strengthen you, keep it for the time after the interrogation. They only do that so we can last longer. Bread provides energy very quickly and so they are just baiting us. Do not eat it now, you'll lose consciousness faster and you can go back to the cell."

Joe followed the professor's advice and took only a small sip of water. After a few minutes the guard came again and pointed at Joe. "You're the first, come with me!"

Joe followed the guard. It went down a long corridor, then they came to a lift. "Hop in. But fast."

Joe obeyed, he felt like a dog being kept on a leash and having to obey in between. He always did what he was told. "Get out and go straight ahead. I will pick you up after the interrogation. Do not die."

"Do not worry, I'm not doing you a favor," Joe said cynically. He had never seen this guard before. He fervently hoped that he would meet the one guard who was probably friendly to them. Joe walked down the hall. For intimidation, pictures of ancient times had been hung on the walls. You saw people on torture chairs. It seemed as if the eyes were coming out of their sockets in pain. He saw terrible pictures of people with severed legs. Others had their tongues torn out. Joe could not continue. He felt himself getting sick, his stomach tightened and everything became improbable around him. He surrendered to the dark green carpet that graced the corridor. Since he had not eaten for two days, only bile juice came up. Unfortunately, he did not become unconscious, even if he had wished it so much. He shivered, trembling all over. His teeth bit his lips, they were already bleeding. Joe did not realize he was wet in the pants, he had never been so scared. The window of time, the chase, everything had been harmless compared to the fear he now felt. Two guards came and pulled him jerkily into the room. The room was bare and almost empty, there was a recliner and a computer in the corner, and behind it was a soldier. Joe struggled with his last strength, trying to fight back, but he had no chance. At that moment, all he thought about was survival. He wanted to see his Vivi again and put an end to the whole thing. Would he have been sure that he would no longer be able to stop the New Germany, he would probably have killed himself. But Joe had hope, and if he could not do it, another would come.

Joe was now strapped in the chair, around him were small, inconspicuous cameras mounted. One followed every movement of his head, the others were fixed on him. The guards left the interrogation room. The soldier at the computer desk tapped a few buttons and Joe heard over a loudspeaker how the people started screaming. Apparently, they broadcast the show live. He could not see what was happening around him, because his head was against the ceiling and he could only move it slightly. An assistant came in and pushed some kind of plug into his spine through an opening in the chair. It felt like a knife cut. The assistant began the interrogation: "Joe Dexter, born in 1984, charged with time-manipulation. Are you guilty?"

Joe answered with a no.

"That was the wrong answer, Mr. Dexter."

Suddenly, Joe was wide awake, feeling a beginning of pain in his forearm. Seeing nothing, he thought someone would put a scalpel there and start cutting slowly. The pain became more intense. Was his arm cut off? Joe screamed and bit his lip until they burst open. Desperately, he braced his body against the straps holding him. The crowd outside yelled. The pain was indescribable, but he did not pass out. Why did not he lose consciousness? With all his strength he tried to pull away, trying to pull the straps out of their anchorages, but all without success.

"Stooooooopppp! Please, I really do not know anything! „He shouted wide-eyed. From one second to the other the pain disappeared. The assistant asked, "If you do not know anything, why were you able to use one of our means of transportation?"
"By accident, we found it by accident. It was easy to use."

Joe tried to speak as clearly as possible, which he did not quite succeed. He tasted his own blood, which flowed from his lips and heard the crowd cheering and raging. They screamed with enthusiasm.

"You swine!" He said. Then he heard the assistant shouting to the soldier, "Go on, he'll talk."

The pain started again. This time, Joe lost consciousness after a short while.

In her cell, Mary and Vivi followed the torture scene live on a large flat screen. They heard the background noise of the cheering crowd, broken by Joe's shouting, a terrible carpet of sound. Vivi rolled tears down her cheeks. "Those bastards!"

She could not get more out of her mouth, she hit the wall with her fist and screamed. Couldn't they finally stop? Joe was innocent, damn it. They had been thrown into this time without a choice.

When, a while later, Julian was taken to the torture chamber and suffered the same agony, Mary did not feel much emotion. She did not know who the man was. He kept yelling her name, which confused her, but she did not know how he knew her.

When the interrogation ended, the force field in Mary's and Vivi's cell was suddenly deactivated. A security guard came in and whispered to them, "Come on, I'll take you to your men."

Vivi, who had previously slumped on the floor and cried, immediately jumped up hopefully. The guard motioned her with a gesture of calm. He led her down a long corridor and finally stopped in front of a force field. Joe, who had since recovered a bit and strengthened himself with his piece of bread, saw his wife come before the force field was deactivated. His heart began to beat faster and he felt a warm beam that passed through his body.

"Vivi!"

Now the professor became attentive and recognized his wife. He jumped up filled with joy. The guard stepped into their cell and ordered the two men to be quiet. Joe and Vivi were already in each other's arms. Julian slowly approached Mary and held out her hand.

"Mary, it really is you!"

She looked at the professor unaware, "Who are you?"

He had guessed. His wife did not recognize him anymore. But he would have solved this problem quickly. He was quite sure he had calculated the frequencies correctly.
"Thanks!" He whispered to the guard, who had turned away and closed the forcefield again. He winked at him from the outside.

"I said you can trust me," he said quietly, disappearing down the hallway.

Joe and Vivi whispered eagerly and hugged and kissed each other.

Vivi said that nothing had happened to them. They were just kept in the cell and even had food and water.

"You women are spared them for some reason. They probably need the women to give birth to the clones, so they will not torture you," Julian said.

Mary stood at the window, staring into the distance. She did not speak to the others and was in a strange, apathetic state. Julian had not dared to make any further overtures, but was busy preparing his tools. He opened his artificial vein and held it to the force field. At the same moment, the material formed into the desired object. He took his earpiece, cleaned it, and used his tool to handle it.

"So, let's just dare. It's set to pass the frequency to the chip."

The professor activated the device and stood next to Mary. When he carefully put the earpiece into her ear, she looked at him skeptically, but did nothing.

"I'm going to pair the device with Mary's chip," he explained. "Do not worry, I will not hurt you," he said affectionately to her. Then he turned on the frequency. It did not happen at first. The frequency was so high that the human ear could not perceive it. Nevertheless, everyone listened intently. Did it work? Or not?

"Oh my god, Julian. What are you doing here?" Mary began babbling. Vivi and Joe looked at each other in triumph. It had worked! Vivi clapped her hands with joy.

"My little stupid man, what do you think, did you lose your mind? Are you tired of life? What are you doing here in the stronghold of the New Germany?"

"This is my wife, that's truly my wife!" The professor beamed and wrapped his arm around Mary's neck.

"Now just shut up, sweetheart. I came to save you, stupid little thing!" He replied in the same tone as his Mary.

Vivi had to laugh. Again the professor and his wife fell into each other's arms and seemed reluctant to let go of each other.

"Oh my gosh, I missed you so much!" Said Mary.

"Hello Professor? Professsoor?" Vivi grew impatient. "Don't you want to disable our chips?"

With a heavy heart, the professor parted briefly with Mary. He also deactivated the chips of Vivi and Joe and in the end his own. At that moment, the guard appeared with a tray.

"Tomorrow will be the next interrogation. Here you have bread and water, chew the bread carefully." He set the tray on the floor and left the cell.

Joe took a roll and bit tentatively. He was so hungry that he wanted to devour it. But he had understood the signal of the guard. The other three prisoners took a roll and broke it carefully. In the middle of Vivi's rolls, they found a very small, hard object: a small earpiece that looked a little different than the one already known.

Joe took it and stuck it in his ear. Nothing happened.

"How do I activate it?" He mumbled.

"You just have to remember that you activate it with your mind," Julian replied.

"Okay, I'll try."

He concentrated on the device and it switched on. Before his eyes a description and a plan appeared. The content read: "Tonight at exactly 2:00 am you will throw this earplug into the recycler. You will see the time by the clock in the corridor. But do not go too close to the force field, it is especially strong at night. The recycler will break. Once this is done, call for the security guard. One will come to replace the device. In the new device are some little things hidden. You can open the secret compartment by tapping the right side wall three times. Behind it are four flight backpacks. It is the same equipment worn by the soldiers who jump out of the peace birds. Be careful, I had to slim her down a bit. The fuel only lasts for five minutes. If you miss landing before, you crash. In addition, the recycler includes a force field deactivation. Once you have received the new recycler, wait for the next patrol, then turn off the force field at the window. They then have exactly six minutes to flee before they are discovered by the next patrol. One minute is meant for destroying the force field deactivation. You should not leave any traces. Put this back in the recycler. It will destroy itself there. Go to the window, put on the 'wingsuits' and just jump out, the suits will open automatically. You also guide them with your thoughts. To do this, before you deactivate the force field, you must plug in earplugs. These are also in the recycler, one for each of you. As soon as you are in the air, the automatic flight guidance system takes over. You just have to control yourself for the first few seconds. Beware of Haunebu 1. Unfortunately, they are numerous in the air and guard the building from the outside. The Wingsuit is programmed to take you to a nearby meeting point where a rebel informer will be waiting for you. If they need to detour, for example, to escape a Haunebu, they should make it in 4.5 minutes. The meeting place is in the middle of the city. The code-word reads, 'Roswell landed'. Only say it after the informant asked you, 'Who landed?' If you make a mistake, they'll shoot you right away, otherwise, the rebels believe you to be spies of the New Germans. Do you understand that? Adhere strictly to the rules. The informant will keep you safe for some time. After 30 minutes you have to get out of the city, because after that the power field around the city will most likely turn on. So nobody comes in or out. Give the earpiece before its destruction to everyone in the cell. Everyone should familiarize themselves with the process so that they are prepared to flee. Now I wish you good luck. Maybe someday you will see each other again. Oh, just by the way. Wing-suit I call the parts so that you can imagine what to expect. In reality Hot Things, StuKa backpacks. The New Germans have named these after the Stuka aircraft from the World War. Stupid but I just wanted to let you know.``

Joe passed the earpiece and squinted nervously at the clock in the hallway. Tonight you would either escape or die.

Flight

Joe looked at the time. It was now 01:00a.m. clock at night. Shortly before, the professor had been taken out of the cell for another interrogation and brought back unconscious. He was still lying motionless on his mattress. If he did not wake up soon, their plan would go to pieces. They drizzled him with water they had kept, and Mary stroked his forehead uninterruptedly. Still he did not move. The nervousness rose in unison with the advance of the clock hand.

"Julian, wake up, we do not have much time left, come on," Joe whispered. The professor did not move.

"What should we do?" Vivi said desperately.

She got no answer, no one seemed to know what was to happen. When it was 1:45a.m. and their last hope was dwindling, the man stirred.

"Julian!" Mary shouted in relief. "Oh, I'm so glad you're awake again!"

"What happened? Where am I? It is over?"

"Yes, it'll be over soon, Professor, in fifteen minutes our escape is to begin. Can you do it? We've put a little bit of bread aside for you to get your strength," Joe said.

They handed it to him and the professor enjoyed the bread. "It is good."

"Are you ready for our mission, Professor?" Vivi asked.

"Do not worry, I'm fit," Julian grinned.

At that moment a patrol marched past. The prisoners tried to sit on their mattresses as unobtrusively as possible. Without expression, they stared at the walls until the two soldiers disappeared.

When Joe looked at the clock again, it showed almost 2:00 am.

"It starts, people!"

They had agreed that Vivi should call for the security guard. The others pretended to be asleep. She took the earplug and threw it into the recycler. The device started to hum and smoke. Carefully Vivi stepped a little closer to the force field.

"Hello! Does anyone hear me? I need help, hallloooooo!"

It only took a few seconds for a security guard to show up.

"Soldier, our recycler is broken, I need to go to the bathroom!" Vivi said.

The guard deactivated the force field and inspected the smoking recycler. "Hm," he grumbled. "Do not touch it!"

He disappeared and closed the force field. The four of them waited tensely for what would happen. Suddenly, sounds were coming to them from outside in the corridor. The force field was opened, and a new recycler was put in, the old one was disposed of just as quickly. When the soldier disappeared, Julian scurried out of his bunk and knocked three times on the side wall. A plastic door slid along, revealing their escape equipment as promised.

"Everyone takes their backpack and their earphones. As soon as the next patrol is over, we start. We must not waste time, otherwise we are dead," Julian instructed the others.

When the next soldiers disappeared from view, Julian deactivated the force field from a safe distance and threw the deactivator into the recycler.

"Go now! You know what to do."

The professor jumped first, he had no problems flying straight for a few seconds. Vivi and Joe also jumped, followed by Mary.

But Vivi's device did not seem to work properly. She raced to the ground in free fall.

"Joooooooe!" She yelled. Joe watched him fly after her quickly.

"Vivi, what's going on?" He shouted through the wind, which blew hard in his face.

"I...I can not do it, it does not work!" Vivi's voice cracked with panic.

"Just think you want to fly," Joe shouted.

Milliseconds passed before Vivi's wingsuit finally opened, and shortly afterwards the computer took over the flight. They shot through the air.

"Joe, you do not have to scream, we can all hear you well. The earphones are connected," Julian intervened.

"Vivi, are you okay?" Mary asked.

"Now! I almost died in fear," Vivi sighed.

"Amazing, whaaaaat for a speed!" Joe laughed. At that moment, not a hundred yards away, a one-man haunebu flew by.

"Look, there!" Yelled Joe.

"Shit, he's probably seen us," Julian answered. "Go on, increase speed, we'll be there in a few seconds!"

Like arrows, they shot at a white, five-story house. On the flat roof a human stood beside an entrance. That had to be the informant. "Oh, and how do you land this thing?" Joe cried in panic. The answer did not come, everyone was busy not to crash against a wall.

The wingsuits were slowing down, but no one managed to get a clean landing. It seemed as if ~~her~~ their guard had forgotten a little detail because the landing took place without a computer. The thought impulse for landing had to be done. So Joe almost flew into a force field and Vivi bounced off the wall almost two meters from the door.

"Oh, shit," she murmured, holding her aching head. She even bleed lightly on the forehead. "Why did not that damned guard tell us how to land?"

"He probably did not think it was important, for him the technology goes without saying," Joe answered, walking up to her. Nervously, he looked for the Haunebu. But it was a dark night, he could not even see any stars in the sky. This was probably due to the eternal haze. Had they possibly been lucky and the Haunebu had not located them?

At that moment, the professor landed roughly on his stomach and got a black eye as a flying object struck him in the eye. Mary had been the cause, because she had flown right in front of the professor and landed in front of him, part of the engine had come loose and flew in the direction of the professor's head.

"Look, woman!" He railed at her.

"I did not do it on purpose!" She called back.

In the midst of the landing, everyone had forgotten the informant, who stood suspiciously beside the entrance and followed the action. Julian approached him.

"Who landed?" The informant announced.

"Roswell landed," Julian replied.

"Well done, my friends! Come in quickly, we have almost no time left."

Suddenly there was a rising and falling noise, a loud whistle.

"What's that?" Vivi asked, startled.

"What you hear is the alarm, they have discovered your breakout much too early! We are running out of time, we have to come up with a very, very good escape plan. The force field around the city will certainly be activated soon," the informant shouted to them. He locked the door, which looked like the entrance to a bunker, and told them to follow him. As he ran down the stairs, Joe noticed that he was dressed as they knew it from their time. Only the shoes resembled robotic feet. The informant led them to the basement of the building, where the walls were bombproof.

"We're safe here for the time being. We have to work out a plan," the informant remarked.

"What's up with your feet?" Joe asked irritably.

"Blown away by a mine. Now I have artificial feet, these are more powerful than organic ones and they work very well. It happend sometimes. But it's not bad. It only gets bad when a part of your head is blown away. It's impossible to fix, you could at most clone yourself, and your knowledge lives on in the clone. Nobody knows then that you are dead. But that's what the New Germans are doing. They bet on their clones. They are cheaper and easier to produce. In addition, they are less likely to malfunction. We've been trying to make good robots for some time, but unfortunately we're missing material."

"Do you not have an escape plan? And by the way, what's your name?" Joe asked.

"Just call me Informant. That is sufficient for the time being, in the case of a re-capture you know nothing, and that benefits you in turn. I had a plan, but now that the force field is already activated, it will not work anymore. I had a Hover vehicle, but now we have to come up with something new."

"Hm, are there still underground stations in New Berlin?" Said Vivi.

"There is, but all the tunnels have been sealed. After the explosions, the rats in the underground shafts multiplied for some inexplicable reasons. They were radioactive, contaminated, and invaded the cities. You just could not get the problem under control. Fearing the rats and communicable diseases, they decided to close down all approaches," the professor replied.

"Would it be possible to open one of the tunnels?"

"Hm, that's even a brilliant idea," the professor muttered. "When the force field is activated, there is no escape route above the earth. We could try to open a tunnel, but nobody has done that yet."

"Why not?" Vivi asked.

"Why should you do that?" The informant replied in place of the professor. "We can move well above. I've been here in town for two years now. They have not recognized me yet. You just have to pretend that you are one of them. Go to their festivals, watch torture from time to time - and they already have no idea. I always have my ear chip with me and watch some old classic during the show."

"Do you happen to know where an old subway station is?" Vivi continued.

The man nodded.

"Take us there!"

He hesitated a moment, until he said energetically, "Follow me!"

"Wait, wait!" Mary called. "I'm supposed to go down to those smelly critters? What if they are still contaminated? We all get sick!"

"Sweetheart, now just hold your beak," the professor said affectionately. "Rats or death by the New Germany, that's how easy it is."

"Why does this shit always happen to me?" Mary complained.

He smiled sourly and said laconically: "Quite simply because you're a professor's wife."

"Do you want me to calm down?"

"No, but that's a fact, and you knew exactly what you agreed to do with me."

"God, I really do not understand why I love you so much!" Mary sighed. But inside, she had already given in. She would follow her husband no matter where he took her.

Joe and Vivi listened to the two, smirking, while they argued and laughed in between over the scramble. "You see, Joe, what's in love, that teases. This saying is true to his call."

The old subway station

A few minutes later, the group was again dead serious. They once again had a life-threatening mission ahead of them. They had to walk a short distance on foot in the streets of New Berlin. Although it was in the middle of the night and pitch black, there was still a chance to run into the military team. The city was on alert, they had certainly sent a search party.

Carefully, the informant stepped into the street and peered in all directions. The air seemed to be pure. He beckoned to the others and ducked against the walls of the rows of houses, they crept through the darkness. Nobody dared to turn on a flashlight. Rather, they stayed close to the walls lest they reveal themselves to a soldier. Luckily, the old subway station was very near. After a few minutes, they arrived at an old building. A dimly lit sign bore the following inscription: "Former subway station. In memory of all the people who tried to save themselves."

"What happened here?" Joe asked the informant.

"It was just before the power plant in Germany exploded: The authorities had issued a warning. 'Everyone should try to find shelter in the mountains.' Some thought they could run downstairs. It was suicide, everyone was killed. Enough of the old stories... Let's go inside. The building is not monitored. And they do not visit, people have other things in their heads, the main sport of everyone is torture. After that come virtual games and everything else that has to do with computers. People do not read anymore and do not go to school anymore, most of them do the same every day."

The informant seemed to sink into nostalgia for a few seconds, then he picked himself up and stepped first into the run-down hall. Since you could not even see his hand ~~inside~~ beside his eyes, the informant switched on a flashlight. No one could be seen. The hall was dusty and exposed to slow decay. They walked down dozens of steps, littered with pieces of falling plaster, and came to the rails. On one track was an old subway train that had just been left standing here, but the tunnel was concreted in both directions.

"Well, how do we get through the wall now?" Joe asked skeptically.

"Maybe the train is still operable," Julian said.

Joe started laughing, "And if you can, can you start it up, Professor?"

"Not me, but you might. In your time these vehicles were still in operation."

Joe's laugh stopped. "I've never steered a train in my life, but I can try it. Anything is better than getting back into the clutches of the New Germans."

"Do you just want to break the wall by train?" Mary spoke up. "Is that not dangerous?"

"There's some risk, of course," Joe replied. "I could die in the cab, the New Germans could hear the impact, the rats could swarm out through the hole..."

"Joe, it's not funny!" Mary interrupted.

"Forgive me, it is not. I'm really scared, but do you have any idea how else we could push through a wall?" said Joe.

Mary was silent. After much back and forth, the five decided that Joe should try once, if he could ever get the train going . Maybe he could turn on some sort of autopilot and then jump off early enough. Determined, Joe climbed into the cab. With a flashlight he lit the cockpit and looked at the fittings.

"Let's just press Start," he mumbled. Nothing happened. Joe called out, "This thing's not working!" His head disappeared back into the cabin. Joe looked around and saw a lever that said, "Electric or diesel."

"What? This thing runs on diesel too?" He wondered. He switched to diesel and pressed again to start. The cabin was suddenly submerged in a pleasant light and the locomotive began to hum softly, then a bang sounded and the engine was running. Again he called out of the window, "Hey guys, it's up to you, imagine it's on!"

But when he went to turn around, his arm caught on the throttle - and suddenly the locomotive began to roll.

"Oh, shit, and now, what am I going to do?" It shot through his head. He called for help and tried to push the throttle back, but it was stuck. Joe shook the lever wildly, but he could not do anything, the train gained speed. When it was only about 100 yards to the concrete wall, Joe ran as far back as possible and held on tight.

"If only that works!" He closed his eyes. Vivi and the others stood frozen beside the track, watching the moving train. They had watched Joe run back through the lighted cabin. But with the rear cars in the dark, nobody really knew what had happened to Joe.

"Joooooooe!" Vivi shouted in shock, tears spilling into her eyes. Mary also screamed. Parts flew through the air as the train hit the wall and shattered it with a big clamor. It felt like the whole building was about to collapse. Stones rolled, dust whirled through the hall and the train came to a stop. The light in the cab kept burning as if nothing had happened. However, the cab was now on the other side of the wall and sent through the broken wall a beam of light, in which the faces of the baffled troupe could be seen.

"Impossible, the tunnel is open. I hope nothing happened to Joe," the professor muttered.

Vivi ran and climbed into a car that was still on her side.

"Joe, Joe, are you alright?" She called into the interior. It was dark on the train. Since she received no answer, she ran to the next compartment, where she heard a groan and a movement. She lit her flashlight and recognized Joe, who was lying on the ground and holding his head. When he saw her, he scrambled to his feet and rubbed his forehead. Vivi aw a small torrent of blood on his head.

"Somehow I'm mad," he greeted her. He tilted to the side but got up again and tried to leave. Vivi stood there wordlessly, hoping it was not too bad. After all, he was still alive. "It's going to be awesome," Joe stuttered, staggering off toward the door. He stepped out of the car, and when he surveyed the people standing at a safe distance next to the track, he suddenly became sober.

"Where's the informant?" He asked the group.

Astonished, Julian and Mary looked around. Nobody had taken care that the informant had turned back during the whole excitement and nobody knew where he had gone.

"Well, it does not matter...the main thing is, we found our entrance," Joe said. Vivi stepped out of the car after him and made sure everything was okay with him. It seemed Joe was ~~the~~ like an old man after the first shock.

"What now?" Said Mary.

"Do not be so impatient now, Mary, you'll see your rats soon enough," the professor provoked.

"Damn, I promise, if I see even a rat, I'll kill you."

"Oh, great, then we can fight again," he smiled.

"What's the matter with them?" Vivi grimaced. "Just be glad you're getting along and keep your mouth shut. Come on, come in!"

They climbed over boulders through the hole that had formed in the wall. It was dark inside, but they found an emergency generator that powered the tunnel lighting. The LED lights, which ran like long queues along the ceiling of the tunnel and lost themselves in a curve, faintly lit up. It seemed it was leading heir way deeper and deeper.

"Where are we going?" Vivi asked Julian.

"No idea," he answered. "Look, there's a turn-off, looks like a maintenance tunnel, let's go through it."

They made their way to the maintenance tunnel, but after a while Joe stopped abruptly. "What's this? Professor, come here!"

But Julian leaned against the wall and rubbed his forehead. "Oh, my God," he muttered.

"What's going on, Professor?" Joe asked.

"I've just had a deja vu."

"Everybody has it once."

"But mine are special. Every time I have one, I know it's a memory of my father or grandfather. One of my ancestors has been here before."

"What, here? What had they done here?" Joe said.

"I saw a door, a black, inconspicuous door."

"Yes, I can see them too, and that's why I stopped."

"Where?" Julian asked.

"Over there, look!" The two ran.
"Wait for us," they heard from behind, but they did not care. When they arrived at the door they read an inscription: "Penemuende 2. Authorization only by Fritz Schneider."

"That's your family name," Joe said. "Do you know the person?"

"I think that's what my grandfather meant."

They looked at a small box with buttons. It looked like the door could only be opened with the right code.

"Guess what!" Joe called to the professor. "Let's see how good your déjà-vu is."

The professor entered a code and lo and behold, the door opened and a voice was heard: "Welcome, Mr. Schneider. Nice to see you're back."

The bunker of the professor

Mary and Vivi arrived and looked in amazement at the entrance.

"We're probably safe here for the time being," Julian said. "It will not be long before the New Germans discover the broken tunnel. The noise was deafening, that must have been overheard. However, they will assume that we have escaped through the tunnel and position their men at the other end to intercept us. If I'm not mistaken, this place offers everything we need for survival. So we can just wait until the force field is deactivated again. At some point, they'll have to turn it off to bring food and other goods to the city."

They entered through the entrance and the door closed automatically behind them. No one would be able to open it from outside without typing in the correct code. The entrance was bombproof. Shortly after they entered, the lights came on automatically.

"My grandfather must have created this place before the big explosion," Julian muttered. "He knew there would be a catastrophe."

On a table in front of them in the room was a notebook. Curious, Joe stepped closer and opened the first page. Dust whirled through the air. He read aloud: "March 5th, 2079: Dear relatives, old or young. The Anti Technicians and I have created this place so that we and our descendants have a place to shelter from war and disaster. We suspect that there will soon be a global disaster, because everyone is crazy about energy. Everyone is safe down here, the room is protected against all kinds of beam weapons and bombs. This place is also the secret hiding place of all my knowledge. My library contains my research and research on the Vril, Thule and aeronautical engineering.

"At the front of the corridor is a control panel. From there you can serve the whole complex. From the switching computer you can get to the individual sections. In room C4 is my greatest pride. Unfortunately, we were only able to acquire a few ships and almost all were destroyed by the New Germans. But the Haunebu 3 in room C4 is functional. It is fast and armed. Only a few small repairs would have to be made. I really hope that you will find all this someday. My current research task is about how to pass on your knowledge. If the hypotheses prove to be true, my son Hannes should have knowledge of everything after the download of the knowledge data and be able to pass this on to the next generations. My son is too young now for me to explain all this to him. So I hope that my experiment works and this room is found later. It is possible that the New Germans kidnap me or harm me otherwise. Then I will have no opportunity to show this place to anyone. My life is in daily danger."

Joe looked up and ran his fingers through his hair. "You said the knowledge transfer experiment worked," he said to the professor. "Why did not you know about this place?"

"It seems some knowledge cells have been corrupted on download," Julian replied. "This explains the Déja-vu. The data are available somewhere, but can not be retrieved cleanly by the brain. You might have to resume research and refine the method."

This explanation sounded plausible and so Joe turned back to the book and kept turning the pages. On the next page he read:

"27th of November 2079: I came down again, but I have only little time. As suspected, the explosion has occurred. I and my little son survived because I happened to take him to work and we were in a bunker north of here. We stayed in this bunker for more than a month because no creature could survive outside. I have not found my wife since the disaster. However, I have not lost the hope that she could escape to safety. However, more than half of the anti-technicians in my troop have died. Few had stayed down here in the bunker.

"Since the explosions, the party of the New-Germans has become strongly radicalized. They behave as if the world belongs to them and have begun to implant citizens with a chip with which they can control every individual. If I get to that, I will try to figure out how to disable this chip. Maybe it's already too late. I see how it ends with us."

Joe paused and looked into the faces of his companions, who had been listening intently. Then he read on:

"Supplement from the 2nd February in 2080: The subway tunnel is teeming with rats since the explosion. Luckily our bunker is well insulated. The New Germans have decided to constrict the tunnels to get the plague under control. They no longer need the subway as they use high-tech flying discs. These means of transport have radicalized technical progress. We anti-technicians resist the high-techization of the New Germans. At the political level we fight for the maintenance of the underground. But if we get away with it is very uncertain. I just wish that my descendants will find this bunker once and use it for the better. If this is being read by a family member of mine, my wish has come true. Finally, I just want to urge you to be careful with all the devices. There are also Tesla coils beneath. These generate a tremendous amount of energy, so be on the alert. Professor Fritz Schneider."

Julian's eyes were wet as Joe stopped reading. "He was a good man. May he rest in peace," he said softly.

"Gosh, so your grandfather foresaw everything. He must have been enormously intelligent," Joe said admiringly.

"And I inherited that intelligence," Julian grinned.

"Do not be too modest, Professor," Joe said cynically.

Vivi went to the central control computer. "Amazing what equipment we got 60 years after us," she called back. She turned on the computer and the hologram of a woman appeared.

"Hello, what can I do for you?" She said.

"Open all locks to each room," Vivi said.

"Command is executed."

Six gates opened. Their location was displayed on the monitor.

"Look at that, Professor," Vivi shouted.

Julian, Mary and Joe gathered around the computer and studied the layout of the complex. Then all four went to the first room.

"What's that?" Mary wondered. In front of them was a metal cube about three meters long, wrapped in glass. There was a sign on the glass.
Mary read aloud to herself: "The last remaining non-atomized iron. Serves to make vrils."

"What's a Vril?" Vivi asked.

"A Vril is the drive type of a hound bus," Julian told her. "This block and other resources could be used to build world class flying disks. My grandfather is was really awesome. That is exactly what we have always lacked. We just did not have the right iron."

The room they were in was over 20 meters long and at least as wide. The iron block was centered in the middle, and on the side there were work coils and a large machine.

On a worktable, Julian found the following note: "A few days ago, we managed to get a smelting machine into the bunker. Unfortunately, the antitank technicians are not currently smelting and portioning the metal to use it for the production of drives. There are too many other things that need to be done right now. Professor Schneider."

On another table next to the cube were several documents with records of machines and their structure. Among the writings was also a lexicon with various technical terms. Julian came across another note. It seemed a bit like his grandfather was preparing a scavenger hunt. Everywhere they found news and clues that were addressed to them. He must have expected that one day a family member would find his life's work.

"Dear descendants, I am glad that you have found the metal, now you will be able to build 1,000 such ships, because the propulsion is not great. Do not waste the iron, you will not get any more. Well, technically, you probably can not decrypt them right away. But the blueprints of the Haunebus are in my laboratory, so it should be easy for you, my descendants, to build flying disks, as you carry my technical understanding in you. The key to understanding the technique is taking time to study the moon. In my library you will find astronomical works. It is enough if you look at a picture of the moon. It consists of many craters, which give a pattern equal to the number four. Please note only the huge craters, which are named on all maps of our terrestrial satellite. Each crater has a different size and each of them represents an electrical component at the same time. On the individual components of a ship are numbers as well as a half full or whole moon. If it is full moon, the number on the component is divided by the number four. At half moon you divide the number by two. So you get the relationships of the circuits ordered by numbers. Professor Schneider."

"Wow, what a genius!" Joe was fascinated. "The anti-techs will use the plans of your grandfather to decipher the functionality of the Haunebu 3 and build more flying discs."

"Yes, it seems we have to take on technical progress and beat the New Germans with their own weapons," Julian said.

As they entered the next room, they were almost no longer astonished. They were in a hall and in front of them stood a Haunebu class 3 in full gear, the logo of the empire was still as new. Even the metal had not ~~gotten~~ a single scratch.

"Where did he get the ship from?" Joe asked.

Julian had already found the appropriate note and read the description aloud to everyone: "Dear descendants, I found this ship during an expedition in Thailand. It seemed to me as if it had been used by the New Germans for a reconnaissance trip. As the soldiers indulged in a fine meal and subsequent massage, I and my team managed to take over the airship and fly to Europe. The maximum speed is so high that we could have covered the distance in a matter of minutes, even before the New Germans had even noticed anything about the loss. Although we had to ignore the international speed limits, no one could complain because the ship was of course registered in the army. Since it was night in New-Germany at the time of flight, we were able to hide the Haunebu unseen in the bunker. It is the most modern airship I know today. It can carry a load of several thousand Lift tons. The diameter is 50 meters, the height 30 meters. Maximum speed: 20,000 km / h.

Armament: four plasma fusion lasers. Crew: a maximum of 25 men."

The four looked at each other speechless with enthusiasm. In the other rooms they found a weapons arsenal with several hundred weapons, countless antique books, generators, and a strange-looking coil. Of course there was also a fitting note about it.

"I've been able to boost the coil's performance, or as you know it, with a Tesla coil many times over. The high voltage generated by this modified Tesla coil would be sufficient to pull a hole into the atmosphere. Only switch it on if you have to switch off power plants or similar. If you let them turn on too long, all life would be destroyed. Maximum ten seconds - it has the same effect as holding your arm in a microwave for ten seconds. Although I have installed a small protection to prevent this, but beware is the mother of the porcelain box. Do you understand me?"

Vivi, who had moved away from them, came back. "Joe," she said, "I found something. Just look. Here." She handed him a map of the entire facility. It extended over an area of 30,000 square meters below the center of Berlin. "Why did not the New Germans discover this station?" Vivi asked incredulously. "It is huge!"

"I can give you the answer," Julian said. "It seems that knowledge cells have activated in my brain after seeing it all with my own eyes. Previously, the knowledge had lain unused in my brain, but through the impulses that are sent through my eyes to the brain, the information from my brain can be decrypted and understood. I suddenly know how my grandfather built this facility, though he never told me about it."

Six eyes looked at him tensely.

"Go ahead!" Joe said.

"The anti-technicians come from a professional group of construction workers. They were specialists in the field of blasting and tunneling. When the entire subway in Berlin was renovated in 2069, a special team of 45 men were involved in the project. The men were privately members of a secret order, which later called itself 'the anti-technicians', this order had the motto, Knowledge is Power. In addition one must say that they were not generally against the technology. On the contrary, many of them were experts in the technical field. But the technique with which the New Germans experimented was repugnant to them, too unnatural and abstract. Although the New Germans were still a relatively insignificant political party at that time, they represented interests that were ethically very questionable. Even then, they fought to provide every citizen with a chip in order to gain full control over the population. Of course, they proclaimed all this as purely safety-related measures, for example, to detect criminals and terrorists early and arrest them. The chip should only serve the protection of the people, was their credo. But the opponents quickly recognized the true interests of the New Germans. They accused them of wanting full control over each individual and a dominant power interest. The secret Order of Anti-Technicians began to rebel against the New-Germans. Since they already knew that the New Germany could become powerful and dangerous, and a war in the immediate time could no longer be ruled out, they took advantage of the redevelopment project of the Berlin subway to run a second project unnoticed in parallel. They built a protective bunker in a side arm of the tunnel, which should also serve as a production hall for weapons. While the regular construction work began at the other end of the tunnel, the bunker was lifted and its foundations solidified. The excavated material was always mixed with the rest of the rubble and did not cause any suspicion. The government was told that they had underestimated project costs and needed millions more. The loan was released. After six years, the secret bunker had been completed, three years before the remediation project was completed," the professor concluded.

"That's almost incredible. These anti-technicians must have been real geniuses," Joe said admiringly.

"First and foremost, my good grandpa. He drew and constructed the blueprints," the professor added.

"But Professor, what's this?" Vivi pointed to the floor plan.

"Interesting, interesting," Julian said. "I knew there must be a second input or output somewhere. So he's it's here then..."

The others also took a closer look at the plan and recognized a small tunnel that led away from the bunker. It was written with: "Escape tunnel. Length: 80 kilometers. Getting Around: Tesla Vril Transporter at 500 km / h."

"Do you know what that means, Joe?" Julian asked.

"Oh, yes, we can get out of New Berlin."

"That's right, but first we have to make some arrangements. The escape tunnel has an exit that leads directly into the tunnel, which leads out of the complex of anti-techs. Of course my grandfather took care of that. You already know the said tunnel. Also, we left the anti-tech complex by him a few days ago. But the antitank technicians do not know anything about this connection, let alone this bunker, which you can reach through them. I want to show this place to some of my people. The anti-technicians should help us to cut the iron, melt the pieces and build Vril drives. To some clever minds, I also dare to decode the technique of the Haunebus. Using the plans of my grandfather and the Haunebu 3, which serves as a prototype, we should be able to build more flying discs. The production hall in the bunker is huge. Joe and Vivi, you will go to the anti-technicians tomorrow and report back to them. Lead twenty of my people to this place. I write you the names. I will stay here with Mary and review my grandfather's work and plans. Soon we will be able to build airships and weapons. If the rebels hear that, they will be thrilled! Now let's see that we find something to eat here. And then we'll sleep a few hours, we have plenty to do tomorrow!" In Room C2 they found a kitchen and a large store of groceries. They took food packages and drinks and ate them greedily. Then they went to room C6, where a shower, toilets and separate bedrooms were found. Dead tired, they lay down in the comfortable cold foam mats and fell asleep shortly thereafter.

Return to the Anti-technicians

Joe and Vivi did not wake up until 10:00 in the morning. The professor and his wife were still wrapped tightly on their sleeping mat. Vivi was the first to use one of the showers. There was even hot water.

The two had a cozy breakfast. The coffee was heavenly, but the food packages took some getting used to by early 21st century citizens . But both enjoyed being able to be free again. A little later, Mary and the professor also appeared in the kitchen. They looked rested and happy.

"Good morning, you two," Joe greeted. "As you can see, we are almost ready for our mission."

Mary also prepared breakfast for herself and her husband, and the professor gave Joe some final explanations and tips. Then Joe and Vivi set off for the escape tunnel.

Meanwhile, the professor scanned the control computer for information about the complex. He found interesting data. The building armor consisted of steel two meters thick, alloyed with a ten-centimeter-thick layer of lead. The bunker was nuclear safe and fully automatic armed at the entrances. Two plasma lasers each were located at the two inputs. There was also an emergency exit, which they had not found yet. The bunker had three internal, exhaust-free Tesla Thule generators with 50 each megawatt of power supplied. However, only one was in operation, as the control application indicated. There they could also read all other current values: "Power consumption: 150 Kw.

Life support systems: three. Thule converter: 250 cubic meters of oxygen per hour. Maximum crew of the complex: 200. Currently present: 2. Food supplies for 200 men: eight days."

The professor studied the hologram of the bunker model and noticed that there was a sort of gate above room C4. "What's the purpose of the gate above this room?" He asked the computer.

"The gate above room C4 allows the departure of the completed Haunebus. Caution: If the gate is opened, no consideration is given to the buildings above it. Only open in case of emergency."

Meanwhile, Joe and Vivi had already arrived at the lock for the Tesla Vril van.

"Attention, please make a safety check before the emergency exit is opened," came a voice. Vivi went to the console and told the computer to do the diagnosis. "Tunnel safe," was the answer, "initiate emergency sequence."

A door opened and in front of them stood a vehicle about three meters high. It was mounted on rails and it was probably a maglev train. "Great, let's go," Joe said.

"What are we waiting for?" Vivi grinned. "In and out!"

They sat in the train and Joe pressed the start button. The acceleration from 0 to 500 lasted just three seconds, both were strongly pressed into their seats. The railway stopped automatically at the station of the anti-tech complex. The journey took only a few minutes.

"Oh my God that's awesome," Joe said as he staggered out slightly. "That was at least 4-5 g of acceleration force, which is four to five times the body weight," he explained.

"You can say that again. My eyes went black," Vivi said.

They quickly found the exit and typed the code they had received from Julian into the small device mounted in the wall next to the lock. The gate opened and they stood in a dark niche in the tunnel to the anti-tech complex.

For a long time they did not have to go to get to the same gate, which a few days ago they had left the complex of anti-technicians, with the aim of reaching the Haunebu of the rebels. Slightly disappointed, they now stood in front of the closed gate. They were back in the same place, the escape from New Berlin seemed another failure. And yet they had gained new hope. The professor's bunker contained solutions that could enable them to make their way to America. However, it was still a long way to go. The first challenge was to get into the anti-tech complex. On this side of the gate there was no input device for a PIN code, let alone a door trap. It looked like it could only open from one side. They were on the wrong side.

While they were still undecided before the portal and discussed how they could get into the complex, the door suddenly opened as if by magic and they saw the leader.

"What happened?" He asked curiously. He had skipped the greeting.

"We were captured by the New Germans," Joe replied. "Just before we finished our mission, they surprised us. The Haunebu is destroyed. They dragged us to their headquarters, tortured us and captured us. But one of the guards was a disguised opponent of the New Germans. He helped us to escape. In search of a way out of the city, we came across a huge, underground bunker built by Julian's grandfather. There are raw materials and plans there to build Haunebus. You will not believe it until you have seen it with your own eyes. A Tesla-Vril transporter leads out of the bunker directly into this tunnel. But enough talk, we have no time to lose! Can you mobilize twenty men who can spend a few days in the bunker? There is much to do! Maybe we have a little chance of survival again."

"That should be possible. Follow me! Did you have a meal? While I organize everything, you could first strengthen and rest first."

It only took a few hours for the leader to organize a select troop. They were equipped to spend a few days in the bunker and were full of energy. Joe went ahead and led them to the niche, which served as a passage to the escape tunnel. They had never noticed this before. The niche was hidden in the craggy rock and no ray of light came through there. After the fast ride in the Tesla Vril van, the troop walked to the bunker entrance, curious. Julian had entrusted the PIN to Joe and they passed unhindered through the emergency exit back to the complex.

Only a few rooms away, the professor in the library leafed through ancient books, reading a few passages here and there, and getting a rough overview of the past.

When Joe and Vivi arrived with the anti-techs, the professor was torn from his reflections. "Hello everyone, did you have a good trip? May I introduce our new arsenal."

The enthusiasm was written in the face of the anti-technicians. "What should we do, how can we help?" Someone asked.

"First of all, I'll take you through the premises and show you everything. Then we work out a plan with the responsibilities. Everyone works in his field of expertise. We have to build Haunebus and plan to escape to America. In addition, we need people who are responsible for the food supply. Fortunately, we are connected to the anti-tech complex through the escape tunnel. The delivery should be easy. Others can be used for security and surveillance. The New Germany are definitely looking for us meticulously. Who knows how long it will take them to discover the entrance to the bunker?"

With Julian at the helm, the men set off. But in the middle of them leaving, the professor quietly turned to Joe, "Where is my wife? Mary?"

"No idea," Joe said, "I last saw her in the armory. But that was a long time ago."

The professor left Joe on the lead and went to the armory. In fact, he met Mary there, leaning against the wall with her head against a wall.

"Mary, what's up?" He asked worriedly. "Are not you feeling well?"

"Leave me alone."
"What is wrong with you? Why are you so irritated and angry with me all the time? Do not you love me anymore?"

"Of course I love you," she answered, her head cocked.

"What is it then?"

"I'm just scared. I am afraid that we will lose sight of each other again, fear that you will be tortured or die. These damn New Germans! The whole situation scares me. I wish we were in America. Do you understand that?"

"Oh yes of course. And believe me, everyone is scared," the professor said and sat down next to her. He gently put his arm around her.

"That may be, but unfortunately that does not help me any further."

"We've never been so close to a possible escape, Mary. We'll build airships that take us to safety," Julian reassured her.

"I want to leave quickly. Preferably today. Why did not my ancestors emigrate? They would have had a nice time in America."

"Well, they probably had no reason to emigrate then. And then you would not have found me," he said softly.

"You're such a nice man. Luckily we are together again. Say, do you ever want children?" Mary asked.

"As?"

"Yes, you already understood me. I would like to have children. For a long time. But I always thought you did not like them, so I left it alone. My Professor, we can ~~all~~ tell each other, how long have we been together?"

"Ten years."

"And how old am I?" Mary challenged.

"You're 35, sweetheart," Julian grinned.

"Well, you see, it's not impossible to have children."

For a while, lost in thought, they sat tightly entwined in the corner of the weapons depot. They both pictured ~~his~~ their future. At some point, Julian broke the harmony and asked, "Tell me, Mary, can you still remember anything from when you were addicted?"

"No, I can not remember anything. Why do you ask?"

"I was just wondering if the New Germans did anything to you. But that is not important anymore.

The important thing is that we are together. Eventually, that too will come to an end. When I was alone for so long, I never knew if you were alive; I thought they had already murdered you long ago. Now I am very happy that they did not do it. Can you still remember how we met? Back in the disco, you danced, you were so cute, I just had to approach you."

"This disco in the bunker was not really a disco."

"Well, what else?"

"A little party with music."

"Then stop that. When you kissed me the first time, I felt so good about my heart, it was love at first sight."

"Well, second, my dear."

"No, no, that's not true. How can you be so sure?"

"Well, quite simply, you're a professor. And a professor rushes nothing."

"I'm not a real professor. I only got the title because I knew so much as a child."

"Yeah, you've always been the smartest of them all," said Mary, smiling.

"Yes, I was always teased for that."
"Be happy, if you were not the one you are now, you would not have me. Very easily."

In that way, the conversation continued until Joe came in and explained that the tour was over.

The Research Station

"Well, gentlemen, I hope you all got full!" Julian stood in front of the 24 people in the dining room and had taken the lead again. "Unfortunately you have to finish your break now, we still have a lot to do!"

The professor knew they were running out of time. If the New Germans had the slightest suspicion that such a station was present underground, it would not be long before half the army stood before the doors. Precautions had to be taken, the entrances better secured and the escape tunnel upgraded. After a good 70 years without maintenance, not everything was in top condition. There were brittle walls and here and there some leaks where moisture seeped through. Thanks to the best quality of the building materials used though, the bunker was still stable and adequately protected.

"First, we'll rehabilitate the walls and reinforce all entrances. We do not know exactly how long we could withstand a potential attack. The two outdoor cameras, which are almost invisibly hidden in niches of the tunnel and fortunately still work, have recorded a few disturbing shots. A few hours ago, a troop of New German soldiers marched through the tunnel. They have discovered the broken train and the broken wall of the tunnel and have to assume that we have escaped through the tunnel. They have passed us through the main tunnel and are likely to continue at the exit of the tunnel. All too well that they do not suspect that we are still in there. However, we must expect that they could somehow locate us. Our only advantage is that the whole base is at a depth of almost 200 meters and there are only five access points. However, if they find out where we are, they will try to seal off our escape tunnel with access to the anti-tech complex and starve us to death. Or they will be able to open the gates. I want all of my grandfather's research to be put into the anti-tech complex and thus to safety. The material must never fall into the hands of the enemy. We will now go to the lab together and decide who is responsible for which task. Leo and Hannes will come with me afterwards. We'll look at the blueprints of Haunebus and create a project plan for the creation of a new flying disk. Once we have the planning on paper, we will portion the iron with the laser. Until then, the rest of the antitank technicians will have brought the research and books to safety and rehabilitate the fragile areas in the bunker. Then all our attention is devoted to the construction of Haunebus. We will upgrade. And as soon as we are ready, we plan our escape to America!"

The men cheered Julian. New hope was kindled. Soon they would be able to lead a life in freedom again. Their ancestors had paved their way. Now they just had to use the resources right.

In the lab, Julian shared responsibility with the leader. Some men served as guards, others took over the food and goods transports between the research station and the anti-tech complex and others, who were skilled with their hands, did the repairs. Missing material was brought by the anti-tech complex. Each of the men was equipped with an earpiece so that everyone could communicate, no matter where they were. They estimated that they could start building the first Haunebu in two days. Albert, who was also the leader of the anti-technicians, was responsible for reviewing all ongoing work and taking care of the workers' concerns. When everyone knew what he had to do, they started.

Since Vivi and Joe were not immediately assigned to the tasks, but were considered guests, Vivi retreated to the library to read the books a little and Joe joined Julian.

"Hey Doc," Joe said to Julian, "are we going to take a look inside the ship?"

Hannes and Leo, who were to study the blueprints of Haunebu together with Julian, were as pleased with the idea as Julian himself. They went to the production hall C4, where the gem stood.

"Isn't it great," Julian remarked proudly as they entered the room.

"You say so!" Joe confirmed.
"How long will it take us to make such a ship?" Hannes asked.

"I do not know exactly," Julian replied, "I expect our workload could be up in two months. Now that we have the metal and the knowledge, the biggest challenges are solved. There is only one problem left at the end: the overflight to America. But we'll manage it."

The four men entered the ship, where they saw a strange sight. Inside, it looked like they were in space, the walls were dark, as was the floor. There were no windows, just a few doors and a console in the middle.

"The ship is piloted from here," the professor explained. "It does not need windows, everything is built up holographically."

"So you have your knowledge of holograms?" Joe asked. "Because your grandfather worked with it them?"

"Must be like that."

"But where did the New Germans get that knowledge? It's going to be huge," Joe said.

"I was never fond of the New Germans either," Julian smiled. "However, hologram technology has become very well established in the 2060s. This was a worldwide technological advance and the New Germans simply used it intelligently for their purposes."

"Vivi once said something about Vril and Thule, but I've never really cared."

"Well, in retrospect, you're always smarter. Now you can make up for everything. Let's take a look around!"

Joe opened an inner door. "Those were the crew cabins," he said.

"Yeah, looks that way," Hannes said.

After examining the entire interior of the ship, Julian and his two men made plans and Joe looked for Vivi.

He found her in the lobby, where the control computers were.

"Well, Vivi, what's new?" Joe asked.

"It's unbelievable, this technique is just insane. Do you see these little dots here?" She pointed to some small spots on the big monitor of the control computer.

"Oh yeah."

"These are rats. This complex is fully monitored by the computer equipment. Every living being is located and displayed here. Should the New Germans approach, we would see this immediately and an alarm would be raised. In rats, the alarm is disabled because he would otherwise start too often. But you could also activate it. Every living being is depicted on a uniform scale. A rat is much smaller than a human. So you even know what to do with it. If you then tap the dot, a pop-up will appear, revealing details."

She tapped one of the small dots and a picture of a rat appeared with information about height, weight, and location.

"Here," she went on, "that's us: two points, also green. However, bigger than the rats. Here are the entrances to see. They are red, it means that all doors are closed. Here at the emergency exit also lights a green light, you see? And this is the suspension railway. It moves and just leaves the complex. The anti-techs have already begun to get rid of material. What I find even more interesting is this gear here. No one has taken notice of this until now. It's another escape tunnel that leads north out of New Berlin. As I can see from the system, there used to be another base in Peenemuende, about 260 km from here. Through this escape tunnel you reached the road to Peenemuende. There, the first Haunebus had to be completed and tested in a secret location, probably the professor has transported the ships from the research station to Peenemuende, because this tunnel is the largest, it has a diameter of ten meters, well, not enough for a Haunebu, but maybe it was transported in individual parts and only assembled in Peenemuende. In the tunnel is a shuttle." Vivi gasped. She had talked so quickly that she forgot to breathe. Joe had no time to comment on the findings, she continued:

"The problem is, I do not know what's in there today. The system does not provide information about whether the breakpoints is still operational. We have to ask the professor, maybe he knows something about it. Peenemuende is located almost at the northernmost point of New Germany, directly on the Baltic Sea. If we leave from there, we can escape without flying over German-German airspace!"

Vivi set out to tell Julian about her latest discoveries. With Hannes, Leo and Julian in tow, she came back to the control computer. The news she had already got rid of on the way. Very interested, Julian glanced at the map and the escape tunnel. When asked if the base still existed, he shook his head.

"No idea, I've never been that high up north. I have no memories of Peenemuende in my head."

"If there's another departure station, you might be able to flee to Britain from there," Joe suggested. "And then from England to America."

"England has not existed for a long time. It is under the control of the New Germans. They are not extremely active there, but we would have difficulty flying over this airspace."

"What would you suggest?" Joe asked.

"About Denmark. Fly around England and then directly across the Atlantic to America. We have to provide the Haunebu with a new drive and a new camouflage. It's just too slow, and we would not last long without camouflage."

"Well, get to work, Professor. I will get some more books. Will you come with me, Vivi?"

"Yeah," she said, following Joe into the library.

After reading for about an hour, Vivi broke the silence.

"What I do not understand, Joe: Look, according to the plan I found at the beginning, the whole station has an area of 30,000 square meters. But the area on which we move is not even half as big. What about the rest?"

"No idea. We probably have not discovered all the doors and rooms yet. It is best to study this plan again and try to orient ourselves. We can also bring Mary to her, she can help us to look for more rooms."

And they did. Joe informed Mary and motivated her to join them. She was not enthusiastic about the job, but she assumed that since she had nothing to do right now she might as well. Julian was madly busy with the construction of his Haunebus and left he alone. Vivi pulled the card into the library and together they bent over it, trying to match the floor plan on the plan with reality.

"That's the room we're in," Vivi said. "C5, that's the library. It's also at the front door."

"There should be another room right behind it," Mary said, pointing a finger at a field beside the library.

"And also here, next to the sanitary facilities," Vivi said. "The two unknown rooms are connected. This is probably going to be a door." Vivi ran her finger over the map as Joe looked around the room.

"According to the plan, another door would have to be next to the corner to the north-east, leading to an adjoining room," said Mary.

"But why is the adjoining room overlapping the library, that does not make sense," murmured Vivi. "The floor plan reaches into the library, the rooms can not be in one another."

"But on top of each other. Therefore, the side rooms are marked D2 and D3. They're one floor down!" Mary shouted.

At that moment, Joe looked at the floor. Was it possible that there was a trapdoor somewhere ? Instead, he noticed a control box on a low dresser. He pressed a button and a layer of the floor slid silently on its side and cleared a staircase. In the basement, an emergency generator jumped and dipped everything in a soft light. They descended the stairs and saw a hallway and a door in it. Mary walked first to the door and typed in a code.

"I learned a little something from my husband too," she called to Joe and Vivi, giggling.

As she pushed open the door, a nasty stench reached her. She grimaced. At the same moment the light also went on automatically in room D2 and she saw an underground garden. Or at least what was left of it. Everywhere there were dried plants in artificial beds at hip height. It smelt of rotten earth and compost. Joe and Vivi had entered the room behind her, staring at the mess as well. Slowly they moved through the rows between the plant beds and approached a computer terminal. The computer was in stand-by mode and started up when Joe touched it.

A flashing alarm message appeared on the monitor: emergency shutdown. Defect in the ventilation system.
"Oh, that was the reason for the system's exit. There was not enough oxygen left," Vivi thought.

"Hey, Professor, come over with your two technicians, have a look," Joe said with his earpiece to Julian. He described his position to him.

As they waited for Julian, they studied a board set up beside the first set of beds. It was again a message from the professor's grandfather.

"Dear descendants, I have created a self-sufficient garden here. The vegetables are genetically modified, it needs very little water and light. In addition, it is easy to maintain, it grows until it reaches a certain size and then remains fresh until it is harvested. The computer system should monitor the garden and remedy faults on its own. Once you have harvested the vegetables, you have to cut the stems, so the plants will grow again. I hope the system works and you will find a thriving vegetable garden. However, should be something defective, you will first look at the filters. Although they are self-cleaning, according to the manufacturer for 200 years, but these are just calculations, since the filters have not been on the market for more than 200 years and consequently nobody was able to prove it. Professor Schneider."

At that moment Julian entered with his two men and the three marveled at the garden hall.

"Something went wrong," Julian said, "otherwise we could eat tomatoes and cucumbers now."

"The computer reports a defect in the ventilation system. Let's try cleaning the filters!" Mary said.

It took less than ten minutes for the ventilation to start whirring. After Hannes and Leo cleaned the filters, the system automatically restarted. Of course, the current harvest was dehydrated and unusable, but if they actually had to use the bunker once to stay safe for a long time, the plants would be quickly restored.

Julian stepped to the control computer and switched off the operation completely. To the people in the room he said, "The garden is great, but not our first priority.

We hope that we can leave the bunker soon with a few flying discs. We have to focus on that. The gardens have been resting for many decades, leaving everything as it is, but we must devote ourselves to the current challenges."

The others agreed with him and Hannes and Leo returned to the C floor to work on the Haunebu plans.

Grinning, Julian said to Mary, "Would you like to try something new, my love?"

She looked at him questioningly.

The Tunnel Towards Peenemuende

Julian had already invented the plan. Grinning, he looked at his wife and said, "It could be dangerous. We will leave Berlin through the escape tunnel and take a vehicle to Peenemuende. I want to know what's over there."

"With what vehicle?" Mary asks.

"There will be one at the end of the tunnel. I have a clue," the professor answered.

Sighing, Mary agreed to come along. She did not like the idea of driving around on the surface of the earth and going into the territory of the New Germans, though not too tempting, but that Julian would go alone, she found even less great. So the professor and his wife went to the tunnel. Although Joe and Vivi had expressed an interest in coming along, Julian said he did not want to risk them being caught by the New Germany. The second time the punishment would be a lot higher, as they were now also accused of flight. He said that down here in the research station they were safe for the time being and that he did not want to risk life unnecessarily. He had not noticed Mary's outraged look.

The monorail in the escape tunnel was intact and brought them within seconds to the end of the tunnel. When Julian gave the order to accelerate, both were pressed into their seats, as their colleagues had been told. Staggering slightly, they got out of the vehicle and looked around the tunnel.

"Great, now what? Everything is concreted here," Mary said.

It actually looked as if they had ended up in a dead end. Julian scanned the walls. He was so sure they would find a vehicle.

"Let's go back," he said.

"Are there rats here?" Mary asked.

"If there's no exit here, they've starved long ago," Julian reassured his wife.

They ran through the dimly lit tunnel and behind the first turn they actually found a door that could only be opened by entering a PIN. Without hesitating, Julian typed a combination and the door slid open. Behind it was a kind of garage. They saw a hover vehicle and a heavy transport truck.

"I told you," muttered Julian. "The only problem is that the New Germans seem to have walled up the exit."

"Well, then let's do it another time," Mary said. "Let's get a team that can drill a hole in the wall."

Even Julian had to admit that they couldn't do anything alone and without tools. He had to postpone the excursion to later. Before rejoining the suspension railway, Julian held Mary back and hugged her.

"Mary, let me talk to you now while we're alone. Since we've been together again, I have often noticed that you are melancholy or even morose. I feel like you've a burden about something." He looked questioningly at her.

"I do not know...The first few days in captivity were extremely hard for me and I keep seeing these pictures of the prisoners in front of me. I was lucky that I was fine. But when I realized that this music was slowly captivating me, I thought it was over forever. I just thought of you for the last time, I missed you terribly, and then...at some point I can not remember anything." She paused for a moment. Then she looked Julian straight in the eye and said desperately, "But that's not all...What really worries me is that I feel like I'm pregnant but not of you. I do not know, but my body goes crazy, maybe it's just because I'm so scared. I wanted to tell you all the time, but I just did not dare. I'm so sorry, I have to do a test!"

That was only time to digest hard food Julian did not know what to say for a few seconds. Then he reached out and said, "Darling, I'm with you, no matter what. Luckily, you finally told me what troubles you. You know, we'll do a test now, then we'll see."
"But I do not want to abort, should it really be that way," whispered Mary, "but I do not know if you can live with it, my love?"

"If you do have it, we'll just get a little baby, maybe it's even a clone. Mary, I will always love you and even then, if you should have a strange child, I will stand by you. But it makes me sad. I am angry, these damned New Germans know neither justice nor human dignity. It's time for us to attack her soon!"

The professor took his wife in his arms and they both started to cry.

"Always stay with me, never leave me," Mary sobbed.

"Of course," Julian said softly. "Come on, let's go back to the research station. Surely there's a kind of infirmary with an ultrasound machine."

Arrived at the main terminal, Julian went to the control computer and asked for an infirmary. The computer informed him that it was in room D3 and drew up a map.

"Access via library or lift in room C4," the computer added.

"C4? That's the production hall where the Haunebu stands," Julian said. "I did not notice a lift."

"Lift is installed in east wall, accessible via switch box," reported the computer. Again, a situation plan appeared on the monitor.

The professor studied the plan, and then both set off. They found the built-in lift in the wall and drove to the D-floor. The hospital room was right next to the self-sufficient garden, they had not paid attention to it before.

They were impressed at how clean and highly modern the sanitary station was. Apparently no expenses were spared. The professor looked around and searched for an ultrasound machine or a body scanner.

"Lie down on this bed," he told his wife, and Mary lay down. She revealed her midsection and Julian prepared a gel.

When he switched on the device and ran the ultrasound head over her stomach, it turned pale, because the scanner showed the outline of a small body. Ironically, the computer gave the age of four and a half months, but the child was smaller than a fist, although it would have measured at least 18 cm in at this stage. It also seemed as if it was not moving. Julian switched the scanner over to the organs. The scanner displayed an intact brain, but the child's heart did not beat. So Mary had a clone in her with a brain that still worked, but the rest was dead tissue. The professor felt more comfortable.

"Mary, you are pregnant, but the child is dead," he said. "It must have been dead for more than a month."

Mary stared at the scanner's monitor. She was relieved and worried at the same time.

"Can you get the fetus out?" She asked.

"We have a surgical robot here," Julian said. "It should be possible. Let me see what types of operations are programmed."

He worked his way through the table of contents and selected Obstetrics. He quickly found the right program.

"Are you ready, honey?" Julian asked.

"Yes my love. Start with it."

The professor rolled the robot to the bed after Mary
bared. He covered her with a surgical drape, leaving
only the spot on her stomach free. The robot was
easy to program. Julian entered the necessary
parameters and the robot began with the disinfection
of the abdomen and a local anesthetic. There was a
small incision in the abdominal area that was barely
visible. When the operation was over and the cut was
clean, Mary breathed.
"Did you feel anything?" Julian asked, standing awake
the whole time.

"No, everything went well." She glanced at a surgical
bowl containing a bloody lump of tissue.

"Oh, this baby looks awful. Get rid of it!" Mary
commanded.

"Where should I put it?" Julian asks helplessly.

"How should I know that? Are there recycles here?"
Mary asked.

"No, they do not go on until later."

Julian looked around the cabin of the infirmary again
and found opaque plastic pouches. They were labeled
with bio-waste and you could seal them with a device.
So you could pass the bag to the normal garbage and
it would be burned.

After Julian had cleaned and tidied everything, he
hugged his wife. She would have to lie in the hospital
bed for three or four days and recover from the

operation. He pushed her and her bed into the elevator and took her up to the dormitory. It was not long before Mary fell asleep.

The exploration of Peenemuende

After one and a half months in the research station, the work was almost completed and the men had portioned all the iron for the production of drives and built the first engines. So that the metal could not come into contact with oxygen, a protective cover had been built around the block and the laser and the metal operated on in the protective atmosphere. The individual portions of iron were also packed in their own protective covers. Only when they were put into operation, you could refrain from the protective cover, as they were embedded in the engine in a force field, which it continued to protect. The original Haunebu 3 was reconditioned and ready for use and the items of other ships of the series 2 and 3 were built. The men had also brought all the valuable books and writings to safety.

Luckily for them, the New Germans had not tracked them down so far. They must have assumed that the fugitives had somehow come out of New Berlin through the subway tunnel. There was a search in all of New Germany. However, the enemies of the state had been spotted to their displeasure in no other region. It was assumed that someone had planned and carried out the escape externally very professionally. Of course, there had to be other groups that had an interest in the time traveler. The rebels were the first on the list of suspects. However, they still had no proof.

During the past six weeks, the research station had also been completely renovated and better secured. Now only the reinforcement of the defense was missing. The plan was to disassemble the original

Haunebu 3 and to transport it together with the already made individual parts of the other Haunebus to Peenemuende. The iron was to be split in half, with one half also to be brought to Peenemuende. The anti-technicians, who were already in the research station, would relocate to Peenemuende and complete the first Haunebus for the passage to America. At the same time 20 more men would be are transferred from the anti-engineering complex to the research station. Their task would be to make more Haunebus and engines and at a later date also to Peenemuende to create more. So they could halve the risk of falling into the hands of the New Germans with the valuable material. The leader of the anti-techs should stay at the research station and coordinate all the tasks, while Julian should prepare everything for the first flight with the remaining men in Peenemuende. Once the airships were efficient for the crossing, the first 20 men could settle for America.

In the meantime, the tunnel that had been laid out in the direction of Peenemuende had been opened so far that the transporter could leave it. The exit had been camouflaged, so it still looked like it had been walled up. The tunnel ended in an abandoned piece of nature, not far from a dense forest. However, it led to a road on a nearby motorway entrance, which lay in the direction of Peenemuende. The road had deteriorated and was worn by erosion. Moss had settled on it. The truck would still be able to get over it anyway, it had huge tires like a bulldozer. However, to this day Julian had not been able to drive to Peenemuende on the Hover to explore the area. Before he would bring his men there, he had to inspect the situation himself. It was possible that the base was totally destroyed. In that case, they would have to look for a different solution.

With an instant coffee in his hand Joe addressed the professor again about the project: "Professor, what about Peenemunde?"

"Yes, I just wanted to come to that. Actually I wanted to drive out for weeks, but the construction of the Haunebus has taken all my attention. But now I could afford to quit shortly. Originally I wanted to go alone with my wife, but meanwhile this idea seems very reckless. There must be some reason why there are no New Germans there. We have to put together a team. However, I want to keep Vivi out. The women should stay here at the research station. But you, Joe, I would like you to be the guide."

"As a leader?" Joe asked in astonishment.

"That's right, Joe. I would like to give you some responsibility after we arrive in America. So I've decided to give you the mission Exploration Peenemuende. I will be there, but keep myself in the background. I want you to take command!"

Joe felt a little uncomfortable. Of course, he had never done such an endeavor, and it seemed he had to go through it without Vivi at his side. He did not know how his wife would react when he revealed to her that he would go into the unknown on his own.

"I'll have to talk to my wife first," Joe said.

"Yes, I'll leave it to you, talk to her. If she says no, I understand that."

Joe got up, ~~and~~ nodded, and left the kitchen.

"Hello, Vivi. All right with you?" Joe tried to put on a loose tone when he found her bent over a book in the library.

"What's wrong? You look depressed" she answered. Apparently his strategy had not worked. His wife knew him too well.

"Yes, that's how I feel. The professor has asked me to be a guide in the exploration of Peenemuende. But I can not, I do not want to leave you."

"Joe, I'll leave you the choice. If you want to go, then go. We will all have to fight in this wretched world. I'll wait for you, my dear."
"Alright, I'll accept. And I will come back, for sure."

"Yes, Joe, I know."

After talking to Vivi and having her support his plan, Joe felt a lot better. Now he was even looking forward to the mission. Julian was also glad when Joe came back and told him he was coming.

"But Joe...like I said, it could not be completely harmless. Maybe we have to fight. I definitely take the men who have the most combat experience. We will take weapons. We have to expect everything," said Julian.

"I'm in, as I said," Joe said firmly.

"Good," the professor said. "Let's go in two days."

For two days, Joe enjoyed spending time with his wife. They read books, talked and had fun. Until the day came, where Joe should go again into mortal danger. When he said goodbye to Vivi, tears came to his eyes.

"Good luck, my dear," she told him. "And don't you dare not come back. I'll be waiting for you."

They were a troop of eight men. Any more would not fit in the hover vehicle. All were connected with one ear device, the weapons were in the hold. One of the men steered the vehicle, Joe and Julian sat behind and discussed the strategy again.

"Most likely, the base is abandoned. I am absolutely unaware that the New Germans have an active position there. Exactly this point, however, seems puzzling to me. Why didn't the New Germans besiege this place and use it for their purposes? Was it strategically unimportant for them? Or do they have another secret?" Julian puzzled.

"We'll find out soon," Joe answered.

The good thing was that Peenemuende was not far from New Berlin. With their hover vehicle, they could cover the distance in a few minutes. The highway was almost empty. They just met three vehicles. It seemed as if they were venturing into the remotest corner of New Germany.

Peenemuende itself resembled a ghost town. The hover vehicle could even measure a slight radioactivity. But not threatening. Quickly they found the old base of anti-technicians and the abandoned airfield. The area looked like it had been 100 years old
 No one had been here for years. The relief of not meeting any New Germans was great. Slowly, the hovercraft rolled over the driveway and approached a building on the airfield. The hologram showed them in high resolution the environment in a 360° angle. Everything was lonely and abandoned. That's why they were all the more shocked when suddenly something crossed the square. The hologram showed a kind of machine. Not even half the size of a human, but it was moving at breakneck speed. When ~~she~~ it had disappeared behind a corner of ~~the~~ a house, the men sat silently in the vehicle, waiting to see if something similar would happen again. Another ~~thing~~ object rushed across the scene. Silently they watched the situation until one of the men said, "Sir, we are waiting for your orders."

"Please, do not call me sir, every one of you has more experience of war than me. I suggest that we first activate all our radiation protection in clothing. There is low radioactivity out there. The goal of our mission is to find out as much as possible about the place and the technology it hosts. So let's get to work. Grab your weapons and find out what kind of machines we've just seen. Let's go."

In the troop was a fighter who was just 16 years old, but already at this age, this boy knew more about the art of war than some veterans in Joe's time. Joe had already taken the boy into his heart at the research station, for he liked his attitude ~~to~~ towards life. He had learned that the soldier had a girlfriend, in bunker two of the anti-tech complex, and that he loved her very much. In times of war, stable values such as a strong relationship and a loyal partner were probably very important. The boy intended to marry his girl. He had also told Joe a lot about life in the anti-tech complex. There was democracy in the bunkers, and the leaders had only the task of recruiting and instructing new ones. There were bunkers all over New Germany, in which anti-technicians lived. The supreme organ of the anti-technician consisted of four elders. Each had been allocated an area: food, family support, defense or maintenance. These elders were chosen by the anti-technicians in a poll and remained in office for two years until they could assert themselves in a next election.

When Joe got out of the Hover vehicle, he stayed close behind the boy. He wanted to keep a close watch on him, taking care that nothing happened to him. A pale daylight enveloped them. The trees were barren, the landscape was different than in the other areas Joe had seen in this future version of Earth. Everything was pale and adapted to the haze of the sky. The ground was not overgrown with moss, but a colorless earth. At some distance they could see the gray sea and the colorless horizon that was built into the sky beyond. In addition, it was deathly quiet in Peenemuende. Not even the surf of the waves was noticeable. Curious, the men looked around. The fast-moving thing that had previously been visible in the hologram had disappeared. Nothing moved.

They saw an old, abandoned airport in front of them and a few buildings. Joe gave the order to head for the first building. It was a hangar, as it turned out. Amazingly, it was in very good shape.

"Secure the environment!" Joe ordered. The men heard his orders over the earphones. Four of them stood guard at the entrance, the other four entered the hangar. Inside, Joe took a closer look. He spotted a desk with a computer on it.

"it's not going to run after all these years," he thought, because it looked like someone had already bothered. A cable had been torn out. Joe took out his scanner and turned it on to power the computer. But as soon as he had switched on the device, he heard alarmed shouts from the guards, that were replaced by gun salvos. Joe was getting cold. He watched some things approaching at great speed outside. They looked like little robots hovering just above the ground. Although they were apparently just machines, ugly and made of metal, they looked very threatening. Some had already reached the building, but the shots of his men did not fail. As fast as the things had come, they moved away equally fast. Joe called out to see if everything was alright. One of the soldiers said yes, but said, "Chief, we have company here. I think we should get out of here."

"Hold your position for a while, please. I've got something to look at!" The power from the scanner worked perfectly, and when Joe turned on the computer, he immediately saw a news program. Someone had sent plans and information from here. The sender was also unique. The imperial logo in the message was unmistakable.

"Julian, look at this!" Joe shouted to the professor, who also inspected the hangar. "I found a correspondence of the New Germans. The first message looks like an invasion plan!"

Julian hurried to Joe and began to read:

"01.05.2081: Today we started the construction of the first cyborgs. They should take over the invasions on the following goals:

2082: invasion of Russia
2083: Invasion of Great Britain
2084: Invasion of China
2085: Invasion America
2086: invasion of Africa
2087: invasion of the rest of the world"

Joe clicked on another message:

"Addendum of 12th of August 2081: We have to retire, the cyborgs seem to have malfunctions. It is no longer possible to control them. They develop a momentum that is dangerous or even deadly. We lost some of our men. The mission is canceled. We will irradiate this place with a nuclear weapon. Let's hope that all cyborgs are destroyed by it. Unfortunately, we will not be able to live here anymore. Our invasion plans must wait. We must continue to clone our forces, for better or worse. Addendum end."

Then Joe and Julian discovered a message that was very different from the others. It had arrived almost 60 years later.

"Unbelievable how sturdy these machines are!" Joe thought through it.

"Entry of soldier Mark Hauser on 09th of July 2139: 'Me and my team were summoned here by Bunker Haunebu Two to explore this place. To my misery, I was not told that there are cyborgs here. They are small but effective bio mechanical robots. They resemble dogs, but they have small laser weapons that fire extremely fast. Most buildings are intact. The nuclear weapons used by our ancestors have contaminated the area but have not damaged the infrastructure. Amazingly, even this old computer works from the pre-deluge. Although I had to feed it with external energy to get it to work, the message delivery seems to be intact. Even the cyborgs are almost not around the corner, it seems. I found out, that these robots can retain and recharge their energy through radioactive radiation. The plan of our ancestors to destroy the robots with a nuclear weapon has probably gone completely wrong. The opposite has happened. The beasts can feed on the radiation. Fortunately, our measurements show that the radiation is steadily decreasing and will probably have reached zero by 2152. By then the cyborgs will lose their energy source and hopefully give up the ghost. We could not kill them with our conventional weapons and we do not want to obliterate the entire area with an atomic bomb.

'Should we manage to reprogram the cyborgs, we would have one of the most robust and indestructible weapons. I hope I can prove my theory by capturing a cyborg and getting into our complex. We'll go outside again later and try to put our plan into action. Causer's end.' "

Joe looked at Julian confidently. "They are weak. The radiation is almost zero. That's why they probably fled so fast when our men opened the fire. Seems like we hit the perfect timing," he said triumphantly.

Joe called the other two fighters who were in the hangar and informed them about the new cache of knowledge. The 16-year-old boy was among them. Together, they discussed how they could wipe out the cyborgs. They had to lure them away from the buildings and then use the most powerful weapon they had with them, the beam torpedo. Since everything was pulverized within a radius of 20 meters after using this weapon , they had to somehow move the cyborgs into the open field. In no case did they want to destroy the airfield. Here, their departure station should be built to America. The only thing that bothered him right now was the cyborgs. How could they manage to lure hem all to one place at the same time?

"Do we have a weapon that releases radioactive radiation?" The boy asked.

"No, but we could use our scanners to simulate a radioactive field," Julian replied. "That way we could lure the cyborgs out. They will surely be greedy for energy!"

"Great," Joe said. "We'll move far enough away so that the radiant torpedo can not harm the infrastructure of the airfield. Then we simulate a radioactive field, and once the cyborgs are at a distance of about 100 meters, we fire the torpedo. But we have to be very fast, the things move like arrows.

The cyborgs must all be within the required radius. If we can not destroy them all at once, we'll have to use the handguns. Grace to us, God!"

At Joe's command, the eight ran to the hover vehicle. The driver drove away a few hundred yards from the airport, then parked the vehicle at a safe distance from the designated battlefield. Again they experienced an unreal silence. Not even a gust of wind whistled through the dry trees. The strongest fighter was equipped with the jet torpedo, the others took handguns. A short nod of the attendees showed that everyone was ready.
"Let's make sure we kill the cyborgs!" Joe shouted. They stormed into the field and turned on their scanners. Immediately the area shone purple on its display, indicating radioactivity. Tense and trembling with nervousness, the men waited for the effect of the delusion. It was not long before a whirring cut through the absolute silence. A black front approached from the direction of the airfield and moved towards it. The men were shocked by the high number of cyborgs. There had to be over 50 of them. Apparently their plan achieved the desired effect. The cyborgs craved radioactive energy. Julian stared at his scanner which showed them highly concentrated. This measured the exact distance of the first cyborg in the line. They were still 220 meters away. Then 140...

"Fire!" Yelled Joe. The beam torpedo roared through the air. The intensity was indescribable. A wave of pressure threw the fighters on the ground, earth and rocks lurched like missiles in all directions. Although the target was over 100 feet away, Joe was bleeding from the cheek for a small stone that had struck him.

A short time after the big bang came again there was dead silence. The air above the target area was darkened by the pulverized ground and dust. You could not tell if the cyborgs were gone. The men rose and stared intently into the cloud of dust and pointed their scanners. Suddenly, two cyborgs sped out of the darkness and headed straight for them. They shot wildly and hit two men, who immediately fell to the ground. The anti-technicians returned the fire and hit the cyborgs, who were then scattered in pieces and left lying on the ground. With raging hearts, the anti-technicians watched the cloud of dust slowly clearing. Were there more survivors? And what about their men? Joe looked after them and was saddened to find that both were dead. But her mission was successful. The battlefield resembled a crater after a meteor impact. Not a single other cyborg survived. They had retaken Peenemuende.

"We did our job. Let's go," said Joe depressed and proud at the same time. He still did not know how to teach the other anti-techs how to lose their peers. But that's the way it was at war.

With a shovel they found in the hangar, the men ~~took~~ dug two graves and laid their colleagues to rest. Silently, they drove back to the research station.

They were already expected by everyone as they entered through the escape tunnel. Vivi hopped around Joe's neck and was overjoyed to have her sweetheart healthy again. The relatives of the two dead men were from the anti-tech complex. Somebody was sent to deliver the sad news.

Joe was ready for this mission. He went to his sleeping quarters and lay down with Vivi in his arms. For the soldiers, he could not have done anything and had the best of intentions, everything had gone much too fast. Still, he did not let the image go away. As he pondered this thought, he fell into a restless sleep and only woke again when there was a gentle knock on the door the next morning. Outside stood the 16-year-old boy. He asked Joe if he would like to have breakfast with him. Since Vivi was still asleep, Joe gladly accepted the offer and stuck out of the bedroom. As they sat in the kitchen over a powdered coffee, the boy began to speak.

"Hey Joe, do not worry, we're at war. Hundreds of men will still give their lives. It is the duty of a leader to survive. You had managed the mission great. I know you have potential." He spoke as if he were 40 years old.

"Tell me, when did you first pick up a gun?" Joe asked.

 "I have had a gun with me since I can think."

"You have much more military experience than me, you should have command of America in my place."

"No sir. I am too young to lead, but I would like to fight at your side. I will support you whenever you need me."

"That's nice to know. I like you! But why is such a young man like you so willing to go to war? Is there anything better in your life? Your girlfriend for example? Why are you in such great danger?"

"Because my father died in the war two years ago. Look, Joe, I almost see you as a dad. I've been very fond of you over the last few weeks." He stirred his coffee with his head bowed, and Joe felt a great affection for the boy.

Move

Now the final preparations had been completed and after a long time in the underground bunker the men were burning to go to Peenemuende . America was within reach. Joe and Vivi also looked forward to the project excited. Now it started! Everything was organized. With the heavy truck, the individual parts of the Haunebus would be transported to Peenemuende. Likewise, the remaining weapons that had been left in the research station would be taken along. Half of the iron was ready for transport. The men who went to Peenemuende would make the Haunebus there and fly to America. There they would develop a war strategy and wait for the arrival of the next soldiers.

Shortly before Julian disappeared with his entourage through the second escape tunnel, he gave the leader the last instructions:

"Remember, you and the 20 men you'll pick up will only have access through the escape tunnel, which is connected to the anti-tech tunnel. Only I have the access code to the main tunnel. You can only enter the research station through the escape tunnel, the other entrances are closed to you. I will send back Meier, who will drive the heavy truck so that we can bring more Haunebu parts to Peenemuende as soon as they are finished. Meier knows the code for the access via the escape tunnel 2 and will open the lock for you as soon as you are ready for departure. I'll probably come by with the hover-drive before. If anything unforeseen happens and you need to contact me urgently, write a letter and send Meier as a messenger to me. Do not try to send me anything. In

Peenemuende I will develop a secure communication system. Until that works, we have to apply medieval methods. We will go now."

The workers set about filling the monorail with material. Every item of the Haunebus, the iron blocks in their protective covers, tools, weapons and supplies were taken to the end of the tunnel. The train had to go back and forth several times. Finally, everything was loaded into the truck and the dangerous part of the company began. The drive to Peenemuende did not take very long, but there was still the risk that a patrol would fly over it and become suspicious. The only advantage they had was that the New Germans would never suspect they were in a heavy truck.

The ride went smoothly, and as the truck pulled into the airport, Vivi exhaled with relief. Now they were almost at their destination. There was a hangar, which opened manually. Since no aircraft was in it, it was ideally suited as a hiding place for the heavy truck. The technical hangar was right next to it, where they would assemble the Haunebus. Initially they were very careful. Who knew if there was still a surviving cyborg? Julian sent a few men with scanners to search the area. After some time, they came back and gave the green light. It looked like the area was clear. While the anti-technicians still unloaded the truck, Julian, Mary, Joe and Vivi already went to the old station of Julian's grandfather, which bordered on the airport. An old staircase led into the depth and through a short corridor they came to a massive stone door. Of course, this could only be opened with a code. The device used to type this code looked like it was broken 100 years ago, but surprisingly it still worked. Without hesitating, Julian typed in a PIN and the stone door opened with a groan. Since Julian had visited the station quickly at the first exploration, he knew where the common rooms were. This bunker was a lot smaller than the underground research station and probably served mainly as an accommodation for the anti-technicians. There was even a food store with supplies. Vivi yawned.

"People, do not mind, but I'll lie down," she said. "Joe, are you coming?"

The two selected their beds and lay down while the professor and Mary stayed behind and devoted themselves to a board game that had been in the common room. They had not played it for a long time. It was called Chrasch. The rules were simple, and yet it promised an amusing evening. Everyone had to move their character with a magnet, until their character was at the finish. Who took the longest to conquer the course was the loser. In the middle of the game Julian had to get up to let the men in. Over a monitor you could overlook the outdoor area. He had already seen them coming. All material was unloaded and ready for assembly.

"Now? Do we want to go to bed too, Mary?" Julian asked as he won.

"Yes, let's go."

So the couple went to their quarters.

"Can you sleep, Mary?" The professor asked as he lay on his mattress. They were in separate cots, and it was hard to slumber because the last few days had been very exciting and challenging. Now that the transport had gone smoothly and they could soon start building the Haunebus, too many things were just going through his head.

"I'm tired, but I can not sleep either, are you coming to bed with me? Please come to me and hold me," said Mary.

The professor went to Mary. Her blanket was too small, but this did not bother the two. Holding each other peacefully, they fell asleep.

"Good Morning! Wake up, you sleepyheads. Today we have some plans," Hannes greeted the couple in the dorm. "The technicians will start assembling the airships shortly. Professor, we need you for the drive and the camouflage."
"You can go back to sleep, Mary. Just come over to the tech hangar later," Julian whispered to his wife.

Joe and Vivi stayed as well. They did not have any assigned work anyway. Julian got dressed, took a pack of breakfast, and went into the tech room.

"Oh, there you are! Look, Professor, this Haunebu 2 will soon be ready to fly. All parts are already assembled, the technicians could not wait and got up at the crack of dawn to assemble it. It just lacks the drive. We call it Promar. In honor of you and your wife," Leo exclaimed when he saw Julian.

"Bring me a computer," Julian said. An assistant brought him the desired device and the professor began to program the engine. He adhered strictly to the blueprints of his grandfather. He had deciphered the puzzle with the moon and assigned the circuits to the moon phases. After a few hours of work, without even looking up, the professor had written the program.

"That's how it should work," he said contentedly, getting to his feet.

The professor gave the computer the command to start. A glaring, white beam came out of the engine and made its way along the casing, where it built up at the edges of the ship into a spherical enclosure that embraced the entire ship. For those present, nothing was felt, but all saw the light. The ball collapsed and seemed to fill the ship. Now, as the light disappeared, the outer shell shone and the ship began to lift itself slightly off the ground. It floated about 50 centimeters above the ground. The professor and technicians shouted with excitement, "We did it, my friends, we did it!" Julian laughed. The men hugged each other with joy.

The professor opened the door to go inside the ship, where all he had to do was program the force field and the camouflage. "Get me Joe, he should come with me and do the first test flight with me! Go ahead, go fast!" He called out. Excited as he was, the professor could hardly wait to fly the first self-built ship. An assistant ran and got Joe. They arrived after some time back to Julian.

"Couldn't that wait? I was in the shower!" He complained.

"No, my boy, science can not wait. She is like a woman: if you pay no attention to her, she runs away from you. Now come in. We do not want to lose any time!" Julian looked like a little boy on Christmas day. He had shiny eyes and spoke at an unusual speed.

Joe got in and the professor closed the door.

"Are you ready for the first flight?"
"I don't know, no, not really."

"We have to see what speed we can reach," Julian continued, notwithstanding what Joe had said.

"What if the New-Germans see us?" Joe asked.

"We have the perfect camouflage, my boy! Perfect, I tell you! With the help of the Tesla coil it lasts four minutes. Longer we will not be outside. It is impossible for them to locate us. Even if they fly past us at a distance of only a hundred meters," the professor explained.

"Well then, my dear Professor, energize, as the Star Trek movies call it."

"Your wish is my command," Julian smiled.

The ship rose. Not a sound was heard. Only small wind gusts penetrated through the open gate of the hangar. Julian slowly edged her into the fresh air. Behind, the anti-technicians stared after them.

"I'll turn on the stealth device now. You may feel a little dizzy."

A soft chirping could be heard, otherwise everything remained calm. Slowly they gained height.

"We fly to the northeast, a lap across the Baltic, where the New Germans are not very active anyway."

The professor accelerated, but only a slight pressure was felt inside.

"How fast are we flying?" Joe asked curiously.

"2,000 km/h and further accelerating. We now have 20,000 km/h. That's enough. We should not fly faster, we would otherwise come up with the airspace surveillance, the atmospheric interference could reveal us. In addition, we would have flown in a few hours around the world. We are almost in Finnish airspace now. Let us turn back. We now know that this device can fly faster than 20,000 km/h. That's more than enough."

Julian set the new course, and it was not long before they arrived back in front of the hangar. Over the main hologram they could see that the anti-technicians were sitting around a table playing cards. Apparently they had used the test flight to take a short break. Nobody took notice of them. What an irony in such an event, people are sometimes strange.

"It does not seem like even our own people can detect anything. Let recognize us" Julian grinned.

When the ship was visible again and floated almost silently into the hangar, the men looked up in amazement from the game. The professor landed, and as he and Joe alighted, the antitank technicians were already in front of the entry hatch. They cheered and clapped. You could see that they believed in something again. So they enjoyed success, thought Joe.

"I did not think it would work on the first try, it's just wonderful!" Julian enthused. "Well, let's see that we can still arm this thing."

At that moment, Mary stepped into the hangar. Julian hurried toward her and took her arm. He led her to the Haunebu and said, "May I introduce you? That's Promar. It is the abbreviation of Professor and Mary. Our ship, honey!" He beamed at her proudly.

Although not as impressed as the rest of the troupe, Mary smiled. She found it amusing how eagerly her husband behaved. She was also very happy that she had caught the smartest man of all. Now it looked like they had a chance to escape to America.

The professor did not think to rest on his laurels, though. "Up, men, now we're going to build the remaining ships together! And then we bring the next 20 anti-technicians here. I'll then sit down at a computer and program a secure communication platform. Then we can tell the leader that our endeavor has worked out."

The men got back to work and Julian, with Mary in tow, approached Joe and pulled him aside.

"Joe, I want to discuss my resettlement plans with you. I've already thought a few things. As soon as the 20 anti-technicians are here with more airships, a few of them are to bring the women and children of all 40 men to Peenemuende. With a second fleet, everyone will come to America, where we will wait for them. Not all anti-technicians will come to America, some will of course hold a position in the bunker in New-Berlin and observe the situation. Through our communication platform, we will be constantly connected with our people in New Germany. When we arrive in America, I want to give you the command of some of my men. I have full confidence in you. We will contact the rebels and work out a plan of attack with them."

"I'll have to talk to Vivi first," Joe said hesitantly.

"Then do that," Julian said, "I just want to share a few things with you. The top priority of our flight to America is our original Haunebu 3. It will carry our valuable material. Once it is assembled, we load it with the iron. Mary and I will be the crew on the ship. Should we crash, everything is over. The war is then as good as lost. You and Vivi will fly Promar. I'll give you some men and more material. The other men are distributed with their families on the other airships. Do you understand me, Joe? We have to get these ships over at any cost. We fly to the north of America. There is the largest Allied rebel station. We will have enough workers and material on site to process all this metal. We will then bring together a fleet of about 1,000 ships. The first Haunebu 3 is taken to a safe bunker where it is stored. Because I will equip it with some special features. It should, if it comes to that, represent our last defense for the station. But I hope that will never happen."

Moved

Joe could not sleep, although the past few days had been very tiring, as the anti-technicians had assembled the airships and Joe had helped load the finished Haunebus with material. In particular, the iron, which had been stowed in Haunebu 3, had given him a bad sore muscles. Julian, the genius, had actually managed to develop a unique communication system within two days, connecting all three bunkers via the high-speed wireless network that was widely available. He had provided it with a high-profile algorithm that neither a robot nor a human could crack within a reasonable time. The code changed itself every three hours, making it impossible to ever get decrypted. In this way, they had an absolutely safe communication network in which the New Germans would find impossible to hack. Two days earlier, Julian had ridden the Hover vehicle back to the research station and installed the program. He had also visited the anti-tech complex and also connected this building to the system. He had arrived safely back in Peenemuende and they had initiated the system and had a chat with the research station as well as the anti-tech complex. The night before, Meier had been sent to New Berlin just before dusk, so that the heavy transporter was ready again to bring the next Haunebu parts and people to Peenemuende. It would not be long before they finally got over the Atlantic. While all this was pleasurable, the negative experiences that always raged around in Joe's head kept him from falling into a peaceful sleep. The fight against these cyborgs was still too prevalent in his memory. Especially since they were back at the scene now. It was just too much, would it ever end? All he wanted was a peaceful life. Joe looked at the clock, it was midnight. He thought of the boy who was called Lars. Joe hoped that Lars would survive the war and marry his girl. How terrible if a child had to grow up in the middle of a war and knew nothing but the fight. ~~He~~ Lars also lost his father. How terrible that had to be for him. Joe hoped they could all lead a life without war in America. But first there was too much to do.

How beautiful they had it in 2016! There were only problems with the internet connection and the taxes were high. And you were ripped off from all sides. But all that was harmless compared to this. Maybe that was the reward for always messing around? The people were never satisfied. But here were real problems. Every step they took outside was about life and death. Behind every tree, behind every corner, a New German could wait to shoot.

Joe got up and walked through the corridors of the bunker. There was an air-tower here, as at every airport. Joe had seen it from the outside, it was right next to the bunker. Was there access to the tower from down here? He wanted to find out and looked at the bunker card. Grinning, he realized that there had to be direct access. He felt like climbing all the way up, and set off. When he opened the door to the Tower, he realized in amazement that he had not been the only one who had had this idea. Lars sat in front of the glass front on a large armchair. Astonished, the boy looked at him: "What are you doing up here? Shouldn't you be sleeping?"

"That's what you're telling me! What are you doing here, boy?" Joe asked.

As it turned out, Lars was not here for fun, but volunteered for the watch. Joe had not even known there were layers of guards.

"Why did you volunteer for the watch?" Joe asked.

"I do not want to lose good friends again, Joe. You know, this is a big and important task for me. If the New Germans or any machines attack, I can sound the alarm. I certainly will not fall asleep. I got some extra Cola. It keeps you awake and I try to sleep during the day. As you know, enough volunteers call in the daytime."

"How come you did not get attacked all these years in the anti-tech complex?"

"I have no idea, they probably don't know exactly where we are, or they have more important things to do. There is terror in the south, the New Germans are very busy down there, because a few like-minded people are very aggressive there. But as we have learned, they can not last much longer. The New Germans are superior in terms of numbers and arms. Their troops overrun everything. It is only a matter of time before the anti-technicians are attacked here in the north. After all, we could now defend ourselves much better with the weapons from the research station. Nevertheless, we will have virtually no chance. No matter how many we kill, these clones come like ants. They are so many. Kill one, 100 come."

Thoughtfully, Joe looked through the large glass front into the deep darkness. Only a hologram and a computer screen inside the tower indicated what was going on outside. It was all quiet. It seemed that the New Germans had not really made it to the north yet.

"Well, we have the metal and we can make a lot of flying discs," said Joe, still staring straight into the darkness.

"That's the jackpot," Lars smiled.

"How did the professor's grandfather get such a lot of iron?" Joe puzzled. "Do you know anything about this?"

"Well, it started in the 1940s. When the Americans started their nuclear tests, the radioactive dust would spread throughout the atmosphere. So everything we know was easily contaminated by radioactivity. Only the large ships, which had sunk before these tests, were spared from this radioactivity. As they lay underwater, the radiation did not reach them. The grandfather of the professor had been in his early years on an expedition in which ships were searched, which had sunk before 1940. The professor told me everything. The research team had recovered wreckage and transported the iron in a protective sheath to a workshop. There it had been melted down with great care, cleaned and pressed into blocks. Later, the professor's grandfather had to bring this precious commodity to the research station and unite it into a huge block."

Approving, Joe nodded. "Julian's grandfather did a lot in his life. He must have been an incredibly intelligent, important man."

"He was," Lars agreed. He made a few settings on the computer and zoomed in on a picture.

"Look, Joe, back there's New Berlin. Just south of us. Can you see it on the hologram?"

Lars zoomed in a little closer and Joe could see the city, with all its lights shining in the night. In the middle of the city rose the tower, which Joe knew only too well.

"The picture quality is incredible," Joe said, impressed. "After all, we're 260 kilometers as the crow flies from the city." Of course, he'd taken that number from the information on the screen.

"Oh, yes, that's her. I hope one day there will be a hologram showing something better there."

"We all hope so."

"I miss my girlfriend," Lars said abruptly. "She's there now. How long have you been married, Joe?"

"It's about four years now. At 18 we got married. At 19, we emigrated to Germany, where we lived for three years. Vivi worked as a computer scientist and I got a job as a technician."

"Will you try to return?"

"Yes, certainly. I just have no idea how. As I have learned, time travel is still not possible. The New Germans are supposedly very keen on this technique. But so far no scientist has been able to build a working time machine." Joe yawned and Lars took a sip of his Coke.

"So, enough talk," Joe said. "I'll go to my bedroom again. Take care of yourself, boy."

"Thanks, you too, Joe."

The night was not over yet when Joe and Vivi were awakened by loud booming noises. Dazed, Joe tried to get his bearings.

"What's that?" He asked his wife, who was rubbing her eyes in alarm. The question was answered immediately when a voice sounded through a loudspeaker: "This is not an exercise, all the soldiers immediately into the common room, the air-towers were attacked and destroyed!"

Then a siren wailed, Vivi and Joe quickly dressed and ran into the common room, their hearts pounding.

"The New Germans are attacking!" They were received by Julian. "We need to get our Haunebus to safety immediately! Lars sounded the alarm when he saw on the radar that an aircraft was approaching. It fired a jet at the air frame and then disappeared again in the night. Probably, to get reinforcements! We need to get the Haunebus to safety immediately before they bomb our hangar! Go to Promar. A few soldiers are already there!"

"But ..."

The professor was already running.

"Jesus, the boy!" Called Joe. "Lars has to come with you!" At that moment, Joe was feeling cold through his veins. Did Julian just say that the air-towers had been shot at? Lars had been up there!

Vivi screamed, "Come on, let's go!"

They rushed to the hangar where the ship stood, and went inside.

"Professor, where is he?" Joe yelled hysterically.

"I'm sorry, he gave me the order to fly right away, he'll follow you then," one of the anti-technicians answered. "Here's an earpiece for you, so you can contact anyone. The ship is set to manual, the camouflage works. Come on, we have to go."

The soldier closed the hatch of the Haunebus. Eight anti-technicians were on board except for Vivi and Joe.

"Open the hangar door," called the commanding soldier. "Technician, turn on the camouflage. Five, four, three, two, one - Let's go!" The haunebu floated through the open gate. "Come on! Just get away from here!"

The ship rose in the air.

"Damn, they're shooting at our bunker, look, there!" Yelled Joe. Three large airships hovered over the airfield, firing at the bunker and collapsed jet. Thanks to the perfect camouflage, Promar was invisible and could not be located.

"I hope Julian manages to get the Haunebu 3 to safety!" Vivi stammered. Her eyes were wide with horror.

"Get ready to shoot!" Joe heard one of the men call. Apparently the anti-technicians were about to return the fire. A ray of light illuminated the air. A Haunebu of the New Germans glowed, but it remained intact.

"Shit, they've built an active force field around their airships!" Gasped one of the soldiers.

"Use microwave drops!" Shouted the commanding soldier. The anti-tech gave Promar the order to shoot. Almost at the same time they sent a ray torpedo behind and this time it worked. The Haunebu of the New Germans went up in flames and fell to the ground. Thanks to the camouflage, the New Germans could not see where the attack had come from. At that moment, the other two airships suddenly seemed to have vanished.

"They activated their own camouflage!" One of the soldiers remarked. "Let's go!"

On the hologram, Vivi and Joe could barely see the hangar where the heavy truck had stood burning up in flames.
"Those bastards!" Joe said.

"Are we following a new Germanic ship?" One of the anti-technicians asked the commanding soldier.

"Negative. However, they have their camouflage activated, so I can not say for sure," he replied.

"That's good, we'll be in America in a few hours, it's not flying high speed."

"We're on our way to America?" Vivi asked.

"The only place we're safe now!" Was the anti-technician's answer.

"Sir, I'm in contact with Haunebu 3," another anti-technicians said excitedly. "Three ships including this one did it, the professor is in the air. There are two men and his wife on board with him, one is slightly injured. Thanks to the camouflage, they escaped unseen. The airfield in Peenemuende is unfortunately completely ruined. The two half-finished Haunebus and some material that was not yet loaded, are also destroyed. Three men were killed. The professor says that we need to design a new plan, as the 20 other anti-technicians can no longer use Peenemuende as a departure station. Further steps must be discussed with the four elders and rescheduled."

"All right," the pilot said. "But now let's face it, ~~that~~ we can get to America safely, or we can give ourselves the bullet right now."

Joe had been listening with full concentration to communication the whole time. Three men were dead, for heaven's sake. He hoped fervently that the soldier had not meant Lars, and sent out the idea of communicating with Julian.

"Professor, can you hear me?" Joe asked in his earpiece.

"Yes, loud and clear. Are you alright?" Was the answer.

"We're all right, we're almost over the pond," Joe said, adding nervously, "Do you know how Lars stands?"

"Do not worry, he's fine, he's right next to me. He has a splinter in his upper arm, but we'll quickly fix that when we find a hospital in America."

At that moment, a message came in via the communication system, which had also been installed on the on-board computers of the Haunebus. It resounded in all three flying discs at the same time:

"Mayday, mayday, we're being attacked!" They heard the controller's horrified voice from the anti-tech bunker.

Attack

"Carsten, is that you?" The professor replied. "Can you repeat that again?"

"The New Germans are bombarding the anti-tech complex!" Carsten shouted. "We have instructed all women and children and several men to go to safety in the underground bunker. The war-trained soldiers are with me. We have the weapons from the research station and we will defend ourselves. However, the New Germans are far superior to us. We do not know how long our building will last!"

"Julian to research station," the professor shouted. "Can you hear me?"

"We hear you loud and clear. The communication system is world class," the leader from the research station replied.

"What about you?" The professor shouted.

"Everything is quiet, no attack has been registered yet," the leader answered.

"How far has the construction of the Haunebus progressed?" The professor asked.

"We have the parts and engines of two Haunebu 2 and one Haunebu 3 ready," was the response from the research station.

"How long will it take you to assemble the flying discs?" Julian asked.

"Where? Here in the production hall of the research station?" The leader asked.

"Yes, on the spot!"

"No idea...maybe three days. Or two, if we take night shifts. But how could we get the flying discs out of here? They do not fit through the escape tunnel!"

"Leave that to me!" Julian ordered. "Start immediately with the assembly of the Haunebus! And you in the anti-tech complex...send the people in the underground security bunker to the research station. The soldiers should hold the position and shoot back. Try to fend off the attacks of the New Germans as best you can to save time! Do not attack, just ward them off! As soon as the Haunebus are done, you give up the anti-tech complex and you're off to America!"

"We're just supposed to have our building destroyed?" Carsten asked. "Are you crazy?!"

"It's going to go down anyway!" The professor shouted. "Trust me, we have one more trump up our sleeve! It's the only way for you to get out of New Berlin alive! Just keep the New-Germans in check until the anti-technicians in the research station have finished the Haunebus! Have you understood my instructions?"

"Yes, we do," one could hear a positive murmur from the two locations.

Joe and Vivi were staring in horror at the whole communication. Now it was really time. The war had reached the front door. Before they could properly digest the shock message, another message sounded. This time from their own cockpit: "In a few minutes we will land in America. The landing station is informed and awaits us. We almost made it, friends!"

Cheers sounded. The other two ships were already in American airspace. As promised, Promar sat gently down on American soil a few moments later.

At the same time, the following scene unfolded in the anti-tech complex: "Lookouts, can you tell where the New Germans are?" Carsten called over the earpiece.

"Negative, sir, they activated the camouflage. We have no chance to ward off their attack, as we do not see where they are!"

It was deafening. "The left wing! Holy shit! The whole left wing was destroyed!" The lookout post reported. "How on earth shall we hold the position for another two days?"

"Can you calculate the bullet angle?" Carsten shouted.

"Probably already...wait! 41.6 degrees northeast."

"We're firing a torpedo in that direction!" It only took a few seconds for a bright light to come on, accompanied by a loud explosion. The Haunebu of the New Germany, which previously had hovered invisibly in the sky, plunged burning into the depths. The camouflage was out of order and the hologram from inside the anti-tech complex clearly showed how the fireball hit the ground. Cheers sounded. The response of the New Germans was devastating in the truest sense of the word. Another part of the anti-engineering complex was pulverized.

"We have no chance if we can only shoot back after they bomb us!" The lookout post shouted. "I can calculate the angle, but we should retreat!"

"Let's shoot again!" Carsten called back. The man in the guard post calculated the shot angle and passed the data. The shot showed no effect. The New Germans had analyzed the behavior of the anti-tech quickly and changed position immediately after their shot.
"Damn!" Carsten shouted. "Retreat to the research station. Take as many weapons as you can carry!"

The anti-technicians, who were still in the anti-engineering complex, ran in the direction of escape tunnels. While in the research station, they were able to hack into a live cam of New Berlin via the professor's communications system and watch as the anti-tech complex collapsed and burned. It was over and the base was lost.

America felt like a paradise. You could even see single blue shreds of the sky, even though the dusk was already over the land. Vivi and Joe went hand in hand out of Promar and put their feet on the United States in the year 2150. Only a few minutes later, the other two ships landed. Joe reacted joyfully as Lars got out of the flying disk next to Julian. He waved to him collegiality and Lars grinned over both ears. At that moment a soldier was walking towards them.

"Greetings, we've heard the terrible news. We are sorry that your home was destroyed. I am Sean, the leader of the rebel base Echo. You are in the largest rebel station in North America. We will cooperate with you. Did you bring everything?"

"Yes, we were able to save all the material," Julian replied, introducing himself as well.
"At least good news. Come on, soldiers, load the metal, then I'll show you your accommodation! Together we will work out a strategy and plan a major attack on the New Germans. As we learned recently, our rebels in the former Russia have started attacking New Germany. It looks bitter for the Russian rebels, but that will give us some time!"

He showed the newcomers a secure bunker room in which they could temporarily store the iron. After the material was safe, he showed them where to go next. Since they had no luggage anyway, they had installed themselves quickly. Joe was sitting on the edge of the bed with Vivi in her bed, yawning heartily. Only a few hours ago he had been lying on his mattress in Peenemuende. It had been a very short night. And now they were in the much-vaunted America. If it was better here than in New Germany, it would eventually be apparent. For now, they did not really know what was expected of them or what would happen to them. But they did not have much time to imagine the future.

A soldier entered and drummed the anti-techs together.

"Do you know we're from another time zone and it's the middle of the night with us?" Vivi said, annoyed. Shrugging, Joe stood up and Vivi followed him sullenly.

In a meeting room packed with computer equipment, the anti-technicians, Joe and Vivi took a seat and listened to a speech by the leader.
"I welcome you again!" He began. "Although it's late evening, I'd like to say a few words about how we're doing. For many years we have watched the war from a neutral perspective. Since the New Germans are technically far superior to us, we have never considered actively participating. All attacks by rebels in other countries have so far failed miserably. It seems as if New Germany had seized the world power. The entry barriers in this war were too high because no opponent had realistic chances and sufficient resources to compete with the New Germans in this battle. But the situation has changed now. Thanks to you, we now have the iron to build fly ships. When we cooperate, by combining our fighting spirit and strategy with your technical know-how and resources, we can attack the New Germans with competitive weapons. And we have a chance to win and put an end to this war! So let's see that we get to work! Your anti-tech will start building Haunebus tomorrow morning, my men will assist you. The combat strategy you can leave to us. Once we've upgraded enough, we'll introduce you to our attack plans. We have a large army of trained soldiers. We only lacked adequate airships and the necessary

technology. For one of you, I have a special assignment.

The leader looked Joe directly in the eyes. "You're the 21st- century man, am I right?"

Joe had to swallow, then he nodded.
"You are the right man for me for two reasons. What's your name?"

"My name is Joe Dexter."

"Joe Dexter! Are you American?"

"Yes I am. At the age of 19, I emigrated to Germany with my wife."

'Welcome back then, Joe Dexter." The leader grinned. "As I said, there are two reasons why I would like you to take on the special assignment. First, you do not have the know-how of the anti-technician and thus have - forgive me - in the construction of the Haunebus no concrete benefit and secondly you know the technology of the 21st century much better than we do. They are supposed to look for an old base of the Russians, which dates from their time. I will put 20 men aside. Just be careful to bring them back safely. You will be on your way tomorrow morning, your wife will accompany you. You will get one of our hover vehicles. Can you drive with such a thing?"

"I guess so. I was already able to gain experience."

"I do not really care what you were allowed to do, I just want you to find this station. It is located in

Mexico! Now go and rest. Tomorrow will be a busy day."

"It works like in the military. Damn, what's this shit?" Joe asked the professor as they left the assembly room.

"He's right, Joe. If our survival is important to us, then we must not lose a minute. The New Germanies are attacking our people in New Berlin. We have to launch a counterattack as soon as possible."

Drive to Mexico

Joe got a decent breakfast and a warm shower the next morning. He was set aside for 20 men and old plans that they had not been able to decipher before. They should leave in the afternoon and use the morning to study the plans and prepare the excursion. Together they sat outside on an outer wall of the rebel base. As Joe studied the plans, Vivi watched the clouds sweeping over them. The haze was far thinner here than in Europe.

"What should we do, Vivi? I have no idea where in Mexico this base should be. Are you making any sense of these plans?" Joe yanked her out of her daydreams.

Vivi picked up the papers and studied them, frowning.

"I saw a show about there once..." she mumbled. "I know a name on the map...Tutche. Do we have access to a database here?" She looked around searchingly.

The announced hover vehicle was already waiting in front of the building. However, this designation did not quite fit, because the vehicle looked like a hovercraft. Simply bigger and more perfectly shaped. It was about 20 meters long and five wide. The outer shell was like a stealth bomber. There were turrets in the front and back.
"Ask for control of the hover thing!" Joe said. Vivi swung behind the helm and spoke with the computer.

"Joe, all these places do not exist anymore," Vivi said in disappointment when she returned. "The computer can not find any of those names. But I can quite well remember the documentary I once saw on TV, it was all about a Russian station near Ensenada. If we put up an up-to-date map of a 21st century map, we can tell which city is now where Ensenada used to be. The base is only about 80 kilometers from the American border. And there is a mountain called Tutche. Exactly this name stands here on the old plans. The base is disguised as a mine. Maybe we should look there. Oh yes, then there is this huge wall that was built in the year 2017 as a border fence, because we can shoot through a hole, what a joy. Since the President had been hotly debated in the year 2016 about back then saw some problems ahead. With his strategy of America First, he had saved this continent from the takeover of the New Germany. What a coincidence, nobody could imagine that."

"Vivi. Print a map of Mexico!"

Together with Vivi he went to the office of the rebel leader and asked to be allowed to print some maps from the database. Sean let him do it. When they placed a recent map of Mexico on a 21st-century map, the city of Esperanza took exactly the same position as Ensenada used to.
"Esperanza is our destination!" Joe smiled. "You are the best!"

Heavily impressed, the leader looked at the two. In fact, had they, within that short time, deciphered the plan he had spent so much time worrying about.

"Joe, you deserve my respect!" He said seriously. "Good luck on your mission!"

Joe contacted his men and told them they had decoded the location of the base. Now only the supplies and the material had to be loaded, then it could start. The men looked at Joe appreciatively. They had expected to spend days looking for the base in Mexico. Their respect for the two time travelers had increased many times over.

Three hours later, the team was ready to leave and assembled in front of the Hover-drive. Joe took another careful look at the vehicle with the turrets in front and behind.

"Hey, what are those guns, soldier?" Joe asked one of the men in the troop.

"90 meter explosive ammunition. Why do not you know them? They are standard with us."

"Because I'm the new one from 2016. That's why. Did not you get informed?"
"Yes, sir, I'm sorry. Well, these bullets penetrate the body. Depending on the setting, they explode, paralyze or put people and objects out of action by electrical impulses. Very effective!"

"Thanks for the information, soldier," Joe said.

"I'm honored, sir ."

Turning to Vivi, Joe said quietly, "Why do they all call me sir, Vivi?"

"You have the command here, Joe, or did you not understand the Chief?"

He nodded smartly, turned back to the soldiers and said loudly, "Let's get on the road, lads. How long do we need to get to Mexico?"

"A few hours, sir."

"Well then, make yourself comfortable. I can manage here already. You two there - you occupy the turrets. And you ~~went~~ with the cap, go to the scanner."

"Sir, we have not seen any enemies here for years."

"I don't care, now do what I said. Last night I saw our friends slaughtered in New Germany, I will take no chances. Do I have to say it twice? Come on, go to the scanner."
"Yes, sir!"

"Well, let's go to Tutche!" Joe shouted. He sat down at the controls and switched to "automatic". His goal was to enter Esperanza in Mexico.

"Hey Vivi, are you scared ?" Joe asked his wife, who was sitting in the driver's cabin next to him.

"A little. Who knows what awaits us at this base. What should we actually do in this bunker? Find old nuclear weapons of the Russians?"

"I have no idea either, the job is just finding the base," Joe said.

"For some reason this will be strategically important. It just leads to a tunnel. I saw on TV that it is almost 1,000 meters below the surface. It is warm down there at about 45° Celsius. First you have to drive through a mine, then, at the bottom, comes a lift. They showed photos of this bunker, it looked very comfortable, maybe we can set ourselves there. We just need air conditioning." Vivi laughed. "Then we could have children there and be happy."

After she said that, she suddenly became very serious and quiet.

"What's up, honey?" Joe asked.

"You know, Joe...I should have told you a long time ago...I have not had any menstruation for three months. At first I thought, my hormone balance was confused by the time travel. Then I blamed it on the stress. But for a few days now, I've been feeling slightly nauseous, and then I suddenly realized I might be pregnant!"

"Oh my god, Vivi! That's awesome!" Joe stared at her in disbelief, grinning like a toy santa. Will they actually have a baby soon?

"Well, as I said, it can all have very different causes..." Vivi protested.

"When we get back to the rebel station, we'll go to the infirmary and ask for a test!" Joe said firmly. "I can not believe it! If we actually have a baby..." Joe beamed. But then he too became serious and said thoughtfully: "The problem is that I feel that more and more responsibility is being transferred to me. Julian has also indicated that I should take over certain tasks in America, but I do not want that at all. But I am afraid that I currently have no choice. I promise you that should all this be over, I will do everything we can to make us live a normal life and keep our children protected."

"That's fine, Joe. It's good if you have a job. We are already through this. Eventually, this war will end! Now we go to Mexico!"
After a few hours, they were on the Mexican border. Due to an international agreement between Mexico and the US, which was enforced by the last president, the border was open again and you could pass without documentary control, the wall was released for destruction and Mexico and America had a cooperation, both nations worked under the name - New America - together. A single continent of Allies. Now Esperanza was only a stone's throw away. The whole area was mountainous and impassable. Fortunately, the hovercraft did not rely on a good road, but floated over the surface. When they came to a junction where there was a large chalkboard labeled Esperanza - 4 miles, Joe stopped the vehicle. Lost, Joe and Vivi looked around the landscape. There were many peaks that could have been called mountains. Which was Tutche?

"And now? Do you have any idea where the mine is?" Joe asked his wife.

She grimaced and said, "Am I a psychic, or what? Give me the plan!" Suddenly she grinned. "Without me you would be lost!"

"What's that supposed to mean?" Joe asked.

"Do you see these three mountains in the east?" Vivi replied. "The one in the middle looks a bit like a horn, it's more pointed than the others."

Joe followed her finger and nodded.

"There are three marks on the map. I suppose that means mountains, because the right marking is labeled 'Tutche'. The middle one is called 'Cuerno'."

Joe looked at her questioningly.

"Do you need more hints? Cuerno means "horn" in Spanish!" Vivi grinned self-confidently.

"So the mountain on the far right is Tutche!" Joe concluded.

"No, the left one!" Vivi said. "On the map is north is above. We see the mountains from a different perspective. You have to turn the map by 180°, then it coincides with our position."

"Why do you always make me feel stupid?" Joe asked, gritting his teeth.

"I love you!" Giggled Vivi.

Joe ordered the hover vehicle to set course for the left mountain. When they reached its foot, they saw old wooden signs indicating a mine. A narrow path led into a ravine. It looked like they would need to hike.

"We're finished for today. This is where we set up camp, men," Joe announced to the soldiers in the back room of the Companion over the earphones.

Due to the proximity of the equator, it was relatively early dark in Mexico, so Joe thought it was most sensible to start walking the next morning to the entrance hatch to the mine. The soldiers set up their tents in a sheltered place. Three men stayed in the hover vehicle, one supervised everything with the scanner and the other two sat by the guns. Joe ordered the guards to be replaced every two hours. He and Vivi also set up a tent, and when they lay in their sleeping bags after eating a vacuum-packed meal, they talked for a while with the light of a saving lamp camping lamp

"Joe, can you crawl into my sleeping bag?" Vivi suddenly asked.

"Do you have enough space?"

"Yes, and yes, those are huge things."

Joe gladly accepted Vivi's request and crawled into her sleeping bag. "Look at you, you are so beautiful. Thank you for keeping me with me all these years. I am glad that I have you. Without you at the side, I would not know what to do. I need you."

"Yes, Joe, me too."

They kissed each other and finally came close for some time.

As the sun squeezed through the haze, the two were awakened by a soldier. "Good morning, sir. Ma'am. We made you a breakfast."

"Jesus, I should have woken you up! I guess I must have overslept...Hm, that's not exactly an exemplary behavior," Joe said apologetically. The soldier grinned in amusement and moved away from the couple's tent.

"Vivi, already awake? Did you sleep well?" Joe asked.

"No, not at all, you were snoring all night, as if you were trying to clear a jungle. I kicked you and shoved you, but you just kept on sleeping. If that happens again, I'll get a bucket of water. Then you would certainly awake!"

"Now stop it...what can I do to make me not snore?"

"A lot ~~of~~. How many times have I told you to get surgery? But a man does not listen to a wife."

"As soon as I have time, okay?"

"You've been saying that for two years."
"I promise it. When our situation has returned to normal, I'll do it for you. And now come on, we'll get up."

They got dressed and made a makeshift start. Then they went to the community square in the middle of the tent city.

Outside, everyone was already ready to march.

"Hey, Chief, awake already?" Called a cheeky soldier.

The others laughed.

"Do not lose your respect, soldier! Otherwise I'll leave you here!" Joe told him, but he had to grin himself, which defused the situation.

Joe and Vivi ate breakfast and then split up. Three soldiers remained as guards in the camp. The others followed the narrow path into the ravine. After twenty minutes of walking, they saw a cave entrance.

"Hey, look, do you see this mine? Could that be the entrance?" One of the soldiers asked, to which Joe said, "Scan the area, what do you see?"

"Only mountains and a little rubble are displayed. The scanner does not show any details," was the answer.

"Four men are to scout the mine. Come on," Joe ordered.
The chosen ones separated from the group and Joe announced: "We others will stop here. If there's anything down there, we'll go down, but at first I do not want to risk anything."

After about twenty minutes, the soldiers returned from their reconnaissance tour.

"Chief, it looks like the mine has been filled. The corridor is capped off."

"Then we'll see that we clear the way. Take your shovels and get to work. Everyone should help!"

The soldiers obeyed the order and set out to uncover the entrance area, while Vivi and Joe read a book in the warm sun, calmly. After two hours the work was done. Two soldiers came back to report. "Sir, we uncovered a corridor. At the end is a shaft that leads deep into the abyss. Two of our men have climbed down a bit, it looks like we're in the right place here. What now?"

"We'll climb down too," Joe decided.

Together they went to the uncovered corridor and saw the remaining soldiers a little further on, who stood in a circle around a hole in the ground. The lights with which they were all equipped were very strong, generously illuminating the old, damp vertical walls of the hole. Here and there a frightened, fair-skinned lizard scurried across the furrowed stones, which had been hidden from human eyes for many decades. "There are animals here, too," Joe shot through his head.

It was cool inside the rocky mine. Vivi shuddered despite the military jacket she had received. She had not the slightest desire to enter the dark hole, especially since she had no idea what was in it. At that moment, one of the soldiers emerged from the abyss and saw Joe.

"Sir, the shaft is very deep. However, the narrow entry widens with increasing depth and there are intermediate passages where you can stand upright. However, they are empty and not very long. After about 10 meters you get onto a platform and from there there is a mechanical elevator. Clint is checking to see if it's still safe."

A while later, Clint called the troop over his earpiece and told them to come below. As it looked, the elevator was still operable. The men began to descend over the metal rungs carved in the rock. Joe instructed two men to guard the entrance to the shaft and then disappeared in the dark as well. Vivi went last. They decided that four people should ride together in the elevator, so as not to strain it too much. Who knew how stable the cables were after so many years. The elevator consisted of an open cabin with a railing. A creaking metal grille gave them access. Leisurely, the elevator slid into the depths, further and further into the abyss. Apart from the scanty lamp in the elevator, they were surrounded by pitch-black darkness. Vivi felt like she was leading straight to hell. It was pitch black and stuffy. After a short time, the two soldiers, who were in the lift with them, began to mount oxygen masks. They did it to them. However, the journey was over faster than they expected. The height difference was only 200   meters, as Joe's scanner revealed, when the lift came to a stop. They saw a steel door and their crew, patiently waiting for them.

"Sir, we're on a sort of middle plateau. There is a door here, but it is locked. We have not discovered another elevator that could take us further down the ~~drain~~ shaft. Very likely the path continues behind this steel door."

Joe examined the door, wondering how to open it when a soldier raised his voice, "Sir, if I can make a suggestion..."

"Speak, soldier."

"Blowing up the steel door would not be a problem. We have enough explosives here. There is also enough space and protection on this plateau to avoid the detonation. If you want, I can prepare the explosive charge. I am an expert in this area."

Joe quickly convinced himself that he did not have a better solution anyway. So they blew up the steel door and released another gear. As they walked for a while, they came to another elevator. However, one did not have to be an expert to find that it was defective. It was crooked and the cables dangled into the abyss.

"Well, how are we going to negotiate the remaining 1.4 kilometers without an inactive lift?" Joe said to himself.

"Sir, if I may speak again..." the explosives expert answered.

"Speak, soldier."

"As far as the 1,400 meters are concerned, we have hover packs, which are backpacks that have been specially designed for such tasks. You can slide down with it without problems. The hover packs were developed in parallel to the peace birds. This is our method to land in enemy territory. The advantage is that we stand upright on arrival."

"Well, then let's go," Joe said, secretly sending a thank-you to Heaven that his problems had been solved so quickly. He would give the soldier a small service present. One by one, the soldiers jumped into the black hole that was lost in the depths. They all had their oxygen masks on. It was not the first time that Joe and Vivi were just leaping into the depths with a small, strapped backpack. Therefore, they made the jump very confidently. The hover packs safely guided them down at adequate speed. The deeper they penetrated the rock, the hotter it became. Soon Vivi had to untie her military jacket and on Joe's forehead sweat beads formed. After about 750 meters of descent, they landed gently.

Immediately they stood with their troop in a corridor that had a diameter of ten meters. The dry heat that prevailed down here was reminiscent of a bio-sauna. The men soon sweat in streams. About 20 meters in front of them was a huge steel door. As they approached, they could see a writing in Cyrillic script above the gate.

"Can anyone read that?" Joe asked.

No Answer. "Break the door! And drink enough! That nobody gets dehydrated!" Joe ordered.

The soldiers placed explosives on the hinges. Soon an explosion shook the tunnel. The steel door fell to the ground and the men looked into another dark tunnel.

The Mine

Now they had done it. They had entered the Russian base they had found without any problems, but something did not seem to be in order. They stood in the wide corridors of the entrance shaft, feeling very queasy, as if they were not alone. There was nothing they recognized, but did they have to deal with cyborgs again? Joe ordered the soldiers to secure the area. Some set off to look for a generator, for perhaps it would still work and brighten the tunnel.

"Vivi, doesn't it feel weird?" Joe whispered to her. "It feels to me we're not the only ones here. Maybe I'm just making it all up..."

"I feel the same way, Joe. Besides, I just heard a strange sound," Vivi whispered back.

"It's probably only bats," Joe said. "We'll wait here until the generators are up and running, then we'll have clarity. Besides, I finally need something to eat again."

Joe took an emergency ration out of his pocket. The stuff did not taste very good, but it had enough calories for a whole day. The food looked like a lump of butter, but it was black and wrapped in a protective foil of aluminum-like material, preventing it from being spoiled by cold or heat.

"Joe, I thought I saw something shiny, on the wall," Vivi ordered excitedly. But when Joe shone on the spot shown, only a shadow scurried across the rough rock face. Some of the men came back.

"It's weird, we're 2,000 meters underground, and yet it feels like we're not alone."

"Joe, something really wrong here."

At that moment, the lights went on, telling them that the generators had been found. A little later, the remaining soldiers came back.

"Hey guys, do you feel like we're being watched?" They shouted to their colleagues.

"Absolutely!`` one said.

"Let's go search," Joe ordered. "We'll find out early on who or what we'll come across here. Let's form four groups of five people each. We stay in touch."

"All right, sir !"

Joe, Vivi and three soldiers marched together. All doors were open, even the light was working everywhere and there was a smell of sulfur.

"Look! Back there!" Shouted one of the soldiers.

Vivi was startled when she saw a skeleton on the ground: the mortal remains of a New Germanic clone. And then they found another, and another.

"What happened here? Looks as if the New Germans been here. The logo on their army uniforms speaks a clear language, they are not Russians! Did they attack down here? Apparently they did not succeed!" Joe pointed out.

"For some reason, they blocked access," Vivi said.

"Uh people..." groaned one of the soldiers at that moment, pointing with his finger at a spot behind them on the wall.

As they turned, they saw a tall man who looked like a New German. He was nearly two meters tall and his eyes were extremely light blue. The hair on his shoulders was snow-white. In his hand he held a weapon.

"Greetings. It has been a long time since we saw a human here. Do not worry, I will not hurt you. My name is One, I am the first clone that the New Germans have produced. They used this old Russian base as a laboratory, since it is almost at the end of the world and they were able to conduct their unethical experiments undisturbed. The Russians had previously poisoned them with mustard gas and made it out of the bunker. At times hundreds of clones lived down here. The successful versions were taken by the New-Germans when they left the base. They had created successful prototypes and wanted to continue breeding in their homeland, then use the clones as a~~ lighters.~~ The failed clones were killed. Four of us, myself included, were deliberately left alive. Come along, I'd like to introduce you to my friends!" One said invitingly, motioning for them to follow him. The weapon dangled in his hand.

Joe, Vivi and the soldiers followed the fair-skinned clone hesitantly. He led them through a small labyrinth of corridors and finally opened a door. There they saw three other fair-skinned clones sitting on a couch talking.

"Greetings," came out of their mouths, "we are very pleased to see you."

"We've been down here way too long. Every change in our barren everyday life is a sensation! Therefore, we are very pleased to receive visitors," one of the clones continued babbling. It looked like they were actually friendly and as if they were really looking forward to the intruders. But Joe and his troupe remained skeptical. Maybe it was a trap and the clones deliberately suggested trust.

One resumed speaking and continued, "As I mentioned earlier, all Failed clones were killed, but we four were left alive. We were supposed to serve as trial candidates because they wanted to know how long a clone could stand without food and watched us through cameras installed throughout the facility. However, their plan did not work out because implanting their doctrine in our brains failed. We can think independently and are stronger and more adaptable than any other clone that followed us. That's why we tracked down and destroyed the cameras. The New Germans have never returned, we do not know why. In any case, we have been down here for many years now. We survived for a very long time, as you can see. We need almost no food and can live without water for weeks, you know. We fed on rats and vermin that lives in the shafts. We've collected drops of water that run over the rocks."

"The lower lift to the bunker is destroyed. Probably the New Germans have intentionally cut off the escape route during their retreat. When you destroyed the cameras, the effort was certainly too big for them to return to Mexico again. They could repeat the experiment at any time with clones, which they had carried to New Germany. That's probably why they left you on your own, assuming that you would starve to death soon anyway," Joe suggested.

Concerned, One said nothing for a few seconds, then said, "That's what it's been like. But we have made no move to reach the surface. Both our eyes and our skin can not stand the sunlight. We would die immediately. What's up there? Are the New Germans still in power?"

"Yes, unfortunately," Joe answered.

"Really stupid," said One. "Oh, how rude of me! I did not introduce you to my friends!" He pointed to the first clone and said," That's Number Four. He is the smartest, but also the weakest of us. Number Three is the fastest and Number Two is neither smart nor fast. There were four attempts, used until the New Germans had created a perfect clone, which they could take home. Nevertheless, wrong creations have been created again and again during the further production. But tell us, what are you doing here?"

"My name is Joe Dexter," Joe said, beginning to talk in detail. "I'm from the year 2016. Through a storm, my wife and I were catapulted into this time, we are now being sought by the New Germany and sentenced to death as time manipulators. Initially, we were picked up by anti-technicians and were supposed to visit a rebel base where a flying ship was hiding to take us to America. But the New Germans destroyed the Haunebu and captured us. However, we managed to escape and found a secret anti-tech research station where we made new airships to fly to America. However, before we could finish our plans, our station was attacked by New Germans and we had to drop everything and abruptly start the overflight to America. Now just three ships have made it to America. Our friends, who are still in New Germany, may already be dead, because shortly after our escape the anti-technician complex was attacked. Those who managed to escape to America have now come to a rebel base and are working with the rebels. Together we want to stand up to the New Germans. It will only be a few weeks before they appear off the US coast. We expect the total war. Our people are currently building and upgrading airships in the ~~chord~~ compound. If the New Germans show up before our force is ready, it will not be long before all humans are subjugated. The rebel leader sent us to search for this old Russian base. Although they knew about its existence, they were never able to find it themselves, as it comes from ancient times and there are no current maps that represent its point of view. There are probably rumors that Russian nuclear weapons are being stored here, which the rebels want to find, as a last resort to launch nuclear bombs at Europe, but I doubt that these weapons can break the shields of the New Germany. This bunker definitely had a reputation in our time for serving as a nuclear camp. However, we did not know the purpose of our mission, it's just a guess. So, if there are any weapons here that could serve us in the fight against the New Germans, we would be very happy if you could let us have them."

One shook his head sadly. "There's nothing down here. If there really were nuclear weapons here, the New Germans took everything. The probability is even great that you are right. There are bunkers down here with meter-thick stone walls, which are provided with warning signs for radioactivity. The doors are open and the rooms are empty. The New Germans would not have been stupid enough to let this precious material rot down here. Obviously, they did not mean to ever return."

"Hm, I guess our mission ended down here. Can we do anything for you? Shall we take you to our base?" Joe asked.

"Joe, we would not survive long up there. We got well acclimated down here. It may be a bit boring, but we can handle it. Of course, a bit of delicious food would delight us and maybe a screen or holoprojector to watch movies. We are also interested in antique books, of which there are hardly any and are of inestimable value. So we could kill time. We stay here, however. Life is not better up there!"

"I will remember you. However, I can not promise that I can come back immediately. We all do not know what to expect when we return to the rebel base. But if I can set it up, I'll bring you supplies!" Said Joe. "And now I have to find my men. Thank you for your hospitality!"

Joe ordered his soldiers over the earpiece to the main entrance, which they had blown up. He quickly briefed them on their find, then set off to the way back. The Hover-Packs again transported them safely to the middle platform. Since the second gear was blocked by the lift, they could not use the fast version with the hover packs and had to use the slow elevator. When they returned to the outside world, they breathed with relief and breathed in the air. It was already dark and the night was especially clear.

"My love, look at the stars," Vivi said. "Don't you look gorgeous? Even here there are moments that should never pass." They paused for a moment, looking arm in arm into the sky as their troops marched off.

"Come here, Joe, I want to hold you." Closely embraced, they enjoyed the moments of togetherness and forgot for a moment the war, the suffering and the fear.

"We will survive this war! Look, there! A shooting star, wonderful," said Joe. Slowly they wandered back to the camp, where their troop had already arrived.

"Well, I'll try to reach the Echo base, I'll let them know about the clones. Let's see what they say," Joe told the soldiers. He went to the hover-drive and made a connection to the rebel station.

"Hover-drive Mexico to Echo Base, come, please."

"Echo Base here, we can hear you well. Did you find the bunker?" Joe heard over the speaker in the vehicle.

"Yes, sir, with success, but we've come across a strange find. The bunker is home to four new Germanic clones, apparently for many years. They are the remnants of an experiment. The base has been plundered by the New Germans, there is nothing down there that would be strategically valuable."

"Did you not find any weapons stores ?" Sean asked.

"The camps are all empty. The New Germans took the nuclear material with them when they left the base."

"Shit," Sean hissed. "Then come back to the bunker!"] A lot has happened!"

At around 10:00 pm Joe and his troop arrived at the rebel station. He was looking forward to the Professor and Lars, eager to tell them the news. At the same time he was also curious if there was any information about the anti-technicians in New Berlin. The friends organized a bottle of wine and made themselves comfortable in a common room. Also Mary and Vivi were there and enjoyed it, once again sitting together informally in the circle of friends. Vivi, however, was very reluctant to drink alcohol, considering the baby that might be inside of her. Tomorrow they would know. After Joe told his story with the clones, Julian informed him and Vivi about the current situation in New-Berlin.

It had remained quiet so far. Apparently the New Germans were not aware of the research station. But the anti-tech complex had been razed to the ground. Now the reason for the surprise attack and why the New Germanier had so quickly gotten wind of their location in Peenemuende was known. Meier, who had been sent back to the research station with the heavy transporter, had never arrived there. It was assumed that he had fallen into the hands of New Germany. Meier had almost certainly become the victim of a cruel torture, in which he had revealed his identity and told of the activities in Peenemuende. Fortunately, however, he had kept quiet about what the research station was about. It could however be only a matter of time before the New Germans with their cruel techniques forced out even this knowledge from Meier. The time pressure was therefore enormous and the anti-technicians had since the attack on the anti-tech complex almost no more eyes and worked non-stop. The construction of the Haunebus progressed quickly. The automatic industrial complexes worked very efficiently and very fast. Already the next day - so they had informed - it would be so far ahead and there were enough flying discs ready to accommodate the remaining persons including women and children as well as all the material in the Haunebus.

"You said you had the Haunebus fully assembled in the production hall," Vivi said. "How is it possible to get the Haunebus out of the research station, they never fit into the escape tunnels!"

Julian grinned smugly. "I said I had one more trump up my sleeve."

Now all eyes looked at him intensely. Julian slowly got up and said he would get another bottle of wine. He cleared his throat after giving everyone a treat. "I found a device in the research station that I have not told anyone about yet. At first, I did not know what my grandfather intended. It's a kind of dome, an emergency exit against the top of the station. But to be activated, strong forces must be set in motion. Directly above the research station is New-Berlin. If the dome were opened, all buildings directly above it would be destroyed. For this reason, it was unclear to me why the dome exists at all. After much deliberation, however, I have come to the conclusion that this device has not been made simply arbitrary. My grandfather had built the dome as a last resort in case the enemy invades the research station and it becomes necessary to abandon the base. So the anti-technicians have one last trump up their sleeve and could escape through the dome into the air. Of course, it is unnecessary to say that the research station becomes useless after the dome has been opened, since it is no longer secret and, secondly, it is no longer protected from the outside. So it's really the very last resort, to survive."

"So you want to sacrifice the research station to allow people to escape?" Mary asked.

"Sooner or later, the New Germans will find it," the professor said. "We have no future in New Berlin. Yes, I will sacrifice the research station. Even though it's hard for me to destroy my grandfather's life's work", Julian said, his eyes lowered. "But the life of our people is valuable, too. More than anything else. And the most important books and plans, as well as the weapons, will be able to save our people and bring them to Haunebus to America."

"If it works," Lars said.

"Yes, if it works," the professor confirmed, taking a sip of wine.

"You said to open the dome, strong forces would have to be set in motion..." Vivi remarked.

"That's the way it is. To open the dome, the anti-techs would have to use the modified Tesla coil. Five seconds are enough to pulverize everything above the bunker and paralyze the force field around New-Berlin." Respectfully, those present looked at him.

"That's going to be a big deal," Joe said.

"It's time tomorrow!" Was the professor's answer. "If they escape through the dome with camouflaged Haunebus after the coil has been activated, they can fly to America before the New Germans even realize what has happened. I'll get in touch with the leader in just a few hours and give him instructions on what to do. It's almost dawn in New Germany, we stagger seven hours behind. Around noon they should carry out the mission. If all goes well, be back with your girl tomorrow afternoon, Lars."

The Dome

The nervousness in the research station created an omnipresent tension. Today it was all or nothing. Live or die. The leader had informed all present precisely on the plans of the professor. There were six Haunebus ready. Two 2s and 4s 3s. That would allow them to carry a total of 130 people. They were only 109, but they had loaded material to capacity. At 12:00 noon, they would turn on the Tesla coil. Exactly 4.73 seconds long. The professor had told them that he had calculated exactly the energy that would be produced. One second more and it could be dangerous. The rays would penetrate to the atmosphere. They were only allowed to generate just enough energy to open the dome and destroy everything within a radius of about 50 meters. At the same time, the energy would also deactivate the force field around New-Berlin. The New Germans would need more than two minutes to restore this. They had to use this time window to escape with their Haunebus through the vacated escape route. Everything was planned meticulously. The airships were ready, boarding began at 10:30. Women and children would board first. Two of them would have to go into the dome's control room to hook up the Tesla coil, turn it on punctually, and turn it off after exactly 4.73 seconds. One of the Haunebu 2 would wait for the men and finally flee. There was no dress rehearsal, either it would work or the damage the Tesla Coil would cause would be so great that they all died. Of the best men, two had been chosen to perform the mission in the control room. Now they could only hope that everything went as they imagined.

It only took 42 minutes for all the people to be on board and secured. The activation switch was in the control room and Kaspar, one of the chosen ones, sat next to it and went through every step in his head again. He had activated a timer that would tell him when the time had run out. They had not managed to connect the timer directly to the coil, so a manual deactivation was inevitable. Via ear devices, the pilots of the Haunebus were connected with Kaspar and his companion. They would give them the starting instruction. In 42 minutes it started.

"Kaspar, what about the Tesla coil, is it ready?" One of the pilots asked. A look at the clock. 11:54a.m. Another six minutes to the super-GAU.

"Everything is ready! What about you?" Kaspar replied. His heart almost jumped out of his chest.

"Zulu 01 is ready to take off," he heard one of the pilots.

"Lima 01 is ready to take off," a second answered.

"India 01 as well."

"Quebec 01 too, but we'll wait until you're back, mate. Just swing your asses here as fast as you can. We only have two minutes!"

"If we can not do it, you'll fly without us!" They heard Kaspar.

"You can do it, people!"

At that moment, the timer turned on and counted the last 60 seconds to the ignition. All pilots and their co-pilots listened to the countdown on their earphones. The starting order had been set exactly. Everyone knew what they wanted from him.

"Coil is turned on!" They heard Kaspar's voice.

Seconds later, the occupants of the ships saw only a white, iridescent light and were paralyzed for a fraction of a second. The energy in the control room, however, was so strong that Kaspar was thrown from his chair against a wall. Felix, who had stood next to it, clung to the desk, which was bolted to the floor. He screamed and fought against the pressure, which also wanted to throw him away. With his head covered in blood, Kaspar remained lying on the floor, fearing for a brief moment to lose consciousness and screw up everything.

"Turn it off!" He exclaimed.
Felix grabbed the lever, missed it and pulled it out again. The force field went out immediately. The two men stared wide-eyed at the timer. 5.29 seconds. They had run the coil too long. But they had no time to worry about the consequences.

"To the ship!" Cried Felix.

They charged and wanted to rip open the door, but it did not move a millimeter. Hysterically they shook it, but the steel door made no movement at all.

"Damn it, the energy has created a vacuum!" Gasped Kaspar. The gasket in the door is so tight that we can not open it anymore. The two of them started madly, hammering on the door.

"We've got to pry them open!" Cried Felix. Hastened, they looked around the small control room to see if they could find an object that could lift the heavy door or relieve the pressure in the doorway.

Fainting, they realized that there was nowhere a long, pointed object that was even apt to pry open the door.

The power of the coil had also shown its effect on the Haunebus in the departure area. The moment that the white light went out, the space under the dome became the epicenter of a massive vibration that caused all objects that were not moored to be thrown across the room. For a few seconds, there was a wild shootout in the production hall, except that it was not bullets but items and furniture that were shot. One of the Haunebu 2 was thrown by a pressure wave to a wall where it crashed. The other ships were able to rise in time and fight the resistance. When the pilots of the Haunebus had regrouped, they saw through the holograms an opening that led into the open air. The dome was open. At this moment, the power supply of the earphones seemed to return, because they heard a noise and a gasp, which emanated from their colleagues in the control room.

"What happened? Are they all alright?" Someone shouted excitedly.

"Get away!" Cried Felix. "What are you waiting for?"

Zulu 01 and Lima 01 flew up. At the same time they activated their camouflage. This was not without danger, as they did not even know where the other ship was. But of course you had previously coordinated the flight directions to avoid collisions. When the two ships appeared on the surface, a large plain was visible. The coil had destroyed not 50 meters, but more than 2 kilometers were swept away from New Berlin. The headquarters of the New-Germans, the high tower, however, still loomed intact in the city center. Its upper floors merged with the haze that hung over the city. But the anti-tech did not have time to take a closer look at the extent of the destruction. Through the open force field, they stalked off and headed for America.

Twenty seconds later, the next two ships started. India 01 rose through the dome, but Mike 01 did not manage to stay in the air. The ship stumbled and fell to the ground. Something about the electronics was damaged. In the cockpit different alarm lamps lit up. Due to the fall, the pilot had received a blow in the neck and hung now limp and motionless in his seat. The fifteen passengers were partially injured and everyone in a panic.

There were exactly 44 seconds left for Quebec 01 to take flight.

"Quebec 01 to Kaspar and Felix. Are you on the way?"

"We're stuck in the control room!" They sounded over the earphones. "Go, fly off without us, we can not do it!"

At that moment, everything became white and a second wave of energy made the entire tunnel collapse with relentless force. The research station sank and ~~tore~~ pulled all the debris that lay over her into an open maw. After the dust had settled, the New Germans could look into an oversize crater. They were convinced that a meteorite had hit.

The Training Camp

The rebels in North America had followed the events in New Germany and had contact with the three Haunebus, which had managed to escape. They had already entered the American airspace and would land in a few minutes. Lars struggled with ~~the~~ nausea. The chance that his girlfriend was still alive was 50%. Life would go on, but a piece of his heart would be dark forever. Crying, he retired to his bedchamber when he realized that everyone had gotten out and Isabelle was not there. He was not the only one who suffered a loss. The partial failure of the mission and the associated loss of 44 humans left great emotional wounds on the bereaved. Once again, everyone had been painfully warned that they were in the middle of a war. The positive was that it strengthened their fighting spirit and made them more than ever ready to pay back the New-Germans.

Life in the rebel station continued, and although Joe and Vivi were saddened by the anti-technicians, they were terrified when they received confirmation from the infirmary that Vivi was pregnant. She was already in the 17th week of pregnancy. They decided, however, to keep the news for a while.

The next day, Sean approached Joe. "Hey Joe, come with us, we need to talk to each other."
Joe followed Sean and he could guess what was coming.

"Just a few days ago you came here from New Germany. I can not force you to do anything. But it is true that we need every single person in this fight. They have done very well and I think the first mission has taught you a lot. I have chosen you to command a small part of the first wave of attack. I will give you 50 man subordinates. But first you have to go through a standard training program that will take ten days. I think we have just enough time for that. We have just heard from rebels from Switzerland that they are making good progress with the Russians. Some outposts of the New Germans were successfully destroyed, giving us some weeks to go again. Nevertheless, we must succeed in mobilizing our forces as quickly as possible and launching the attack. We are in the process of testing the new weapons from your research station and developing combat strategies. Soon we are ready for a first blow. Well, now for your decision, I can not force you to do anything and certainly you will want to talk to your wife about it. Do you want to accept my offer? I promise you, at the end of the war, we will make sure you have a good home."

"Sean, I think my wife will say the same thing, I suppose," said Joe.

"All right, Joe, I'll go over the details with you. Tomorrow you will be shipped to Canada. Some of your men will come along and go through the combat training as well. Since we are undisturbed by the New

Germany, we were able to convert a large area to a military training area. They will fight there almost in real time against new Germanic clones. It will only be holograms, but be careful: there will also be some real robots under it shooting at you. You will not be able to tell which are holograms and which are robots. So be on the alert. You will learn how to prepare food, you will get to know different weapons, and you will be trained in some other details. Remember, you have just ten days to use them as best you can. They will decide about life and death. Any questions?"

"What happens when a robot meets me?"

"Then you're dead," Sean said succinctly. "We will be careful at first, but at the end of the training it will be life-threatening for you. Take a look at some pictures here, they will make you careful."

Joe looked at the cruel pictures of fallen rebels that Sean had handed him.

"What did they die of? From the pain or directly from the gunshot wounds?"

Sean just shrugged his shoulder. "In the end, it doesn't matter, does it? But excuse me for a moment, please. I just got a message from the command center. There is new information available. Wait ..."
He closed his eyes to better focus on the earpieces messages, and finally said, "The energy field around New Berlin has been strengthened, probably the New Germany have now realized that it wasn't a meteorite that dragged part of their city into the abyss. My informant tells me that they are gathering their forces. They're up to something. Time is pressing, Joe!"

After Joe had said goodbye to his wife, he and his companions drove north in a hover vehicle. They had received little provisions and equipment. Also a sleeping bag had not been distributed, so they had to cope with a makeshift bed. Vivi had resolved to pass the time at the rebel base by studying the new technology the Americans possessed. The good thing was that food was not scarce in America. Here there was enough delicious food and one did not have to feed all the time on lumps containing protein, which were shrink-wrapped in a foil. With a full stomach, she was better at tackling complex issues.

Shortly after Joe had set off for Canada, the news was heard that new Germanic reconnaissance flying discs were flying along the coast. They did not attack, but apparently only observed. But you could never be sure whether they would come or not. The rebels strengthened their guards and kept a close eye on the enemy targets. It was still too early for an attack. However, if the New Germans attacked, they had to try to keep the defense as good as possible with the available resources.

Meanwhile, Joe had arrived in Canada. The recruits were not given time to recover, and the first exercise was announced via a loudspeaker in the hover vehicle. It gradually became dark as the men got out of the vehicle. They had to make their way to the training area and when they entered the forest that belonged to the training area, a warning shot was fired and a voice sounded from loudspeakers: "Welcome to the camp, you losers! You didn't pass the first exercise! You get out of your protected jeep and don't even scan the surroundings? If you'd scanned everything, you'd know there were four enemy holograms nearby. That would have been your death in the war. You Joe, as commander you should have instructed your people! What is this dilettantish behavior? This lesson should suffice for now. But from now on such carelessness will be punished, I will see to that. And now go to the bunker!"

Joe was shocked. Apart from a ridiculous standard military training in his old life, he had no experience of how to behave in a combat area. So the only thing he could do right now was to just clue the men into it, to be extremely careful. On his way back to the bunker, he made it better. He sent two men with scanners ahead, who tracked down two enemy holograms and fired. Everything went well: They reached the agreed meeting point, where a man stepped out of the bunker.

"Joe, I suppose? So you have made it yet. We watched you, you have talent, you just do not know. And we will promote this talent. But you also have to be ready for that. Here you have a map. In addition, you'll receive from us 40 men. On your map is marked a target, which you should take. Do not risk anything, you do not know what to expect."

Joe nodded.

"Get on your way, Joe," the man said good-naturally, and Joe and the soldiers started running.

When they were out of sight of the camp, Joe ordered his men to stop. He selected a few of them and then leaned over the map with them. They had quickly figured out the direction in which the target was. Their scanners helped them, because they could be used like a navigation device. Finally, you were in the 22nd century and not in the Middle Ages. Joe had to grin. Immediately, however, he became serious again and ordered the men to divide into groups of twelve, with each of the highest ranked should take command. One group should be from the front, one from behind and two from both sides. The group that was to come from behind had the longest way to go. Joe's group came from the front. The three highest ranked people became familiar with their way and then the groups split up. Joe's group also marched on. From now on, each unit was on its own, even though they were all connected via their earphones. Everyone had their scanners activated. Every now and then shots were fired, but none of the men were injured, as they could recognize the dangers early and avoid them. After an hour, Joe ordered all the soldiers of his and the other groups to set up the camp via the earpiece, because it had become too dark to go any further. He chose two men who had to keep vigil and said to the others, "See that you are looking for a good shelter, and do not bother with me, I'll make it somehow."

The soldiers took him at his word. Since they had been trained for years, all had their beds quickly set up. Joe and the seven anti-tech technicians with him were the only ones who did not know what to do. However, the lay people were all divided into different groups, so they could orient themselves to the professionals. In the dark they tried to see how the soldiers solved the problem. But Joe did not find a good place, and since he was very tired, he did not feel like looking any further. Finally, he could not think of anything but climbing a tree, where he tied himself to the trunk with his belt and fell asleep.

He awoke several times during the night and glanced at the scanner. Everything seemed calm, not even animals could be heard. What a silence, he thought, what an eerie silence. He remembered the horror movies he used to see a lot, and he was worried. He tried to suppress the thoughts, but he could no longer sleep. Joe imagined he saw red eyes, then he thought he could hear voices until he was shaking all over. It was the war that scared him. He used to be alone in the forest and never felt scared. Everything was different now. An attack could happen any moment, and though it stayed calm, Joe still could not sleep all night.

When the sun rose, Joe woke the soldiers.

"Get up!" He shouted. "We have to move on."

Irritated, he discovered that the soldiers had built a kind of shield with their scanners. They had retooled the equipment to create a force field. One of them said apologetically, "Excuse me, sir, that we have not told you about this possibility. We have learned to obey our commander full obedience. We could have helped you, but you told us you did not want help..."

Joe nodded. "Thank you, soldier. You're right. As you can see, I'm still a bloody beginner. How should one like me be able to lead a whole troop! You are all 100 times superior to me!"

"You know, Joe, you have the gift of leading. You have a strong charisma, you feel well under your command. And we all think that here. You are not one who is constantly picking on the soldier, and we really appreciate that. We will teach you everything and support you energetically. Right, boys?"

The rest of the soldiers agreed, "That's right!" Joe was now full of confidence. The soldiers had encouraged him to continue and he would succeed.

"So let's move on, two men back, two sides, we'll move slowly. And I beg you, if any of you have a better suggestion, let me know."

They resounded with, "Yes, sir."

They trudged slowly through the sparse forest. Soon after, Joe ordered his people to stop, as he was told by the back team that they had encountered a patrol they had just been able to fend off. Joe asked for caution. They should be slower but also be more careful, and they should not risk anything as they have more than enough time.

The troop began to move again, when suddenly from the left a huge bang sounded. Shots passed close over the soldiers' heads.

"Duck, look for cover. Can anyone see anything?"

"Sir, a hover tank."

"Excuse me?" Joe called through the noise. "Soldier, what do you see?"

"I said: a hover tank."

"Soldier Brown, sneak up on the tank and put in an explosive charge. Meanwhile, Roger and Mike are distracting him."

They managed to distract the tank, and after a while a loud explosion broke the silence of the area.

"Sir, it was just a hologram of a tank, deceptively real and even physically tangible, wow. But now it has gone out. We destroyed the target," Brown reported when he returned.

"Well done, boys, keep it up!"

At that moment, the commander's voice sounded over a speaker again: "You responded well, Joe. Remember, even in battle you need to be prepared for unannounced things. So do not be surprised because we will use more tricks. The End."

Joe wondered beyond measure. As it looked, the whole forest was wired and full of cameras, apparently watching them with eagle eyes. He had thought they were on their own until now.

"Guys, you heard it. Let's be prepared! Slowly I feel like a kid playing robber and gendarme. Let's show it to the robber!"

They kept running, sometimes they could hear shots, otherwise everything was quiet. One of the soldiers recognized something on the scanner and shouted a few words to Joe, who let him hold the squad.

"What's up, soldier?"

"I can not say exactly what it is, but it looks like there are a lot of tiny animals in front of us."

"Tiny animals?" Joe scared. "Cyborgs!" It shot through his head.

"Show me, soldier!" Joe ordered, reaching for the scanner. There were actually many points to be recognized, but they did not move a millimeter.

"They do not move...that could be mines," Joe said.

He sent two of his soldiers ahead and in fact they came across mines all over the place and nobody knew if they were real or not. But no one wanted to take the risk of testing it out.

"We're going to bypass this area extensively. Our final goal is not far away. I just communicated with the other three troops. They are also very close to the bunker."

The soldiers marched on and around the minefield. They regularly looked at the scanners. Team left and right were now almost at the bunker. They were supposed to attach explosive charges while the team was carrying out a diversionary maneuver from behind. When the charges were in place, Joe ordered the ignition. The bunker went up and from the loudspeakers the voice sounded again: "Very good, Joe. They proved themselves. They may now return to the base."

The next days flew by. Joe was exhausted from the strict training sessions, but every day he felt better prepared for the war. At the end of the ten-day boot camp, when he was bid farewell by the commander, the commander said: "We have driven up heavy artillery, Joe. Nevertheless, they fought very bravely. The threat that their lives were in danger was not real, of course. It was only to help you do your best. We don't kill our own people just like that. The Russians with their special forces do that. But we need every man. But from now on they are really at war, I urge you to be careful. The first attack is approaching. The rebel station in North America has informed us that it is making good progress with the production of the ships. In less than two months 1000 Haunebus will be ready and the major attack can be carried out. Now return to the base, your wife is waiting for you."

While this was being discussed, Vivi was lying in her quarters thinking about Joe. What was he doing? Did he miss her? Vivi herself missed him very much and she had had enough of reading books. Luckily she had survived the endless ten days now. Soon he would come. At least she was hoping for it, because they had not been allowed to communicate for the last ten days. The soldiers should not be distracted, they said. She knew how important this exercise was for Joe. If he had not survived them, there would be no reason for them to go on living. The thought of having to raise the baby all by herself made her incredibly sad. She wanted a happy family. She wanted her Joe. She didn't care about the war as long as she could only be with Joe. Two hours later he entered her bedroom and wrapped his arms around her neck.

"Finally you are with me again. I was so afraid for you. Please don't leave us anymore. Never again. From now on I will always come with you, no matter where you go," she said and tears ran down her cheeks.

"But Vivi, I don't want you to go to war with me. Think about the baby!"

"Does it matter where we die? Sooner or later we all die, and I'd rather die in your arms than leave somewhere alone in one of those bunkers. Do you understand that, Joe?"

"Yes, my Vivi. I'm sorry that you had to go through this. From now on we stay together. But let us go to sleep now, we have another long day ahead of us tomorrow. Sean told me before, when I arrived, there would be a weapons training. I will try to get you a good position, perhaps as a commander on one of the ships. I don't want you to be on the open field, that would be far too dangerous for the child and you. But you could be used as a pilot. I'm sure you can still work for two months. You will notice for yourself when you have to excuse yourself. However, you would have to prove yourself. Flight training is very difficult. And the computers are different, but you already know all that."

"I would love to do that and I also have the feeling that I can do it. But let's go to sleep now, I'm totally tired. We can still talk about it tomorrow."

Carriage

Joe and Vivi fell asleep quickly, snuggled up very close to each other. As always, the night passed much too quickly. The morning bell sounded shrill and tore the two out of their dreams. Joe was confused and didn't know where he was for a moment. Half asleep he called for his dog. He quickly realized that it had all been a dream. There was no dog and they were also no longer in their house at the edge of the forest. They were here, in a cold, barren room. After dressing, they went to see Sean.

"Sean, I have to talk to you, it's about my wife," Joe began.

"Go ahead."

"I can't leave her alone in the bunker while I'm out there risking my life. It's her wish to get a job, let her do the flight test in the simulator, I beg you!"

"Just because it's you, Joe. But I will only give her one try. Come on, Vivianne," Sean said.

She followed Sean, who led her into the simulator room. "I will explain everything to you well. All you have to do is dodge the white dots that appear in front of you, it's like a PC game, only much more realistic. Some of these hits they can endure. Here you can see the display. If it is in the red area, all you can do is escape. There is no escape capsule. Every time you are hit, you will feel an electric shock. It becomes more painful with increasing damage. So you will feel it in reality. It is caused by the weakened force field. Begin."

Sean left the simulator room and gave the order to start. Vivi was nervous, but things went very well in the beginning. It wasn't difficult to dodge the points, but after a short time she was hit and a painful electric shock was pouring through her whole body. Adrenaline was poured out, she felt anger in her. This spurred her on to better performances. Bitingly she avoided the white dots and got better and better. Sean watched with excitement and surprised at the control monitor. So far nobody had made it this far without getting into the red area. She was outstanding. The games she had always played at home had trained her reactivity. She had now proven that such games also had their good sides.

When the test was over, Sean came back in. Most astonished he said: "Very good performances, Vivi. You just set a new record. I welcome you to our Air Force."

Vivi had a talent: She had an enormously good ability to react, which had made her an air force pilot in the rebel army. She wouldn't have dreamed that she would ever dare and master this career step in her life.
Since she was now officially allowed to fly, she asked Sean if she could dare a first real flight, and Sean agreed. It was no problem, she could fly, it was said.

Together with Joe and Sean she boarded a four-man ship. Joe sat in the co-pilot seat and watched Vivi operate the ship. He was proud of his wife. The ship rose quietly into the air.

"We will fly north. That's where the danger of being seen is least. The new Germanic people are only off the coast. So far they haven't come any closer, Vivi," Joe explained the new situation, because he hadn't heard anything about the reconnaissance flights of the New Germans yet, since he had almost been cut off from the world in Canada.

"Hopefully you will know what to do if new Germans do show up," Sean said. "Accelerate to 2,000 km/h. Test the ship, it's yours now. Familiarise yourself with it, give it a name."

"I'll call it Joe-One in honor of my husband. Thank you, Sean. Let's see what this thing's got, hold on tight." Vivi accelerated so fast that Joe and Sean were pressed into their seats. She flew the ship close to the ground, but suddenly it stopped.

"What was that now? Vivi, what's going on?" Joe asked.

"I don't know, we're in the air, but nothing's moving."

"The fall protection was triggered," Sean explained. "Vivi flew way too close above the trees."

"She will have to familiarize herself with this ship," Joe said encouragingly. And turned to Vivi: "After a few flying hours you will be a professional!" The rest of the exercise went satisfactorily and after a while they returned to the rebel station unharmed.

No Turning Back

After more than a month of daily training, the first concrete attack was planned. They should sustainably weaken the New Germans. They still had two weeks to prepare. The New Germans' flying disks had remained stubbornly off the coast until recently. It looked as if they had controlled the progress in America. But the preparations were top secret, it was actually impossible for the New Germans to know about the strategies. Nevertheless, there was always the unpleasant feeling of being watched. The troop strength of the New Germans was estimated at 15 million, with the rebels worldwide could muster just two million. According to estimates, the New Germans owned about 100,000 ships, all equipped with the most modern weapons and all of an unprecedented speed. Although the rebels had no chance at that time - soberly - they had been up for weeks to upgrade. The required amount of flying discs was almost reached. It was still better to go to war than to be subjugated by the New Germans. Therefore, the production ran at full speed, as the day of the attack approached.

A new day dawned and Joe and Vivianne sat in the bedroom on the edge of the bed. Vivi was already in the 23rd week of pregnancy and could no longer hide the baby bump. A clear bulge was visible. However, as she still felt very fit, she continued training and Sean let her do it. Today they woke up by themselves, Joe first, because he had a bad feeling. Could it really be that there was no way but to fight and go the path of certain death sooner or later? His dream had always been to live somewhere remote with Vivi, to enjoy the rest of life and to bring up children. They would have a baby soon, but the dream of the beautiful house was still far away. As much as he looked forward to the baby, he felt so uncomfortable because he had to expose his child to the war. He had imagined how beautiful their lives would be if they could live in peace, without fear of New-Germans, bombs and flying disks. Vivi, on the other hand, looked more pragmatically towards the future. It was the way it was and she would make the most of it. Although the war was raging outside, she would give her child as much love and affection as possible so that, despite everything, she could grow up in a sheltered atmosphere. But until that happened, she would go on and fight for the rebels. She'd flown several times since she had passed the flight test and had become familiar with her ship. It was overwhelming to fly such a device, the speed, the acceleration, the maneuvers. All this that Vivi had done, and it had become clear to her that there was no going back: they had to fight. Every single one. Or everything was lost.

It had been quiet in the last few days. Too calm. The New Germans had previously bombed a few positions on the coast, but since then their flying targets had been withdrawn. They left with further attacks coming. It seemed like they had other problems.

Maybe Joe was just nervous because they were sent to South America today for another practice mission. Vivi was there to test her new experiences as a pilot and Joe got to know new weapons and leadership techniques. His team played slowly, it came now and then to a small scramble, but the problem was usually solved quickly and unbureaucratically. Occasionally, Joe was involved in a brawl, but he did not think it necessary to report it to the commander. Slowly he got used to the tough guys in his new environment.

When Joe and Vivi returned from their practice mission the next day, there was news. A message from Russia had arrived. The New Germans had apparently launched a large-scale attack against the Russians. Their goal was to finally level all Russian rebels. The rebels in Russia fiercely resisted and called on the Americans. The stock of Russian rebels was still about 10,000 and it was growing less daily, because the New Germans were fighting with clones, which were replaceable. It had been decided to support the Russians and send a fleet to Russia. The Russians did not have suitable flying discs, and if they did not get help soon, it would look bad for them. The selected soldiers would leave the next day. Joe was not there, they wanted him with him for the attack against New Berlin, which was to be carried out in a few weeks.

Five days later, when news came that the last 10,000 Russian rebels had fallen and the American rebels returned greatly weakened, one could feel something of a slight shudder in the rebel camp. But Sean motivated the troops and drove forward with the planning of the attack.

There were now almost enough positions to withstand an attack of 50,000 ships for a short time. What worried the technicians, however, were the new types of weapons that were occasionally whispered about. It was said that the New Germans had weapons that could destroy enemy troops with a single shot. By complete annihilation - it was understood that a group of 20 men could be dissolved into thin air. Maybe this was just a rumor, because the jet torpedoes had the disadvantage that the explosion was pulverized within a radius of several meters.

At last the final attack plan was ready. The day of the attack was January 1st. Shortly before that date Vivi had to be admitted to the infirmary because of excessive blood pressure. She was diagnosed with gestosis, more specifically, it was a pre-eclampsia, a condition that can only occur during pregnancy. The doctor advised her to rest and forbade her to continue to fly before the birth. She had to take a relieve and stay in the bunker. Terrified, Vivi stared at the doctor. Joe would fly to Europe in a few days and fight. She did not want to be left alone! But the doctor remained adamant. Under these circumstances he could not let her go. She had the responsibility for herself and the unborn child.

In her bedroom Vivi let her tears run free and clung to Joe. If he did not return, everything was over. But she knew that could happen when she was there. There was no guarantee. That's why she wanted to be sensible, at least for the sake of the child. She would take care of herself and take good care of her baby. At the same time, she would wait for Joe every minute and worry.

The day on which everything should take its new course moved closer. At night, Joe could not close his eyes and Vivi clung onto him like a burdock. If she lost him, her child would have to grow up without a father. Joe thought of the young Lars celebrating his birthday today. He was already 17 years on this earth, and he had seen nothing except strife and murder. I hope that the same thing would not happen to her child.

On New Year's morning Joe was awakened by a soldier. The departure time had been set at 11:00a.m.. The units were cleared and Joe was flown to the hangar. Every soldier and every commander had to take along a weapon, provisions and a hover-pack. Joe's force would land on the fringes of Italy, the only country not yet under the complete control of the New Germans. Italian rebels have been trying for days to clear the way for the invaders. Three landing sites had been chosen and Joe was lucky enough to land in Italy, because another troop had to land in Normandy, the same place where the Allies landed during the Second World War. The third landing party had to attack from Russia. Switzerland had been chosen as the center for communication.

Each landing squad comprised about 10,000 men, with 330 troops being made available to each squad. The ships had the main task of securing the airspace, while the ground forces were used against the dreaded clones. It was uncertain what to expect. Although each soldier had a serious training, the clones had martial techniques from nearly 200 years of martial arts. It seemed impossible to win this war. Each landing party was given the necessary information, because no risk could be taken.

Shortly before the soldiers got into the flying discs, Sean made another speech. The men listened through their earphones because there were so many of them that they would never have understood Sean if he had spoken live in front of them. Rebels from all over America and Canada had come together to go to battle together. The two other landing troops started from other stations, one from Argentina and the other from Greenland. Overall, rebels from all over the globe had mobilized. 30,000 men went to war today. The rest of the rebels were ready to move as soon as the number of soldiers decimated. Only together they were able to fight against the huge army of the New Germans.

"Do not trust anyone but your units," Sean's voice said. "You can not even trust the European rebels. Be careful! Let the wounded lie. You will not be able to help most, a shot from a ray weapon is 95% deadly. The nervous system fails in no time. Remember, you will not meet anyone, it's just clones. Go ahead, just like in training! Think of your ancestors, soldiers! They experienced the same thing 200 years ago and have emerged as heroes from history. Now you are the ones who will be heroes soon. But your commitment will be great. Not all of you will be back here at the end of this battle. It is also in your hands, whether this will be a battle that will decide everything or whether it will be just a small pinprick. I wish you all much success!"

Sean tried to make the soldiers believe they had a chance. Many saw the fear in each other's eyes, some had even already taken their own lives, as they were no longer able to cope with the pressure. The only reason Joe wanted to finish this war was his family, his wife, and his child. He wanted them to see how they could grow old together in a house somewhere far away.

Vivi overheard the whole speech from the edge of the great square. Now it was time to say goodbye. She ran and fell around Joe's neck. Secretly she struggled against the tears. She did not want to make it any harder for him than it already was. No, she wanted to be strong! He would come back. After all, he had an obligation as a father! As a farewell, she handed him a small gift that he was only allowed to open on the base. She also gave him a letter.

The soldiers started hymns. Every soldier who believed in anything prayed to what was sacred to him. The clock showed 10:45a.m. and a siren sounded in a loud tone. The soldiers ran, each one heading for his ship, and after ten minutes no human soul could be seen on the huge asphalt. Only the 330 ships were ready for departure. From above, the various aircraft looked overwhelming, standing in rank and file. The rebels had developed eight different types of ships. They looked partly similar to those of the New Germans. Some could be thought of as flying pills, others looked like dinner plates, others were similar to rockets only imagined in science fiction stories. The largest ship, however, could be compared to a sheet of paper flolded at the ends with a span of 150 x 150 meters. It was the command ship whose crew consisted of 250 soldiers. All around it were turrets. On the underside, two tubes with a diameter of about five meters were mounted longitudinally. These would help start the first attempts to deactivate the force fields of the outposts. For a total of 20 torpedoes were provided, these bullets were not made of solid matter. They had not been able to test how they would react, They knew they would do enormous damage without a force field, but it was still not clear how the New Germans managed to shoot through force fields. There had to be a way to penetrate them. Finally, there were the smaller five-man ships. They were fast and maneuverable, but had a very light armament and their armor was minimal. They were good for reconnaissance flights. There were also the vans, they were slow, but well-armed and very well armored. The soldiers had to be able to leave the ship on the fly with their hover-packs. The vans were partly Hover tanks. There were only a few such tanks available, because they were very expensive to manufacture. In addition, they were easy targets for airships. Then there were the destroyers, these were medium-sized, well-armed, well armored and relatively fast ships. They had a crew of twenty men. A destroyer was equipped with five cannons left and five right. At the bottom there were four torpedo tubes and on the roof was a gun. In addition, these were equipped with automatic defense shields. It was amazing how fast the rebels had constructed these ships. The only thing they missed was the opportunity to test the ships and their weapons in action. Nobody knew how a clone would react to a hit. In addition, the Neo-Germanic commanders and some of the clones were surrounded by protective shields. Not all clones, only those who had experience fighting. Before this they had to be particularly careful because they were the best.

A few dozen small ships were taken for diversion, unmanned drones carrying a small, self-firing gun. It could also be programmed to pick and destroy a target.

As Joe sat in the Haunebu, which was about to fly him back to Europe, he tore open Vivi's letter and began to read: "My dearest Joe, I am sorry that I can not be with you during this difficult time. How I would like to have fought at your side. I do not want to die without you, I ask you to come back to me. Whatever happens, come back to me, we'll soon have a young girl, yes, it's a girl who needs a father. It can not be that I'll lose you after four years. Take care of yourself. I will try to locate you. And if I am better, I will come to your aid. My dearest Joe, I dare not say goodbye to you, because you will have to come back to me, whether you like it or not. If you are injured, contact the captain of the air raid fleet. I have a deal with him. It does not matter what I did. However, he will fetch you immediately should you be wounded. He gave me his word. It's not what you think. I will tell you in due course. The deal was hard for me, but I hope you can live with it. Now take care and come back. I'm waiting for you."

Joe came to tears, he was not allowed to fall, he was not allowed to do this to his Vivi and also to his daughter. But what did Vivi mean by deal? What could she have done? In Joe, the worst thoughts came up. He tried to push her away, maybe it was different. But why could not she tell him? Would it hurt him too much?

Major Offensive

The soldiers leaned in their seats and the ships rose silently into the air. Thanks to the ultra-modern drives with pure material no engine noise could be heard. Joe was in a van with his troop. When the aircraft had risen to altitude, he said to his men:

"Guys, we had plenty of time to meet. I could learn a lot from you. We had a good time together, but it was not always easy. We will now make the first strike against the New Germans. Be brave and take good care of yourself!"

He tried to encourage the soldiers, because they looked at their fear. Almost everyone had a family, and some of the women were also soldiers. But there were only men in Joe's unit. Now he commanded a smaller squad of 30 men. The rest had been redistributed and three had committed suicide. Joe knew very well about every one of his troopers. Everyone had a good fight, but everyone had their own specialty to help the troop.

The ships stayed in the air for a while, then the sign was given to accelerate. Now there was no turning back.

As they approached mainland Europe, Joe spoke again. The last half hour had been very quiet. Everyone had their own thoughts and no one had the desire for informal small talk.

"Be prepared and put your hover pack on standby, it can go any moment. Note the green lamp. As soon as it lights up, you have to get ready to jump off."

Some shivered and others even vomited. Joe only knew this image from old war movies, and now he experienced it on his own body, but by now he was greatly hardened and sometimes even thought he had no feelings left. There was only one thought left in Joe's head: When would the first shot fall? Would the New Germans expect them and open the fire, or would the rebels be able to attack first?

A soldier looked out the window and saw nothing but the gray haze. Did the ships of the New Germans lurk somewhere behind this camouflage? Did they observe the powerful mobilization of the airships from the beginning, or were they unaware of the rebel's plan?

Joe fervently hoped that they would have a small edge and that the New Germans had no idea of their arrival, because they had already arrived at the Italian border and so far nothing had happened. But in retrospect, Joe had to realize that this assumption had been false, because the New-Germans let them approach as closely as possible to the defense. Suddenly a huge explosion shook the ship. The lamp indicated red. Something had happened. Joe saw the back of a soldier lying prone on the ground, covered in blood. The ship-internal siren sounded, the first shots fell. Within seconds, Joe heard only explosions. Then the lamp switched to green. The door opened and everyone had to jump, Joe ahead. Immediately the others followed him.

As they raced to the ground with their hover-packs, Joe saw dozens of ships in flames without a single shot. Joe saw a soldier being hit in the air, his hover pack exploded and his guts escaping from his body. As the ships flew several thousand meters, it took several minutes to reach the ground. The soldiers were well equipped and wore state-of-the-art helmets that supplied them with oxygen. Their army uniforms were made of synthetic fibers, which also perfectly protected them from heat and cold. During the flight, Joe almost lost control of his hover pack. One ship after another was simply destroyed. The sight was horrible. The camouflage of the ships was gradually switched off by the electromagnetic impulses and the location of their ships was an easy one for the New Germans.

"Shoot at them!" He gasped.

Finally undamaged ships opened fire. Some flying discs of the New Germans were hit and fell burning into the abyss. Lightning flashed everywhere and the explosions were massive. They were already over a mountain range and would arrive shortly on the ground. Joe saw a soldier failing to turn on the hover pack and he rushed straight onto the rock.

Horrified, Joe pursued the misfortune of his comrade until he himself came down. Within seconds, the rest of his men landed on the ground. Using their scanners and ear devices, they were able to orient themselves and quickly find their way back together. Four men from Joe's troupe were missing. Now they were only twenty-six. Some ships had managed the landing, while the mothership fired incessantly against the positions. It was already badly damaged when it ignited the main drive and started the return journey. For many other ships, everything was too late, they crashed burning over the Alps.

Of the 10,000 soldiers who were to land in Italy, as many as 1,650 had died before reaching the ~~bottom~~ ground. If this continued, it would not be long before they were all eradicated.

Joe ordered his troops to take cover immediately: "You have seen what has just happened, this should warn you all the more caution! Our goal is the outposts of the New Germans, which are located just before the Swiss border. You are only about three kilometers from our current location. So it must be expected that we will soon meet the enemy. They will come quickly. We will try to go where the trees have grown dense. In between, however, there are always open areas. Pay close attention to the enemy ships that circulate about us, besides, we do not know whether the New-Germans own tanks."

"Attention!" Brian heard something. It was the first clone, a single clone in the middle of the forest. Brian shot. He hit the clone, but it did not seem to matter. Only after a few more volleys he fell over.

"What was that? A single clone?" Joe thought. He thought of a scout. "There are sure to be more clones to follow. Always have your scanners in the sights! Remember our training camp!" Joe shouted.

Before Joe could say another word, someone shouted, "Cover, men!"

The soldiers threw themselves on the damp ground. It stank of burnt meat, shots fell. But then Joe realized that the shots were for a neighboring squad. He saw a group of about 20 clones running towards the other party. They did not even slow down when they were shot at. They ran directly into the fire of the rebels. They did not seem to mind. At the same time they shot back, and within seconds all the other group were killed. Of the clones, only two had fallen in the fire.

"What was that? Did you see that?" Joe gasped.

They were only about seven hundred yards away and the individual trees that rose out of the ground were not a serious camouflage. The clones began to run in their direction. Now it would be their turn. It seemed as if panic would break out. But one of the soldiers, specializing in technology, had a self-built rocket launcher with a range of one kilometer. He started shooting, accompanied by the fire of the other soldiers. When the smoke dissolved a few seconds later, they saw several clones that had been brought to the track and lay motionless on the ground. But then two appeared who had survived this huge explosion. That could not happen! The technician continued firing. Just before one of the clones could engage his weapon, he dropped to his knees, head up, and shouted, "Hail, leader!" Then he fell dead.

The soldiers were shocked. Yosoju, the technician, needed four more shots to kill the last clone.

"Oh, shit!" Joe stammered. "What if an army of 100 clones comes up to us? We're being massacred like pigs in the slaughterhouse."

Yosoju was quite pale and said, "I used up almost a third of my ammunition. We'll never succeed! I want to go back, let me go, I want to go home!"

Joe tried to calm him down, but he had no convincing arguments. They and other troops had not even covered 500 meters and the clones had already caused them extreme losses. What else could they do? They could not turn back, there was no ship to pick them up. They had to come up with something. Tom looked at his scanner. It seemed to be calm within 200 meters, but this could change quickly.

"We were told that the weapons would kill a clone as well as a human," said one of the soldiers.

"Yes, that's what they said, these bureaucrats. Let them come here and fight with their miracle weapons!" Yosoju cursed desperately.

"Well, we'll spread out at a distance of 20 meters. They can not eliminate us all at once," Joe said. "Everyone is responsible for a small section. Get your grenades ready. With the guns you will not get far, the armor of the clones is too strong. You only use energy."

Step by step, they went forward. But Joe suddenly stopped. There were dots on his scanner. Immediately he remembered the training camp. He called the mine specialist to check the matter.
"It's actually mines," the specialist said. "But these are different. They look like they have no technology, purely mechanical. I'll defuse them," he said, and went to the first mine. When he had endered it harmless, he

looked up and said to Joe, "These are 20th century mines. Do you know how I know that?"

"No idea."
"These are the only mines that do not go up when fired. If they were electric, they would be too sensitive."

"Where did you learn that?"

"I attended various weapons classes during my training. One course was named 'Weapons and Mines of the 20th Century'. At first, I thought this course would never do me any good, now it has saved our lives. Clever, these New Germans are damn clever. There are few who can defuse such mines."

At that moment Joe had an idea.

"Get me down a narrow path through the minefield," he told the specialist. "You soldiers lay in wait here at the edge of the minefield. Behind these rocks; you can take cover and fire a few shots to direct the clones in your direction. Get ready for an attack. I'll lure the clones to the opposite side of the minefield, and if they're there, run through the path in the minefield. They will follow me and run towards us, but in the hail of fire they will not be able to monitor their scanners at the same time. So they will step into the mines. I hope it works," said Joe.

The specialist cleared a narrow path through the minefield, and when everything was ready, Joe switched his scanner's rayon to 2000 meters and recognized a cluster of 20 clones about 1.3 km north of them.

"I'll be here in 15 minutes with the clones. Get ready!"
He said, then he marched extensively around the
minefield and went to meet the clones. Halfway down
he fired a flare. It did not take five seconds for the
clone group to move on the scanner. They ran in his
direction and Joe started running too - towards the
minefield. He had his scanner right in front of his eyes,
so that he would not miss the uncovered path. As he
walked through the minefield, the clones appeared in
the background. They started firing and Joe ran as
fast as his legs could carry him. He felt a shot close by
him. Then, fortunately, he reached the rocks and flung
himself under cover.

The soldiers fired shots to drive the clones further in
their direction. They were still running towards the
minefield without batting an eyelid. Joe's plan worked.
When the first clones were in the minefield, explosions
were heard. Joe could watch the clones burn and try
to extinguish the fire by rolling on the ground. The
remaining clones continued doggedly and one by one
fell victim to the mines. The soldiers saw clones with
no legs screaming, and at that moment it seemed to
Joe that these clones were just normal people, seeing
how they suffered. Severed limbs lay on the ground.
The images burned deeply into Joe's memory. These
were not just brainless, organic dolls, but creatures
that suffered pain. He thought of the clones in the
mine in Mexico and how friendly they had been
received there. Although one had said that the other
clones could not think independently and were only
puppets of the New Germans, but still they had
sensations. The catastrophic events struck Joe again
with relentless force and he once again desperately
wanted to be in a peaceful place, away from all the
cruelty. For the first time, Joe killed someone, even

though they were not real people. On the one hand, the clones suffered like humans, on the other hand, they knew no fear. In addition, Joe felt shameful because until now he had not gone back to the clones in the mine to bring them food, although this would have been timely once agreed.

The few clones that had been fortunate enough to remain unharmed by the mines were now shelled by the soldiers. Finally, the entire minefield went up in a breathtaking explosion. All the bodies were pulverized. Joe's troupe had managed to kill 20 clones in one fell swoop. That was certainly unique. One of the last clones had shouted something before he died. No one had understood and it had sounded like the Goa'uld from the 'Stargate' movies that Joe used to watch. Was it a secret language?

After this victory, the motivation of the soldiers increased. They had seen that they were not totally inferior. If they were smart, they could get through. On the scanners, they recognized other rebels fighting clones. But their advance was largely pushed back, many had already fallen. Gunfire was heard all around and bullets raced past the trees. A flying rebel group could advance with a battleship up to an air defense and destroy several ships. But then a New Germans battleship came in, and then unmasked and began firing at the battleship. Barely ten seconds passed and the battleship crashed to the ground. The new Germanic ship disguised itself and disappeared. Although the battleship was lost, a gap had been created in the defensive ring, which the rebels could now use. Rebel transporters flew through the gap to Switzerland and arrived in New Germany. There they set off their soldiers with hover-packs. So at least they could shoot a few clones and get into the country where it was quiet at the moment, because it seemed as if the whole defense had gathered at the Italian border. The sky was black with flying disks, it looked like a swarm of bees attacked by hornets. Many rebel airships had activated the hyperdrive, fled, and returned to America. They had to realize it, at the moment they had no chance. The Battle of the Air was largely lost, the New Germans were vastly superior to the rebels, although these also had a modern equipment. This was due to the armor, which was insufficient. That of the New Germans was four to five times stronger. How they did that was unclear, and therefore few succeeded in destroying a New Germanic ship.

Joe ran forward with his troop. They were not allowed to lose any time, the station was only 300 meters away from them. Only four clones were on site. These immediately opened fire. Brian was hit and was killed on the spot, Fritz's head was shot away. Yosoju fired when they did, as did the rest of the soldiers. In the end, the four clones fell, they could not fend off the attack.

After more than 100 ships fled back to America and the rest was destroyed, it slowly became quiet on the ground around Joe. They had passed the Italian border and were now in Switzerland. Joe knew there was a rebel base nearby that could provide shelter. They just had to find it.

"Let's go, let's get on our way!" He ordered his troop.

"Joe, you can not do that to us, and if we encounter such resistance again, we will all perish. We've already lost six men and we have not even survived the first day!"

"And if we stay here, we die as well, soldier. Here we go!"

They marched for over an hour and did not register any enemy activity. The scanner told them that they were now very close to the rebel base.

"Felix, Tom! You will precede to scout," ordered Joe.

They started walking and came back after a while with an encouraging message: "The bunker was held! We did not see any living clones, but there are clone corpses around the bunker."

"Let's go and join the others," Joe said.

They were cheerfully received by the commander. "Welcome, we have tracked your attack, unfortunately we could not do enough for your ships, we were under fire ourselves. An hour ago, 40 clones besieged us. We could kill them though. Why are you idiots attacking from Italy? You should have attacked from France, the way would have been better there, and it would not have been too full of New Germans."

"We did not know that the New Germans are guarding the Italian border so well. Another landing party landed in Normandy and the third attacked from Russia. Actually, we thought we would have been assigned the best landing site, since there is still Switzerland between New Germany and Italy. But obviously we were wrong."

"Switzerland was annexed a week ago, didn't you hear that?" The rebel commander wondered.

"Unfortunately not. There's nothing in the news about that!"

"Oh, these Americans just have the feeling that a country as small as Switzerland is unimportant," sighed the commander.
"Did you hear about the other troops that landed in Normandy and Russia?" Joe asked.

"No, not yet," said the commander. "News reporting in war is sluggish. Well, you will probably know, because you will not get away from here so soon. It will not be long before the New Germans send new clones. You are a tiny little trumpet, do you want to cross Switzerland like that? You would be dead in no time. You were tremendously lucky that you even arrived here! Here you are relatively safe for now. We were able to improve our positions enormously, our defense is very good. In addition, we have a good location here. The guns of the New Germans can not penetrate the mountain. Unfortunately, we are currently tied to this site. Since the annexation, these clones are teeming around us and we have no airships to escape."

"Have you noticed that your weapons against the clones are not enough?"

"Oh yeah. Previously, it was only the officers who were surrounded by a protective shield, but now the clones also get one. Every clone. The New Germans did not comply with the production of the clones, so they have strengthened them so that they survive longer and less new ones are needed. The shield will withstand normal weapons without any problem, unless you are aiming for the generator on their back. The force field does not completely surround it, leaving an opening approximately three centimeters wide. When this is hit, the generator explodes and the clones die instantly. But since it's unlikely we'll hit the hole, we'll have to go with torpedoes or rocket launchers at the clones. However, you still need about three to four shots. Unfortunately, we still could not develop a more effective weapon. But it's not just the clones that bother us. The New Germans are getting more and more tanks. A single clone is enough to drive the whole vehicle. He controls everything automatically by computer. Their latest achievement, however, is Haunebus's Achter series. These are so fast that the turrets almost do not follow. Our advantage is that such high speeds can only be achieved for a short time. After operating for more than ten minutes on maximum power, the generator explodes. It is unclear where the New Germans got this technique from, but a single aft ship is enough to destroy 20 of your ships in just three seconds. I hope you will promote your production and your technique, otherwise we will have lost this war in a few weeks, because then there will be no more rebels. While our attacks do not cause lasting damage to the New Germans, we can give the Americans more time."

"Whether this actually has a benefit is an open question. The rebels do not have the slightest chance. Let's face it, the Americans have massively underestimated the New Germans. In such a short time they can never catch up with technical progress."

"Do not be so negative, Joe. Nothing is impossible."

"You're right, we can not give up! How can I just think about giving up, I have another wife and I'm going to be a father soon!"

"Well, then you have a good reason to keep fighting! Nothing is lost yet. Soon our latest development is ripe for the field. If the results are in accordance with the hypothesis, we will soon be holding a strong weapon in our hands," the commander remarked.

"What are you talking about?" Joe asked.

"We have a cyborg prototype, Joe," the commander said meaningfully. "Should he be as efficient in combat as we suspect, the clones will soon have no chance. He is aggressive and destroys everything that comes his way. Previously, the problem was that the cyborg could only recharge energy if the environment was radioactively contaminated. However, we have managed to install an energy supply for him. In addition, he is programmed so that he attacks only New Germans. If he proves himself in battle, we can produce him. He'll be ready for production soon, the last tests are almost complete."

Joe was not amazed. "You have a cyborg?" He repeated in disbelief.

"You heard right, Joe. His name is Ions. Using the cyborgs, we will destroy as many outposts as possible. We will kick the New-Germans in the ass! But now you all come along, you have to eat something."

Joe and his troop followed the commander of the rebel station while the war was raging outside. The bunker defense worked perfectly, the generators ran at full speed. For dinner there was something stewed. It did not taste bad for war.

"How long can a clone live without food?" Asked a soldier named Felix as they ate.

"We watched the clones with our outdoor cameras and found they sometimes ate a chocolate bar. They never ate a real meal. We suspect they can live without food for several days."

"Well, in fact, clones can live without water and food for several weeks. I know this first-hand, so to speak," Joe remarked in a schoolmaster's tone.

When the soldiers looked at him questioningly, he told them about his mission in the Mexican mine. However, right after Joe came back to the current events: "We need a new strategy," he said to his soldiers. "Until we know exactly how the other two landing parties did, we'll wait and see. But our next goal is to turn off the main defensive position further north. If the Swiss rebels work with us and we can use the cyborgs, we may even have a chance. In addition, after dinner, I will try to contact the headquarters in America. They should send us a few airships for reinforcement."

"As far as I know, the main defensive position at the New Germanic border is specially protected, especially the air defense is very strong, because it has an emergency power plant and a second force field. In addition, the entire complex is guarded by about 200 clones. There are turrets for ground defense within 300 yards," the commander remarked.

"Oh, holy shit," Joe muttered. "Nevertheless, we must try, we can not win this war if we flee."

Later, when he was alone in his night room and tiredly falling to his bed, he suddenly remembered the package Vivi had given him. He felt it in his jacket pocket and pulled out the beautifully wrapped, small gift. Vivi's necklace was in it. Joe put her around his neck. He missed his wife beyond measure. The fact that he could not assist her during the pregnancy and was so far from her burdened him greatly. He had previously contacted the headquarters in America, his point of view and asked for airships and other soldiers in order to advance to the Swiss or New Germany border. He also had greetings to his wife and learned that the other two landing troops had recorded great success. The New Germans had not been prepared for an attack on the French border and had lost over 2000 clones, whereas very few had fallen from the rebels. The landing party, which had come from Russia, had also already managed to advance to New Germany and bombard various defensive posts. The next day the battle would continue. At least that was good news. Tired, Joe fell asleep.

Wounded

Joe got reinforcements from America three days later. Thanks to active camouflage, two aircraft were able to reach the Swiss bunker unseen and be hidden there. The Swiss had started producing cyborgs. The prototype had been tested in the field, had killed 50 clones within a very short time and then returned without damage.

"Guys, we can not stay in this bunker forever," Joe talked to his troop. "Sean has promised to make a transfer to buy ten cyborgs from the Swiss. The commander says they are ready for action in two days. As soon as we have it, we will move to this position on the New Germanic frontier. We have to make it there to turn off the anti-aircraft. Prepare for the attack!"

When the time came, Joe gave another short speech: "Now it's time. We leave the safe shelter and plunge again into the lion's den. If one of you should fall, the others have to go on, whatever the cost. Do you understand me?"

"Yes, sir!"

Some Swiss rebels had joined the Americans and also climbed into the flying discs. As they camouflaged themselves into the air, they could see muzzle flashes everywhere, flashing at the Italian border. An omnipresent noise and a roar were heard. Quickly, however, they left the battle zone behind and flew with activated camouflage close to the ground to the north, until they were only a few kilometers before the main defensive position at the Neo-Germanic border. Immediately next to a river they found a larger meadow where they could park the airships. The rest they had to cover on foot, because first the ground forces had to be wiped out. Then they could storm the turrets and beat the New Germany with their own weapons - that's the plan. If they managed to take the turrets, they could shoot the New-German flying disks from the sky without endangering their own ships. Then they could use the free air space to penetrate with their flying discs in New Germany. A few soldiers remained in the airships, it was connected via the earphones. If necessary, the airships could make an exit or - as hoped - the rebels can pick up after successful takeover of the defense station to penetrate into the country. Joe had set himself high goals.

"Soldiers, we'll divide into groups of two," Joe said just before they got out. "Each should move so far away from the other groups that a mutual cover fire can be guaranteed. The cyborgs are for the time being in our midst. Always pay attention to your scanners. As soon as we look at clones, we let the cyborgs run. Stay low on the ground and keep an eye on your colleagues. We have to be able to count each other. And off! Forward, as discussed!"

The groups were divided and each went into their positions. Carefully, they ran, each soldier paying close attention to his scanner. Tense, they also looked into the sky again and again to see if an enemy ship was in sight. But instead of a new Germanic ship, some of the rebels' ships suddenly flew over them, their signs clearly visible. Was that about the reserve that had managed to break through the defenses at the Italian border?

"Yosoju, scan the two ships up there," Joe instructed the technician.

He obeyed and announced: "Joe, these are Russian rebels, the zoom clearly indicates Russian characters next to the logo."

"What? I thought they were all dead."

"Apparently not."

"They arrive at the right time. Now the New Germans should be distracted."

At that moment they heard shots. Joe saw some Russian soldiers leave their ships with their hover packs. They were tall, well-built fighters, and from a distance they could hear their war cries. The scanners indicated clones that were approaching the Russians. There seemed to be a slaughter of the biggest kind. A loud crash filled the air as the New Germans bombed the first ship of the Russians and threw it burning on the ground.

"Come on," said Joe. There was no better moment than now to storm the main defense. Much of the clones were busy out in the field. The last few miles the soldiers laid back on foot. Soon they saw the turrets sticking out in the sky. A few moments ago it was suddenly quiet, the defensive position fired no longer on the Russian ships. However, these were no longer visible. Did they manage to reverse or were they destroyed so quickly? The latter was more likely. All that remained was to hope that the Russians could wipe out some clones on the ground.

"We'll try to do as much as possible from a distance," Joe said. "Yosoju, that's your job. Tom, take Hans and Stefan. You will form the Attack Team 1. You are the best for this job, the rest of us will follow you. Then on, Yosoju. Your commitment is needed."

Yosoju started the fire on the first turret. Tom helped him and everything was in flames within seconds. The gun turret shot back and the first clones had been sent. Yosoju shot what it took.

"Guys, I need more energy, bring me a scanner, there you go," he shouted. The remaining soldiers fired as well, with firefights on all sides. Hans cried out when he was hit. A few seconds later he was dead. As the clones approached, the cyborgs were dispatched. Efficiently they did their job and relieved the soldiers. Yosoju was still trying to keep the positions under attack, firing one gun turret at a time. Four other soldiers managed to penetrate to the station and install explosive devices. A huge explosion shook the complex and there was no sign of the soldiers. Half the position had invaded and clones came from inside - there were more and more. Although the ten cyborgs were working tirelessly, it seemed that the rebels were not up to the incredible number of clones. There were hundreds.

"Where did they all come from?" Joe shouted. Nobody had time to answer.

Joe was about to give the order to retreat when he felt a thump on his leg. When he looked down, he saw blood.

"Retreat!" he shouted, and in his ear device there was the pilot of the flight ships with an emergency call: "We're surrounded by some 100 clones chance of survival equal to zero, if we are not collected. Get us away from here!"

It was not a minute before the rebels' airships came into sight. The Cyborgs had now killed a hundred clones and yet the New Germans were still in the majority. The rebels succeeded in releasing an escape route and now the remaining ones ran towards the saving flying targets. Joe hobbled away from the battlefield as best he could, trying to ignore the hellish pain. Finally, another technician called back the cyborgs, who had kept their backs off. When everyone was aboard, the ship took off and accelerated to its maximum in an instant. No New Germanic ship caught up with them, which was very amazing. But as the pilots began to study the holograms from a bird's-eye view, it was clear that the New Germanic flying disks were still busy with the Russians.

After some time they arrived at the Swiss rebel station, where Joe was taken to the hospital as soon as possible. A doctor certified him a chance of survival of 15%, because during the flight his condition had worsened dramatically, he had lost a lot of blood. Joe was not the only wounded, and half dead people were carried from the other ships. Most of them, however, had not returned at all.

Joe was operated on and connected to a machine. There were no blood reserves. While Joe fell into a coma, the war raged on outside. The picture of defeat became ever clearer, as there were not many troops left to fight. In the meantime, of the initially hundreds of airships, there were 24 left. Sean ordered to cancel the entire mission and bring back the survivors. However, with most of the rebels scattered somewhere, it was difficult to track them down, and many ships flew home empty-handed, leaving the soldiers to their fate. Because Joe was in a coma, he could not turn to the captain of the air raid fleet to redeem Vivi's deal. But when Vivi heard in America from the Swiss that her Joe was in a coma, she turned unexpectedly to the captain, who was still in Europe. He promised her to bring Joe back to America. The same day the captain arrived at the rebel station in Switzerland. There, the doctor made everything ready for transport and so Joe, who noticed nothing of the whole effort, could fly back to America with the remaining soldiers of his troop.

Of course, when the ship landed and Joe was transported to the infirmary on a stretcher, Vivi was present and wept with joy and grief at the same time. On the one hand she was relieved to have her Joe back, but on the other hand she was worried about his life at his bedside. She was already 27 weeks pregnant and could feel the baby moving.

Joe was operated on again. Modern medicine was

able to reproduce lost tissue from stem cells and implant it to the patient. So Joe's leg, which had been smashed, could be restored. Every day Vivi was on Joe's side. He still did not want to wake up from the coma. A whole month passed before Vivi, who had dozed off beside Joe, suddenly heard his voice: "Where am I? Did we do it?"

Immediately she was awake. She could hardly believe her eyes: Joe was awake!

"Joe, my dear, you actually woke up!" Crying with pleasure, she fell over his neck, and Joe, who did not quite know what was going on, simply held her and enjoyed her closeness.

"I'm not sure...I'm feeling a little tired," he stammered.

"That's okay, try to sleep a little, I'm with you!" She said brightly.

When Joe woke up and got his bearings, he demanded the reports of the attack. It seemed as if they had only been able to inflict damage to the New Germans at certain points. Allegedly, about 50 new Germanic ships had been destroyed and no more than 10,000 clones had been killed. Given that the new Germanic army had a force of 15 million people, this was a joke. Since the attack in Europe, some New Germanic ships had bombed the coastal regions of America, but they had not advanced further into the country. Nevertheless, there was an acute danger that the New Germans could plan a serious attack. Since the iron the rebels had brought from New Germany was almost used up, it was extremely difficult to retrofit an almost reputable fleet.

The highest ranking soldiers were called together and it was decided to unite the entire rebel armies from all countries and form a new formation. So they came to some airships. In a second attack they would be better prepared. They had a plan to produce new weapons, weapons that were more effective against the shields of the clones. In addition, they thought about how to equip their own soldiers also with such force fields. Unfortunately, this technique was still too advanced.

Joe was still too weak, he could not get out of bed, every time he folded. It would be a while before he was fully fit again. Meanwhile, Vivi kept her husband in the hospital company. The baby could be born every day, even every hour.

One Sunday morning, at 09:14, Julie Dexter saw the light of day.

Cease-fire

Vivi and Joe took parental leave for three months. They enjoyed the time with their little family and cared for the baby. At some distance from the base there was a small lake where they often went for a walk. It was late spring and the days were getting warmer. So they spent hours on the lake shore in the sun and sometimes even almost forgot the war. Life would have been perfect. If not soon the next attack would have been at the door.

One day Vivi told Joe what kind of deal she had made with the captain. She told him that she had committed herself to military service and devote the rest of her life to the fight against the New Germans. Her daughter did not know about it and she was still too young to understand it all. Vivi said she could give Julie the care of a caregiver to resume work as a pilot. At first, Joe was reluctant to know his wife was in the field while another person was taking care of her child. A more dangerous job Vivi could not have chosen. But he could not hold her against anything, after all, he himself had been at war and would go again at any time, when a second attack became concrete. So Vivi began to fly again, became familiar with all sorts of ships and became the best of all pilots. However, she flew only missions within the country and no real attacks against the New Germans.

Meanwhile, the rebels had recovered somewhat and the production of new ships ran at full speed until all the iron was completely used up. As more and more rebels gathered around the world, realizing that they would not be able to face the enemy on their own, hope was restored. Why the New Germans did not obliterate America was a mystery to all.

Julian, the professor, and other anti-technicians had not gone to war as soldiers, but had developed the technique in the rebel station, including finding ways to surround buildings with force fields to protect them. They had also deciphered the cyborgs technique that had been taken to America for Joe's ambulance. The ten copies had served as a template to produce more, and now you could count on the 600 cyborgs. Each had the fighting power of four rebels.

But as fast as the rebels were recovering, the New Germans also increased their holdings. Europe became an impenetrable fortress. This apparent balance of power allowed for temporary rest. The New Germans had all of Europe, as well as large parts of Asia and Africa in their power and saw the rebels therefore no longer as a major threat, because the land they wanted was completely in their possession. They had successfully built up their new Great Germanic wealth. They no longer expanded and probably focused on building the infrastructure and defending their new empire.

Two years passed and little Julie grew up. Since there had been no active war effort, Joe and Vivi had never been on a mission for more than a day at a time and had plenty of time to take care of the child. In America, it was decided to reintroduce the state system of democracy, which was done after local votes. So a new state called New America was born. The number of inhabitants increased daily, not only because of an increased birth rate, but also because rebels from all over the world were naturalized. The vision of New America was a state whose population consisted entirely of rebels. After all, there would only be two more world powers. The citizens of New America slowly got used to the state of peace. The alertness decreased slightly, no one looked with ardent eyes on Europe. Although new weapons technologies were still being worked on and upgraded, they were no longer at the same pace as two years earlier.

Joe moved with Vivi and Julie to a small house in Canada where they lived without any consumer electronics. They had arranged with the rebel station that they would be immediately available in case of an attack. But it had never happened. For a while, they felt as if they were back where they had come from - in the peaceful 21st century. They had to hunt their own food, which pleased Joe. He got himself an old rifle from the 21st century. Fortunately, the wilderness of Canada was not greatly affected by the explosions and devastation of the war, there were still enough animals left to survive. They made a garden and cared for themselves all the time. Joe secretly hoped, though he did not want to admit, that he could live here forever. It was what he had always promised his wife.

While still in the hospital, he underwent a nose operation to prevent him from snoring at night. But despite all this seclusion, he could not forget the past. He suffered from terrible nightmares. They tried not to confront little Julie, but it could not always be avoided. From time to time they also quarreled and the scraps flew, but they always reconciled after a short time.

When they returned to New America for a short stay, especially to visit Julian and Mary again, they did not believe their eyes. In this short time many things had happened: new houses were growing, defensive positions had been built, airships now circled in the sky every day, and cyborgs used to guard the people were being found on the street.

Joe went to the Echo base with Vivi to say hello. A friendly young gentleman came to meet them. "Good day together, a long time since we last met." It was none other than Lars, who now had the entire Echo base under his control. Sean had been transferred to San Francisco. "A lot has happened, has not it? I hope you enjoyed it," Lars continued.

"Yes, you can say that. What about the New Germans?" Joe asked.
"Well, I'm the only one here who's prepared for an attack. The others are not worried about it right now. They think that because the New Germans are so quiet, they do not have to fear them anymore. They have lost all respect. And most people forgot the battle two years ago. It will still get so far that the New Germans will one day attack us out of the blue and nobody will be prepared. Almost every day I struggle with the new politicians to finally revive the arms industry. But for them, the war is over. I tell you, the New Germans have a plan. We'll build everything here, and if it's big enough for them, they'll come and get it."

"That's really scary," Joe said. "So many have died from our ranks, we can not just forget this and pretend that everything is alright. I lost many good friends during the battle."

"You are absolutely right. Look, we actually have enough resources to get a decent army going. I think it will be some time yet, but I hope we can finally start fighting in a few years and bring back our country. We have to turn off these New Germans and their leader. I suspect that there are already some spies among us. As generous as the rebels are naturalized here, a few spies are easily infiltrated. The only person I still trust is you, Joe."

Thoughtfully, Joe and Vivi returned home in the evening.
The next day, Julie was gone and nobody knew where she was. Joe and Vivi searched everywhere, shouting for her, but she was nowhere to be found. The two parents panicked. Wild animals lived in the forest, they expected the worst. Crying, Vivi ran through the forest and kept calling Julie's name. Joe, too, was a bundle of nerves. Armed with his rifle, he stumbled through the thicket. Finally, an hour later, he found his daughter sitting on a pile of wood, not far from the house, playing with sticks. Although nothing had happened, cause Vivi and Joe had big dispute. Joe blamed Vivi and Vivi blamed Joe and a long back and forth followed until finally the little girl began to howl. When Joe was poisoned just four days later, because he drank from the stream without boiling the water, the couple seriously wondered if they were in the right place. Joe and Vivi had almost decided to return to the Echo Station when a farmer passed by and gave them food. Luckily he had some medications in the car and Joe recovered. After some time, the incidents were almost forgotten and they appreciated the peace and quiet in seclusion. It was really good to live without technology, without radio, without internet. They had discussions or read a lot. They had taken

various books from the professor's holdings, and so they learned some interesting details about the past: The Second World War had allegedly been started by a society that called itself the Thule Order, an association of magicians and media. This had then used the theories of white and black magic and Hitler helped to power to start the war. It was rumored that he had been in possession of a spear that would give superhuman powers to his bearer. This spear should have already worn the legendary King Arthur and Napoleon. However, nobody could prove the legends. Another book claimed that the UN and the EU had been led by the Illuminati's secret organization. The European countries had been told that everything would serve their own benefit. But when a team of unknown scientists from an opposing secret society, the so-called IDOs, came to the light of the Illuminati, they were large parts of the EU, the United Nations and other organizations fall apart. As a result, there had been a year-long economic crisis.

"Hm, interesting, we weren't there in the 21st century." Joe thought and read on eagerly. He loved conspiracy theories.

The book went on to say that the Illuminati at the time had everything in their hands and that it was a coincidence that they had been exposed. Actually, the Illuminati had had the plan to seize world domination, they were materialistic people without any morals or ethics. But they had overlooked that there were other powers. Although they had been hidden for almost a century, they had been there and had only waited for the day whenthey could seize power again: The followers of the Thule Society which consisted of National Socialists and other like-minded people. After the Second World War, they had retreated to Antarctica and built huge stations there. They called themselves New Germans and developed an unbelievable technical know-how there in more than 100 years and built flying discs and new weapons. In the cold of Antarctica they observed everything and meticulously prepared themselves for day x. When their time came, they had come back to Europe and had taken power. Everything went so fast and nobody had expected it. Their announcement shone with huge holograms all over the world. Huge holograms of beam crosses were projected into all ends of the world and rang in the new time. So it all began. Some world powers tried to destroy the Antarctic station unsuccessfully with atomic bombs. The consequences were atrocious, as some atomic bombs were returned to the launch site and contaminated the country.

Return

Another year moved into the country. In summer the young family collected firewood for the cold winter months and in winter the three sat comfortably in the warmth and Vivi tried to sew clothes.

For some time they managed to forget the terrible past and you could almost think that everything was fine. One night a bear came by and ate all their supplies because Joe had forgotten to lock the door to the shed. As a punishment Vivi didn't cook for him for two days and he had to go fishing and fry the fish on the fire.

The three lived very well. In the meantime, they were also in contact with the old farmer who had given Joe the medication against the poisoning. The farmers lived nearby, which is why they and the young family were able to help each other. The farmer had special grain, it was genetically manipulated, but it tasted good. He even gave them a cow so they could have their own milk. When they visited him one day, Joe told of their life story and the old couple was very upset. However, they were also a little sceptical, they couldn't quite believe the story. Even at the end of the world it was known that time travel only existed in movies. But Vivi knew how to convince them. They sat for hours in front of the fireplace in the farmhouse and discussed about cows and the past 150 years.

The farmer's wife had fallen in love with little Julie and was like a grandmother to her. So Joe and Vivi decided to leave Julie with the farmers in case of another attack. Nowhere else in the world was she as well protected as here. The old couple were immediately enthusiastic about this idea. One day, however, the farmer's wife stood in front of Joe and Vivi's front door and said agitated that her husband had not returned from the field since the evening before. Joe and Vivi had the worst forebodings. When Joe went looking for the farmer, his fear came true. He had died in the field, probably from a heart attack. It didn't take but a month for the old farmer's wife to die. As if the two had felt the approaching fate, there was a will on the table:

Dear Joe, dear Vivi,

You will inherit everything in our possession. You are our only friends and almost our family. Our only son no longer lives. He emigrated to the city many years ago and died in a battle. Now you are the sole heirs. We don't have much money, but we have a gold mine. It is far away from here and we were too old to mine gold. For a long time no more gold was mined and we had to keep it top secret, otherwise we would have been attacked. I hope you can do something with it, because gold is a rare commodity nowadays.

In love,
Fred and Elena

Joe and Vivi were very touched by this letter, but they were also unspeakably sad that the two of them had left. They stayed in Canada for about six months before deciding to return to New America. During this time they visited their gold mine twice and decided to leave their inheritance to the rebels to build engines with the gold. Since the pure iron had long since been used up, the gold would give new impetus to the production of airships. Raw materials such as metal had not been mined worldwide for many years and prices were horrendous. Recycling was the new economy.

So Joe and Vivi returned to the rebel station with their four-year-old daughter. It made Joe particularly proud that Lars was still the basic leader. Joe couldn't have imagined a better job. When he told him about the gold mine, Lars sent a team of specialists to bring the gold to New America.

After the first gold deliveries arrived, Lars gave the order to produce another 500 airships. However, he had not expected to reap strong disapproval from the democratic leaders. They threatened him to close down his factory if he did not stop building up the war. This seemed very suspicious to Lars. After all, rearming served the security of his own country. He had Julian program a security cyborg to spy on the government. After a short time the cyborg returned with explosive facts. Some members of the government were new Germans and had influenced the rest of the government ideologically.

When the scam was blown open, the New Germans tried to escape, but the cyborgs did a good job and shot everyone. So it was possible to start building the airships. The biggest work was done by robots, but the programming and testing was done by humans.

Amazingly, shortly after this incident, the rebels received an offer of peace from the New Germans, which could only indicate that they were on the right track. The rebel leaders had immediately taken the offer as a trap and were again alarmed that the danger was not over. Spies had lived among them for several years and had probably sent countless pieces of information to Europe. They grieved about their own naivety. In response to their carelessness, the rebel stations invested in further warfare methods. They developed a completely new submarine technology that enabled them to get to Europe unnoticed. It was known that the New Germans controlled the airspace and the ground, but they had not yet entered the water for warfare. Another strategic advantage that the rebels could use for themselves. They also possessed thousands of the feared cyborgs, which they could use on the ground.

The motivation to carry out a second, all-decisive attack was increasingly felt, and so it came to pass that the highest ranks of politics and warfare met to determine a strategy and a timetable at a conference. When hundreds of ships were ready again and the soldiers had completed training with new weapons and had been equipped with better scanners, which could now also X-ray, nothing stood in the way of the mission. The rebels had also produced Hover tanks in measure in addition to the flying ships. These were to be transported with the airships. They were fast and well armed tanks whose armor consisted of an extremely strong titanium hull and was surrounded by a force field. In addition, the largest tank, a kind of artillery tank, had a torpedo turret with which a projectile could be fired over several kilometres to the nearest metre. The projectile varied between electro-plasma compounds and compounds with antimatter, which is why enormous forces were released in an impact. Several houses could thus be blown up without any problems within a radius of ~~approx.~~ approximately 150 metres, or more precisely, pulverised. Two medium-sized guns were also mounted on the lower sides of the tanks to target objects near the ground. The tanks were able to travel at around 400 km/h, looking like floating rectangles with rounded corners. Only the guns protruded a little. But this was not comparable to the guns Joe and Vivi knew from the 21st century. They resembled some whisks and some spools with some tubes. Also the rifles of the soldiers needed getting used to and consisted of three parts: The energy part could be fed with a scanner in an emergency. The ammunition part - whereby the term ammunition was understated, because it was a kind of generator for various projectiles - could also be replaced, and then there was the barrel from which the shots came. These weapons were constructed in such a way that they could be combined with other weapons at will or, by exchanging individual parts, they could soon be converted into another type of weapon.

The X-ray scanners could illuminate walls and objects, and in addition they had a resolution that reproduced details razor sharp in a few hundred meters. Technical progress had also been made with the hover-packs. They were modified so that it was possible to breathe under water for a short time. A kind of air bubble was generated around the hover pack that lasted 180 seconds. From a technical point of view, they were definitely competitive. At least they thought so. But the rebel army, despite the global cooperation of the New German Army, was still far behind with all its clones. The rebels did not bring young people under the age of 16 into the army, this was a code of honour, whereas the New Germans trained children from the age of twelve. Despite the better conditions, no one knew how the second attack would proceed. Would they suffer such massive losses again? Would they be able to do more damage to the new Germans this time?

In order to be prepared for a counterattack, the positions on the coasts were massively strengthened. Bunkers were erected in the mountains, in case of emergency the population should be able to seek shelter there.

Vivi began to fly again, but it was no longer a great challenge. The ships flew almost automatically, but in battle they had to be steered. There were also one-man ships, but they could not fly more than 50 metres high and had to be small to maintain maneuverability, so they were classified as ground combat vehicles.

Joe amused himself about how the young people spent their free time. The teenagers played with laser weapons in the forest. It was a game and at the same time a preparation for the war. Of course, the game weapons were an attenuated version of the originals, but when someone was hit, a harmless narcotic was released, which knocked them unconscious for ten minutes. This prevented one from cheating while playing. The girls usually all hung out together in some computer salon for women, where you could create holograms and virtual worlds. But there were also comfortable sofas where the girls could chat about fashion and boys. Since much of the work was done by robots, jobs were scarce and most young people had no career prospects. Unless you were a programming genius, inventor, or fighter.

Little Julie, meanwhile, had turned five. She was a lovely little kid, quite intelligent and a lot ahead of her peers . For some time she went to kindergarten.

Attack

It was the 05th of August in 2156. Each of them went about their business and no one had the slightest idea what would happen shortly. Joe and Vivi sat in a coffee bar and talked about trivial things. Then it happened: the clock showed one minute after noon. Sirens suddenly howled and all citizens were asked to go to the shelters immediately. The New Germans were attacking. The public news systems learned that the first positions along the coast were being bombed. Joe and Vivi had to report to the commander immediately. They ran, picked Julie up at the nursery and took her to the Echo Bunker. The rebel station had a highly secure complex and her daughter would be safe here for the time being. Mary, who was now the mother of two children, would take care of Julie.

With a last fleeting kiss Vivi said goodbye to Joe. She went to the pilots, but Joe had been assigned to the reserve and had to move out only when a certain stock of soldiers was used up. The rebels were actually prepared for a war effort and would soon have launched their own attack. Now the New Germans had come before them.

A large part of the troops was mobilized and already the first airships in the air rose to counter-attack. This time they had working force fields and would not go up in flames at the first shot. The plan was to lure the

New Germans away from the positions so they could wage the war in the air. The rebels succeeded in achieving good results. Vivi sat in her ship and attacked with four others a Haunebu 9, as a radio recording showed: "Watch the turrets of the battleship."

"Attention, they're firing, start turning maneuvers."

"Damn, Number Three, what's up? I need cover!"

"Can not, I'm being followed by a ship."

"Then turn it off."

"I'm trying!"

"I could turn off the four!"

"Well done. Now follow me, we must give the rest to this mothership."

"Vivi, look, there's a sevens behind you!"

"Oh, shit, one of my guns was hit. Number two, help me, take the top!"

The ships engaged in an inexorable battle. Since they were now equally protected, it took longer for a ship to succumb to the damage and crash into the depths. All series of Haunebus were sifted, presumably the old models were still used extra to clear them out, but most of the fleet consisted of newer ships, which were excellently armored. While Vivi tried to attack the larger ships with her unit, ~~also~~ several dozen other ships also delivered exciting duels. They sent torpedoes and the air was like a unique fireworks display. At that moment, contact with number two broke out of Vivi's unit.

"Number two, what's up?" Vivi shouted.

She received no answer, but could see through the hologram how both the Neuner ship of the New-Germans and number two crashed burning.

"Damn, we lost number two."

"Hey Vivi, do not think about it, we've got a pair of eights up our ass," yelled the pilot from number four.

"Those damned eights are just too well armored. Let's go and try an attack on the next sevens."

"Agreed, we'll go from the south to the next sevens. Accelerated!"

"Number three, go from the left. Number four from the right, I'll tackle it from scratch," Vivi shouted.

She headed straight for the sevens, it looked as if she wanted to ram it. Shortly in front of the ship, she lit her entire arsenal, raised her own aircraft and flew over the sevens. Burning it fell into the depths.

"We take off, let the others do the rest, we do not have enough energy left. Besides, we're too damaged!" She called over the radio.

The team flew back to the base and Joe came running up, "Hey, I thought it hit you, our losses are huge.

You're lucky to be able to fly the new series with your colleagues, the old series of ships is being slaughtered like flies in a pile."

"What are our losses so far?" Vivi asked.

"Nearly 200 ships were destroyed."

"How many New Germanis ships are still operable?"

"A few, maybe 20. It will not be long before we can decide this attack. Wait...I'm getting the message that the New Germans are retiring!"

"Finally!" Vivi sighed. "I almost got it."

In the evening Joe sat down with Lars to sum up the day in retrospect. In total, more than 700 ships returned to the stations today, some of them damaged, but still ready for use. The attack had brought some losses, but the balance was consistently positive. The New Germans had gotten a powerful one on the lid.
Lars started a videoconference with other commanders in the country and the answer was the same everywhere. The reaction to this surprise attack had to be a concrete counterattack. That same week, they would leave for Europe with their entire force. Part of the troops would come to New Germany with the submarines, the advantage of these submarines was the ability to drive through the hover technology in the countryside. Slightly slower, but still efficient. They would be loaded with cyborgs that would be the invasion force once the submarines had surfaced on the coasts. Over 35,000 cyborgs were now operational. Rebels around the world were notified

and mobilized. Long before, the cooperations had been maintained. Everyone was networked worldwide and ready to fight together when the time came. Again they wanted to attack New Germany from three sides simultaneously. The Russians would come from the east, the submarines from the north, and the fleets from the west.

"The Russians have all been fooling us, they still have a few thousand men ready to fight and we thought they were all dead," Joe told Lars when the video conference ended.

"With that they really shot the bird. But are we glad that it is so! The help of the Russians gives us massive support."

"How many tanks do we have?" Joe asked.
"1,000."

"All right, we'll send everyone into battle. I can't say how all this will turn out, and we have to reckon with daily counterattacks.

After the meeting Joe went to Vivi.

"Hey honey," he said, "did you get it? We will start an invasion. You'll probably have to go to war again."

"Yes, Joe, I've committed myself."

"Then I will also go. I will be there for the invasion. Our child is in good hands, Mary is a good nanny. We'll give the new Germans a blow they won't soon forget."

"Joe, I will miss you and be terribly afraid for you. Promise me that we'll see each other afterwards, never give up and stay covered by the cyborgs, okay?"

"Don't worry, I'll take care of myself. You and me, we'll come back!" Unconsciously, they both looked at the crib at the same time, where Julie was sleeping blissfully.

"Look, the little one. She seems to dream happily. Come on, let's let her sleep. Let's go outside and take a look at the stars," Vivi said. They went together to a meadow near the Echo base, sat down and looked up at the sky.

"You know, Vivi, I was terrified when you were up there fighting. I thought I'd never see you again. I hate this war, even if I take part in it. I only do this so that at some point everything will finally be over. Why did all this have to happen? We have lost so many good colleagues and friends. And I wasn't even really conscious when Julie was born."

"Oh, the little one. It's been a long time now," Vivi sighed nostalgically.

"Oh, yes, five years. It has changed a hell of a lot during this time. Do you remember when we were in captivity? Back then we were together for a few years. Or do you remember the festival in the old days, when we talked to the guys about the band Kraftwerk and you were very drunk afterwards? Did I ever tell you what it was like in this time slot? You were unconscious the whole time!"

"Yes, you did. But it's been so long, tell it again!" Vivi looked at him expectantly.

"It was strange. I was no longer wearing a seatbelt and yet I could not get out of the car. I was fully conscious, everything was dark around me, then I saw these colored balls. My God, Vivi, we have experienced so much together. What am I glad to know you?"
"The first time we saw each other, Joe, I thought, What's that guy? I imagined my future husband in a different way. But then, after a while, it grabbed me. I fell in love and thought of you every minute. Do you remember how we secretly sneaked out of the apartment at night to meet in the woods? My parents have never heard anything. Or can you still remember how we came up with the stupid idea of getting a bottle of whiskey on a DVD night? I had a headache the whole following day and I just felt sick. I had drunk so much tonight that I telephoned everywhere and even asked a colleague if we were building a UFO together."

"Oh, what we got for a bang," grinned Joe. "What would you do if we were back in our time?"

"I think I would enjoy life more and listen less. We had it really nice."

"Yes, Vivi, you're right."

Joe put his arm around his wife. She closed her eyes and enjoyed the moment. "Hey, Joe," she said softly.

"Yes?"

"I love you."

They hugged and kissed. After that, they went back to their daughter and went to sleep.

The next morning, they woke Julie.

"Mum, dad, do you know what I dreamed? I dreamed of the moon, and a man came by ship from the moon, then he saved your life when you were in combat. ~~Is~~ Isn't that great? So you do not have to worry. He will save you."

Vivi smiled melancholily. If only it were that easy.

"Honey, there's no one on the moon to save us," she said.

But little Julie insisted, "Yes, yes, I dreamed it. An old man with a lot of people saved you."

"I'll have something to eat," Vivi said, not focusing on the dream any more. "Go quickly to the storeroom, Joe, and get us some stuff to make something out of."

While Joe went to get breakfast, Julie sat down on the bed and began to cry.

"What's going on, sweetheart?" Vivi asked worriedly.

"I'm scared for you, Mama, I do not want to lose you," she sobbed.

"Dear, I know, but we have no choice! If not every single one of us goes to war, we will not survive long, and I do not want you to fall into the hands of the New Germans. You know, they did a terrible thing with us. I want to save you from it. Mary is taking good care of you, sweetheart. Everything will be alright, okay? We'll come back, everything will be fine," Vivi tried to comfort her daughter.

Julie rubbed her eyes and nodded.

"Always remember what we taught you," Vivi went on. "Trust only Mary, Julian and Lars, have you heard? Always stay close to Mary!"

Joe came with the food. "What's going on?" He asked, seeing Vivi and the baby on the bed.

"Oh Joe, Julie is having a crisis.."

"Come here, Julie! We know that you are afraid, but we will come back to you, I promise you. Then we go back to our house in Canada, get a sibling for you and spend the rest of our lives there, is that good?"

"Oh, that would be great. But when I grow up, I want to fight too," Julie said.

Joe and Vivi had to laugh.

"I think the war will not last that long. But I'm sure you're a good fighter," Joe said.

"Come on, you'll have to go to kindergarten soon. Take a roll!" Vivi told the little girl.

"Oh, or you'll be late," Joe agreed, "what are you doing in kindergarten?"

"We paint pictures of airships."

"That's great," he said, turning to Vivi. "And what's your schedule of the day, sweetheart?"

"I have to test the new series of nine again. The weapons do not always work as well as they should. Then we have another problem with the sevens series. The drive sometimes turns off for a short time."

"Well, you can fix that problem, dear. Today I will look at the positions on the coast, I want to get a picture of what it looks like. Then I have to evaluate some holograms that we got from the Russians. I also have to go through the invasion plans with Lars, split the units, and so on. Have you read the review of the new shields?"

"Yes I have."

"I have not gotten it yet. Are they good?" Joe asked.

"I think so. They can handle a lot."

"Do you know what pleases me most?"
"Let me guess. The cyborgs?"

"Exactly. Our technicians were able to design them so well that they became much faster. They have excellent armament and are extremely well armoured. I think we can take ~~them~~ on the new Germans really well."

Insight

The days passed and already the attack stood before the door. The nervousness was omnipresent again. How many people should lose their lives this time? Would their efforts bring anything?

On the day of the attack Joe stayed in bed for a while before getting up and held his wife tight. It was 08:00 in the morning and the day promised to be sunny. But this did not interest the thousands of soldiers who prepared for the fight. It seemed as if the end of the world was just around the corner. Lars had been awake for hours. He followed and coordinated the events. Music sounded from the loudspeakers to calm the soldiers. Many were hopeless and afraid to die. Would they ever return and see their families? It could all be over soon, but the war could last for years.

Vivi and Joe were also restless. What would become of little Julie if they did not return? Slowly they rose out of bed. Julie had already got up before and gone outside. Now she came back and shouted excitedly:

"Mommy, Mommy, the ships are being positioned outside. When will Daddy and you have to leave and when will you come home?" Julie didn't seem to fully understand that it wasn't a game.

"Julie, I don't know exactly when we'll be back yet," Vivi said. The tears rolled out of her eyes. "Be strong, my love."

"But Mommy, I don't want to lose you, I love you so much."

"Yes, darling, I know."

Joe sat next to his wife. He didn't say a word, he could see how badly she was.

"Mommy, I don't want you to go."

"Julie, but we've got to, the New Germans will kill everyone else."

"But we're safe here."

"Yes, but for how long? Look, the army needs every soldier. And your dad is a very good soldier."

"I don't care, you can't leave!"

"Come, let's go outside," Joe interrupted the two.

Joe took his wife and daughter by the hand, and all three went outside where they had a spectacular sight. As far as the eye could see, the three saw only ships and soldiers.

"Come on, let's take a look around," Joe tried to say as casually as he could.
They walked past the soldiers and admired the ships. They happened to meet Lars. "How is the little family?" he asked.

"Well, still quite well."

"Joe, I didn't sleep much last night and one thing kept me particularly busy. Remember, Joe, when I told you about my father?"

"Oh yes, I know that."

"I don't want you both to be in the attack. I can't ask you and Julie to do that. There are enough other soldiers. I can't do that to your daughter. I don't want you to do the same thing to me. She should be able to grow up with you. I suggest that you retreat to Canada."

"And what shall become of you? You need every man," Joe protested.

"Joe, two more or less do not carry weight. See that you get out of here. I know that some won't like it. So be careful that nobody sees you. I have already assigned your teams to other leaders. On the park field B4 is a hover vehicle ready for you. There is food in the hold. I have had to watch enough times, as dozens of men have fallen, in the most cruel way. If I had to tell your daughter that you are dead, I would not bring that to my heart. It's better this way. I'll give you a transmitter so you can follow the events. I will fight in your place, because nobody is waiting for me here. There are enough people here who can do my job if I do not return. Nevertheless, I hope we will meet again. Now I have to go, here's the transmitter." He handed the item to Joe and went on without further explanation.

"Vivi, he's right," Joe said. "Let's get away. We have lost a lot, but our family is still intact. Let's go while we can. Let's get our things packed!"

They went to their dorm and began to pack their few belongings. Until just a few minutes ago, Joe had been convinced he was going to war, maybe even death. And now the tide had turned. He was incredibly relieved. He would have given his life out of solidarity and given up his family. Nobody would have thanked him. He would have just become another victim of the war. Would it have been worth it? What was more important in the world than the people you loved? Out of pure sense of responsibility, he would have made war on his family. A senseless war that fueled the greed of psychopaths and killed innocent citizens. No, he would not place his family on the cannons. Joe looked up. Was there really someone up there,who watched all this? If there was a God, he would surely be shaken by the cruelty of the creatures he created out of love.

"Maybe I should pick up my Bible again," Joe mused, realizing in the next instant that he had none left. It was left behind in the old days. There was no faith in this world. The people had forgotten God. It was only then that Joe realized he had not seen a single church in the new era. Never before had a human being mentioned a word of God. It was bleak and terrible.

The Joe, who had once fought so hard to defeat the New Germans, was no longer the Joe he once was. It was as if Lars had opened his eyes. He suddenly saw everything differently. He did not want to take revenge anymore, he did not want others to go to war, it was just pointless. What if they won? The war would not stop, it would go on and on with the malice of the people. Why couldn't you just make peace? Why did you want to destroy life and destroy nature? He found no answers to all these questions.

"Let's go," Joe said as they finished packing.

Joe, Vivi and Julie ran. As they passed Lars' office, Joe paused to tell Vivi and Julie to wait. The door was open, but Lars was not there. Joe went in and wrote a farewell letter for Lars.

Hello my boy,

So now we are gone, away from the war. If there is a god, he will protect you. I will never forget our time. You have taught me a lot, last you opened my eyes. I will pray for you, it will be the first time that I will pray for someone. I hope for you that the attack will be successful. Watch that you come back. You are always welcome with us in Canada. Do not be shy to drop by, you know where to find us.

In love,

Joe, Vivi and Julie

When the three left the building, no one paid any attention to them, they were all hectic and worried about their own worries. Soon the signal would sound and the soldiers would have to board their ships. The submarine crew drove with Hover-cars to the coast and boarded ~~there~~ the boats there.

Before they got into the vehicle, which was ready for them as promised, Joe looked back again. They would never come back. Perhaps they would remain prisoners of that time forever, but they would never return to the rebels. They would live a simple life in

Canada, take care of themselves and ignore the war. If the world powers did not destroy the planet with their amazing weapons, they would grow old in Canada. It was the right decision.

When Joe and his family arrived in Canada, they found their old house exactly as they had left it.Far and wide there was nobody to be seen. Vivi began to unpack her bags and Joe went outside. He knelt in the woods and began to pray. He prayed to the god of his childhood. He should protect everyone and let the attack go well. When Joe got up and looked at his watch, he noticed that he had spent more than an hour on the forest floor. He had tears in his eyes and shivered. The soldiers were already in the air and would probably arrive in Europe in a few minutes. Joe went in and picked up the transmitter.

He heard music play. It was the music that had been running on the starting field all the time. He heard the soldiers sing, they sang together a song that they had rehearsed before, a song about love and war. It read as follows:

"It's time to go, we say goodbye, and it's all over, we'll give everything to win."

There was no sound of mourning in the song, but Joe knew there were many thousands behind the song crying.

Then Joe heard the announcement that the first airships had arrived off the European coast. Nervously he went in a circle. A few minutes later, the Fleet Command's message came in:

"Attack started. First enemy ships fired, they return the fire."

Joe listened to how some rebels were able to eliminate new Germanic aircraft, but also in their own ranks losses were reported. The submarines had arrived and had the cyborgs storm into the country. The attack took place on several fronts, from north to south. The forces of the Allies were gradually butchered, they had no chance. It seemed like there would be no second Normandy. The defense of the New Germany was terrible.

Joe put it down, he did not want to hear about it anymore. He switched off the transmitter. He would eventually know what would happen . Joe went to the living room where his wife and daughter sat. Vivi was reading to Julie from a picture book. When he entered, both looked up and tried to smile. The fear was written in his face, because they knew secretly that the war was already lost. They guessed what was coming soon to everyone.

"Daddy, you don't have to be scared, because now the man is coming from the moon and will free the world." Joe and Vivi looked at each other puzzled and did not understand why Julie said that sentence out of the blue.

Special thanks to

- Corinna Schild – You are the best wife!
- Kevin Wieser – You are my best friend!
- Andrea Rohpeter – Thanks for your help!
- Kay Radzik – Thanks for your help!
- Leo Kopka – Thanks for the awesome Cover!

Remember 1945